The Candleberry Tales 2

The Candleberry Tales 2

Santiago, Here We Come!

KARL D. LEHMAN

RESOURCE *Publications* • Eugene, Oregon

THE CANDLEBERRY TALES 2
Santiago, Here We Come!

Resource Publications
An Imprint of Wipf and Stock Publishers
199 W. 8th Ave., Suite 3
Eugene, OR 97401

www.wipfandstock.com

PAPERBACK ISBN: 979-8-3852-7459-8
HARDCOVER ISBN: 979-8-3852-7460-4
EBOOK ISBN: 979-8-3852-7461-1

VERSION NUMBER 03/26/26

For my big brother,
Robert Miles Lehman
(1951–2011)

I always looked up to you.

Contents

Preface

HAVE YOU EVER LOOKED out the window of a tall building and watched the world pass beneath you? When I do, I feel I have become an observer of the people, cars, trucks, and buses below as they scurry about the daily activities of life (unless, of course, it's rush hour).

And so it is with *The Candleberry Tales* series. You, the reader, can step outside of faith's daily practice and observe believers go about day-to-day life in their own worlds. For a few brief moments, you watch from above the characters interacting with each other, enjoying deep fellowship, having arguments, finding reconciliation, and a few doing some very bad things. My hope is that the fanciful circumstances and exaggerated behavior in the space of these short stories help you, the reader, gain fresh perspective on the walk of faith in our complex, polarized, and anger-filled world.

Throughout history, humor and satire have been tools used by writers to get to the heart of serious issues of their day, whether it be Chaucer, through *The Canterbury Tales,* poking fun at the foibles of various professionals and elites of the fourteenth century, Erasmus with *In Praise of Folly*, pointing out the failures of church and society leaders at the time of the Reformation, or CS Lewis making light of hypocrites through *The Screwtape Letters*, published in 1942.

Longstanding issues that face the church can become extremely contentious and can fester beyond control. Take, for example, the *Filioque Clause*. I read a Protestant scholar's recent complaint that the famous clause should not have been in a reprint of the *Nicene Creed* that was included in a new study Bible.

What on earth is the *Filioque Clause,* you ask? Seventeen centuries ago, bishops and Christian scholars from across the Mediterranean world gathered to iron out thorny theological disagreements. After two meetings, one in Nicaea (AD 325) and another in Constantinople (AD 381), and with the resulting requests for reimbursement to cover meals, lodging, and mileage costs, they drafted the famous creed which included a reference to the Holy Spirit proceeding from the Father. You can imagine that a few of the theologians did not supply the requisite receipts with their cost reports, and given the slow nature of the ancient postal systems, spent years, if not decades, seeking to secure their payments from the ecclesiastical accounting departments.

A few hundred years later, folks in the Roman or western church, without any input from the folks in the east, added "and from the Son" (*Filioque Clause*) to the *Nicene Creed* and thus created a very divisive east/west issue. By 1054, after flinging back and forth condemnations and excommunications, the eastern and western churches, in a very un-First Corinthians manner, split, in part over the theologically loaded *Filioque Clause* (The Great Schism). Bad feelings continued to fester to the point that in 1204, Crusaders made a stop in Constantinople (the headquarters of the eastern church) and went on a horrifying killing, pillaging, and raping spree equal to that of the worst sacking recorded anywhere in the Old Testament. Today, nearly a thousand years after the ignominious east/west divorce, I was surprised to see that feelings over the *Filioque Clause* remained quite raw. And then Pope Leo XIV said the clause no longer mattered.

Even Bible translations have become a source of division within the church of our age. There are "test verses" that the faithful use to determine whether or not the translators are among the faithful or the faithless. Millions and millions in Bible sales hang in the balance, putting pressure on publishers to get it right when appealing to their particular chosen audience. If that were not enough of a headache, a plethora of Christian social media influencers are there to tell the followers of Jesus which translations they should pass over like a plague of locusts.

Indeed, battle lines have been drawn. I know of two groups that instead of going into the world to create disciples, decided it better to take on billionaires in public debate, hoping for solid wins that would lead to a trickle-down effect upon the masses. Perhaps the fact that one debater was deemed conservative (and wanted to go after progressive billionaires) and the other a progressive (aiming for a victory over a conservative), meant that they would balance each other out, ensuring that there was no net gain in new believers.

Many issues facing the Church of the twenty-first century are too serious and heartbreaking to lend themselves to satire and humor; a prophetic voice is more appropriate when confronting violence, abuse, racism, child exploitation, and poverty. That being said, other challenges do make appropriate targets for humor and satire, and the themes you will find in this collection of parables draw their inspiration from our contemporary practice of Christianity in the United States. Take as an example, the growing number of believers caught up in the Headship ideology, a movement in which proponents not only prohibit female ordination (as many denominations still do), but have gone further and do not allow women to teach, counsel, or undertake any profession that would put them in a position of leadership over men. Some even advocate for the repeal of the right of women in the United States to vote! Whether it be a business hyper-focused on monetizing the Holy Scriptures, wary residents in a small town having to accept the kindness of foreigners, or overly domineering men learning the hard way to accept and value the leadership of women (or to flee), you will find these and other indomitable, ignoble, and inglorious characters in this book.

Also, in *The Candleberry Tales 2* is the story *For A Peck of Oats*. In it, you will learn of a decommissioned saint whose feast day was removed from the calendar in 1969. If after reading this story you believe the decision should be reconsidered as do some, feel free to join them and write to the Pope at, Secretariat of His Holiness Pope Leo XIV, 00120 Vatican City (The Vatican does not accept email).

And, in case you were wondering, there is no historical record of reimbursements being requested by the attendees at the ancient councils of Nicaea and Constantinople. Welcome to the world of satire.

Acknowledgements

I WANT TO THANK the people who have made *The Candleberry Tales* project possible: my publisher Wipf and Stock, who believed in *The Candleberry Tales*; Dr. Justo L. González and Dr. Catherine G. González, whose encouragement kept me going through years of rejection and for their input into several of the stories in this volume. I also want to thank my pastor, Reverend Tom Hagood, for his support of the first volume of *The Candleberry Tales* through endorsement and book club promotion, and my neighbor Barbara Seal for her enthusiastic book club promotion. I am so appreciative to my sister Nancy L. Ryan, with whom I share what some consider to be an odd sense of humor, for proofreading the first drafts of this book; and my son Jorge R. Lehman-González for our thoughtful conversations about theology and faith. Finally, because Jesus himself said the last shall be first, first and foremost, I want to express my deep gratitude to my beloved wife of more than thirty years, historian Dr. Ondina E. González, for providing me with critique and editing of my writing, offering significant content suggestions, hearing my story ideas *ad nauseam*, and for giving me endless support and hope through the creation of *The Candleberry Tales* series and what ultimately will be its thirty-six parables for modern humanity.

The Prologue

"So, ARE YOU SCHENGEN passengers?" the neat and starch-stiff airport officer asked the Reverends Dave Tucker and Ben Boyle. "If you are, you must stay here!"

Dave, Ben, and the other ten O'Postles were in the Madrid Barajas International Airport, hoping to get started on their pilgrimage to Santiago de Compostela. But instead of walking the famous Route of Saint James, they would be sharing a comfortable bus ride along modern Spanish highways.

"I've never even been arrested," Dave said to the airport officer. "And we're all law-abiding Christian ministers of the gospel." Dave pointed to the group of pastors waiting with their carry-on bags a few yards away. "None of them has been arrested, either. And to be a minister, we had to undergo extensive background checks." Reverend Tucker was very tired after a long flight from the busy, crowded, and chaotic Atlanta Hartsfield airport. He was also getting anxious about being deported. "Oh, I forgot, we've got one independent pastor, so I'm not sure about him."

"I ask you again, are you Schengen?"

"No one ever told us we were shenanigan passengers," Dave said. "Like I said, we're law-abiding ministers of the gospel."

"I've never been categorized as a criminal," a nervous Reverend Ben Boyle whispered to Dave. The two ministers were trying to figure out how to get from Terminal T 1 to their baggage and were, apparently, in the wrong area.

"I think we're in the area for criminals," Dave speculated. "Why else would he keep asking about shenanigans? Maybe one of us has been in jail before. It had to have been Ed."

"Ticks me off," Ben added. His face was turning red. "I just want to get out of the airport, and I refuse to be labeled as a criminal. I ain't never even had a speeding ticket!"

"Ben, go ask Ken what this is all about. He's been to Spain before."

Before Ben even started walking, Reverend Ken Leslie had already come to find out why they were being delayed. "What's going on?" he asked Dave. All of the lines were moving, and he couldn't understand why they all were not already in one of them and moving too. "Is there a problem?"

"They're giving us a hard time because they think we're criminals," he replied.

"That makes no sense," Ken said. "Why in heaven's name would they think that?"

"He keeps asking me if we're shenanigan people," Dave replied. "The best I can figure is that they think we're jailbirds."

Ken looked at the airport officer who seemed as confused as he was. "Is there a problem, sir?"

"Are you with these men?"

"Yes, I am." At that moment Ken wished he wasn't.

"This area is for Schengen arrivals. If you are, you stay here. If not, you need to be over there." He pointed to several lines on the other side of the terminal area. *"Qué tontos, no puedo hacerlo más claro,"* the officer thought to himself.

"Thank you, sir," Ken told the airport officer. "Dave, we need to be over there," he said, speaking in a tone that one would use in a children's sermon. He pointed to the same area to which the officer had pointed. "What made you think this area was for criminals?"

"That's what Dave said," Ben replied.

"I don't know, Ken. Like I told you, he kept asking me if we were shenanigans and I didn't want us to get deported."

"Dave," Ken said. "It's Schengen and not shenanigan. Schengen is the name of a treaty that allows folks in the European Union to freely move from one member country to another."

"So Spain doesn't think we're criminals?"

"No." Ken waved to the other nine ministers and pointed to the area where they needed to be. Once there, they found the line was reasonably quick.

"You've never flown internationally, have you?" Ken asked Dave.

"I've been to Puerto Rico," he replied.

"That's still the United States."

"Well, in that case, no."

"Then, relax. They're used to confused and disoriented American tourists here." Ken gave Dave a comforting pat on the back and said, "Let's get through immigration and customs, get our luggage, and then we can pick up the bus, okay?" Ken smiled at Dave. "And I'll do my best to be patient with you fools," he laughed.

"Thanks, Ken. I really thought we were gonna be deported."

After roughly ninety minutes, the Twelve O'Postles of deep South Georgia's Early County were in the airport parking lot, ready to board a brand-new, fifteen-person comfort-class bus that Dave had rented from a company he found on the internet. Called Cargado, this van rental business was the creation of the Spanish billionaire entrepreneur and visionary Juan Cargado. He created a special fleet of fifteen-seat, glossy-pink passenger vans for American tourists, the name of which he had splashed across the side of each bus. In bold pea-green cursive letters, it read, *Lleno de Americanos Tontos.* With Spaniards overwhelmed and angered by the explosive number of tourists, the brightly colored van was outfitted with an AI box that both directed the driver to less crowded areas and alerted residents about the passengers who were on board. Cargado also had vans for Germans (glossy yellow with *Lleno de Alemanes Exigentes* on the side) and Brits (glossy pea-green with *Lleno de Británicos Ruidosos*). Spaniards, especially those who reside in cities that get a steady supply of foreign visitors, absolutely adore the program. Vans for other population groups that Spaniards found irritating awaited capital investment.

A Lutheran, the Reverend Ken Leslie, was replacing Dave as their customary driver for this pilgrimage. Ken was the only O'Postle with a Spanish bus driver's license and the only one with experience operating a van through the narrow streets of Iberian cities, something he got a few years back while serving as a mission volunteer in Spain. Ken's role was to transport Spain's five Lutheran pastors back and forth to Hanover in Germany for monthly meetings and team-building retreats.

In addition to the Methodist pastor Reverend Dave Tucker and the Lutheran Reverend Ken Leslie, the Twelve O'Postles also included three Baptist preachers, Reverends Ben Boyle, Billy Barker, and Bob Bending; an Episcopal Rector, the Reverend Sarah Priestly; two more Methodists, the Reverends Jim Mayer and Sue Moyers; two Presbyterians, Reverends May Presley and Princeton Newport, III; Reverend Ron Morgan, himself a Christian Church (DOC); and former mortgage banker Ed Steale, an Independent and nonaligned minister.

Ken pushed the electronic start button, revved the engine, and led the group in a new Lutheran-based hymn written for this special pilgrimage to Santiago. Roughly following the tune of *A Mighty Fortress Is Our God,* they sang with great joy-filled sarcasm:

> Has our liturgy gotten too stale, is it time for major reform?
> Our hymns are all from centuries ago, is it time to sing something new?
> Who says that this is so, was it some hired pollster?
> Yet some members remain, would change make them all go?
> So let's keep things as they have been.

"Who's got the directions?" Reverend Princeton Newport asked. "We're in a foreign country, and I don't wanna get lost."

"I do. And don't worry, I know how to get us there," Reverend Leslie said. "The bus is outfitted with this way-cool AI program that automatically directs us to where we need to go. See?" Ken held up a box that he pulled from its dashboard docking station. It had a screen that displayed a map with specific directions. But once he removed the box, the bus shut down, the lights turned off, and its on-board loo door was locked with Reverend Ron Morgan inside.

"Help," he yelled. His voice was muffled and could hardly be heard.

"If you're okay with it, I am too," Princeton said.

"Where's Ron?" Sue asked, a little worried. Before anyone started to look for him, Ken reinserted the AI box into its docking station and restarted the bus. The lights switched back on, and the bathroom door unlocked itself.

"Why'd you lock me in the loo?" Reverend Morgan was angry.

"Sorry," Ken said. "I didn't realize that would happen when I pulled the AI box." Ken hit the accelerator, exited the parking lot, and, following the AI directives, headed out of the airport complex.

After roughly thirty minutes, they were leaving the Madrid metro area. Looking at the highway signs, however, Reverend Newport became a bit concerned. "You sure about those directions? We seem to be heading south. I thought Santiago was west."

"I'm just following the AI program's directives. It alters the route when the main highways get backed up or a place gets too many tourists. I'm sure it'll take us on the best route."

"Well, okay," Princeton said. "Did you tell the AI program that we're not like other tourists?"

"I think the program will get us to where we need to be." Ken felt very confident.

"Who's got the first story for this part of our journey? Dave asked.

"I'm up first," Reverend Ron Morgan said. "I call my tale, *She Is Risen, Indeed,* and my text is John 10:10, a text we should all know by heart. With a twist, I'm using the Geneva Bible as my translation. My congregation gave me a copy of it for my birthday, and I like it a lot."

"Is that a new translation?" Reverend Ed Steale asked. "I've never heard of it."

"Nope, it's an old one, quite old in fact. It came out in 1560," Reverend Morgan said.

"Has it got all those thees and thous and haths and 'eths like the King James?" Ed asked. "I much prefer more modern versions."

"A bit more of them. I think."

"I'll stick with the New International. I like to understand what I'm reading."

Reverend Morgan walked to the front of the bus. He smiled at his fellow clergy members. "My story has mystery, archaeology, and mummies," he said, describing the tale. "And most importantly, it is about having life in abundance."

"I tell you, after Holy Week, I could use a little less abundance," Reverend Priestly said. "I'm feeling hung, drawn, and quartered."

"Me, too," Dave added. "It was nonstop all week long."

"Way too much abundance," May laughed. "I am so ready for a break."

"On with the story." Dave was ready to hear Ron's tale.

She Is Risen, Indeed

The thief cometh not but for to steal, and to kill, and to destroy: I am come that they might have life, and have it in abundance.

(John 10:10 Geneva Bible, 1560)

It is rare that someone remembers seeing Constance B. Dalrymple. Soft-spoken and unassuming, she has managed the books of St. Fillup on the Bypass Episcopal Church without a single error and without missing a single day of work for ten years. Always clean, always tidy, always dressed in a twinset and pencil skirt from her favorite shop, Ann Taylor, she keeps the church business operations running smoother than the nighttime waters of Lake Allatoona. Yet, most people who come to visit the church's rector, the Reverend Imani Austen, walk right past the hard-at-work Constance without ever noticing her; visitors can easily recall her workspace but are hard-pressed to remember what Ms. Dalrymple actually looks like. Constance didn't get out much and, to no one's surprise, lived all by herself. She was a complete mystery to everyone.

Last December, at the St. Fillup's employee Christmas party and secret Santa distribution, Constance received a gift that would change her life forever. Always held on the second day of December, no one knew how transformational a simple secret Santa gift could be—not Reverend Austen, not anyone at the party—especially not her secret Santa, Sabbath school superintendent Maggie Dean—and not even Constance herself, no one.

Two weeks earlier at the November staff meeting, Maggie had drawn Ms. Dalrymple's name from the secret Santa name basket. When she saw that she got Constance, her heart sank. "Oh no," she thought. Constance was the one name that no one wanted to draw. No gift in the past decade, as far as anyone could remember, had piqued Ms. Dalrymple's interest, let alone any curiosity; not a CD of holiday music, a box of premium chocolates, a bottle of sherry, a basket of fruit, fancy stationery with matching envelopes, not even a book of poetry; nothing did the trick. This year, however, Maggie believed she had a hit. One day last summer, Maggie had seen a deeply focused Constance quietly reading the rector's copy of the *Journal of Bible and Church Archaeology*. "Wow, you really like archaeology," she said to Ms. Dalrymple.

"Yes, Maggie, I do find it stimulating," Constance replied.

At the December 2 gift distribution, Maggie handed Constance a square white envelope. "I hope you like it," she said as the other partygoers looked on with low expectations.

"Thank you, Maggie. I am sure I will like it," Constance said in her gentle voice. Constance folded the envelope and slipped it into her purse. She smiled at Maggie. "I'll look at it more carefully when I get home." She then took a small sip from her cup of punch and sat quietly for the remainder of the party.

Feeling disappointed over her response, Maggie said to herself, "Oh well, another Dalrymple dud. Why do we do this every year?"

Mrs. Dean did not know it at the time, but her secret Santa gift would infuse into the St. Fillup bookkeeper a rebirth in spirit more powerful than anything she had experienced from the best team-building exercise or motivational speaker in any of the previous ten years (and there had been many). Later, reflecting upon the astounding transformation of Constance Dalrymple, Rev. Austen would call to mind what Paul had written in Romans, ". . . be transformed by the renewal of your mind." Indeed, every staff member and every person who attended St. Fillup on the Bypass Episcopal Church would soon see that there was something drastically different about Constance B. Dalrymple.

Saturday morning found Constance enjoying her coffee and a warm walnut muffin while seated at her prized, yellow-topped, chrome-legged kitchen table. Inherited from her parents, the table was the only kitchen table Constance had ever known. It sat in the back of the only kitchen that she had ever known in the only house in which she had ever lived; a very tidy yellow-clapboard, single-story bungalow that had belonged to her parents. Using her grandmother's letter opener, she carefully opened the square white envelope that contained her secret Santa gift. Constance, always frugal, saved the envelope and put it in the reed basket where she kept used envelopes for lists, notes, and reminders.

"Maggie Dean has given you the gift of a one-year subscription to the *Journal of Bible and Church Archaeology*," Constance read aloud, softly. "This must be the journal's motto: *Haec phrasis est pura nuga; volebamus videri sapientiores quam tu.* It sounds Latin; I wonder what it means?" The letter was signed by Chief Archaeologist Dr. Johnson Jones Johnson. Also, in the envelope was an article about recent discoveries in the catacombs of ancient Rome. "Oh, how fascinating," she whispered. Constance smiled for the first time in several months. There was still one thing left in the new subscriber packet.

"Hmm, what's this?" she wondered. It was a flyer filled with pictures of catacombs, Roman sarcophagi, and a few ancient wall frescos. The other side of the card caught her attention. In bold Roman font, the title bar read, "The Chance of a Lifetime—An All-Expense-Paid Trip to Rome With an Exclusive Tour of the Ancient Christian Catacombs led by the World-Renowned Archaeologist Dr. Johnson Jones Johnson." More details about the trip, including the hotel, airfare, and transportation, as well as a link to a website where the reader could complete the online entry form, were noted in fine print. "Someone will be very lucky," she thought to herself.

Constance finished her breakfast, cleaned the dishes, gathered the envelope contents, and put them in the empty gifts-received folder in her filing cabinet. It was 9:30 a.m., and as with every Saturday of every week at 9:30, it was time for a trip to the grocery store.

While driving to Crowgers, the only grocers she had ever frequented, she couldn't stop thinking about the all-expense-paid trip to Rome and the exclusive tour. The thought of going on such an adventure left her giddy with excitement. She felt like a playful puppy jumping around a grassy backyard, a sensation new to Constance. While pushing the cart up and down the aisles, completing her grocery list on the back of a used envelope, the exciting pictures of the Christian catacombs as well as the thought of being led by Dr. Johnson Jones Johnson gave her goosebumps. Then, waiting in the checkout line, her eye caught the latest issue of the *Hollywood Stories* magazine on the large display of periodicals. Its cover included a picture of Harrison Ford from the movie Indiana Jones. She imagined herself being led through ancient Roman tunnels by a dashing brown-fedora-wearing archaeologist. "Enter the contest, you fool," she thought to herself. "What do I have to lose?"

Once home, Constance put the groceries away, folded her reusable bags, and put them in the reusable bag basket located in her kitchen pantry. Without wasting another moment, she went straight to her gifts-received folder and retrieved the *Journal of Bible and Church Archaeology* gift subscription documentation. She found the contest entry information and went to her computer on the desk located in the corner of the parlor.

On the journal's website, she saw more fascinating pictures of archaeological sites; she found the page for the contest entry and started to complete the online form but then stopped. Constance heard her mother's tired voice in her head. Her heart sank; the message was paralyzing: "You know you won't win, so why bother?" Then, her father's voice entered her mind: "You can't get something for nothing, and if it can go wrong, it will." She remembered him saying that to her whenever she made a decision. And things did go wrong for her father, like the time he was pulled over for speeding; his just-purchased, too-good-to-be-true deal, previously owned, top-of-the-line Lincoln had been stolen the week before from a New Jersey mob boss.

Like a nonstop audio loop, both messages kept playing in her head, over and over. Letting out a sigh, she looked around the parlor and remembered being in the same room with her parents, sitting on the same furniture, and watching the same television shows week after week. Constance turned back to the computer screen and looked at the ancient frescos that covered the walls of the catacombs. At that moment, she felt a powerful, irresistible draw from the magical spirit of archaeology; it pulled her out of the monotony of her past and present and into a mesmerizing world that she so much desired to experience for herself. "No, I probably will not win, mother. But I am going to try."

Constance completed the online entry form and clicked the submit button. "And yes, father, if I win, something will go wrong." She printed her entry receipt, gathered her gift subscription and contest entry documents, and started to file them in the gifts-received folder. She stopped herself, smiled, and instead filed everything in the vacation folder. "Sometimes you do win, and sometimes something does go right," Constance thought to herself.

Old Rome is congested, even without tourists (and the occasional *Journal of Bible and Church Archaeology Review* contest winner). Taking a taxi from the Roma Fiumicino airport to her hotel located on the Via Santa Caterina da Siena, Constance found riding in the back seat of a speeding Fiat Panda zipping through the exceedingly narrow streets in the heart of the old city an experience she did not want to repeat. "I'll walk everywhere, if I have to," she thought to herself. "I'm glad I brought my sensible walking shoes." Speeding through the crowded streets, they dodged pedestrians, oncoming traffic, outdoor café tables, sidewalk vendors, and construction workers, finally reaching their destination on a road not much wider than the Fiat itself.

Wet from rain, the taxi's tires had difficulty gripping the historic millennia-old cobblestone pavement when they got to the hotel; they were going so fast that the little Fiat Panda came to a sliding stop a few dozen yards past its front door.

"Didn't we pass the hotel?" Constance asked the driver in her soft voice. "Can you please back up?"

"I-a no can-a backup, Signora," the driver said. "The street-a, she's a one-a way the way I'm-a going." He turned to look at Constance. "You walk-a that-a way," he said, pointing to the way they had come.

"Can't you go around the block?" Constance quietly pleaded. The rain was starting to get heavy, and she didn't relish the idea of walking.

"It would-a forever take-a," replied the driver, shaking his head. "It's-a too much-a maze, and we-a have no block around-a to go."

When Constance got out of the car, she realized that the taxi driver had placed her suitcase on the front seat; it blocked the meter. "That'll be-a one hundred-a Euros, only cash-a, please. You get-a suitcase now," he said, patting its top. She didn't see him clear the meter totals. Constance pulled her suitcase from the little Fiat and walked around to the driver's side.

"A hundred Euros is a lot of money," she thought to herself, handing the driver a one-hundred Euro note through the open window. He kept looking at her with his hand open. "Tip, I guess," she thought. She handed the driver another one-hundred Euro note, asking for eighty back.

"With a big grin, the driver said, "Thank-a you." He sped off, leaving Constance standing in the rain and without any change.

"I have a lot to learn," she said to herself. "Nevertheless, something always happens." Constance hurried to the hotel; the wheels of her suitcase made a loud clackety-clack sound that echoed off the buildings on the narrow street. Not only did she look like a tourist, but the loud noise she made drew the attention and stares of everyone, inside and outside. She also found it hard to simultaneously walk fast and keep the suitcase balanced; several times it flipped on its side when a wheel hit a spot where a paving stone was missing. The moment Constance got to the hotel, the rain stopped; she was thoroughly drenched but still in good spirits. "I sure hope the room's nice, with a hard bed, and a hot shower." Pulling her suitcase up two ancient marble steps, she entered the hotel through an ornate seventeenth-century doorway.

"You must-a be Signora Dalrymple," the hotel manager said with a warm smile. "We heard-a you coming up-a the street, and we are-a so glad-a you are-a here." He was standing behind a very old counter that had been part of the very old hotel since it first opened for business on the second day of December in 1612. "You are-a very much-a wet, Signora."

"And exhausted," Constance said. "I hope my room is ready."

"We have-a for you-a the best-a room on its-a floor. It's-a no charge since you-a are winner. Dr. Johnson Jones Johnson, he has-a for you taken care of-a everything, he and the Journal."

"Thank you." Constance felt greatly relieved, though she was now starting to shiver and longed for a hot shower.

"He-a will in the morning be here-a to pick-a you up, 9:00, maybe-a little before or maybe-a little after." The manager handed her a very large, old iron key. "You have-a room 2-12, floor duo, room numero 12."

"Where's the elevator?" Constance asked. She was exhausted and didn't want to use the stairs.

"I'm-a so sorry; we-a do not have-a the elevator. We are-a too old." The manager pointed to the ornate marble stairs. "I hope-a you not-a mind."

Room 2-12, though small with not much light, was beautiful. She went to the window and opened the blinds to look outside. About five feet in front of her was the brick wall and the open window of the building next door—a parochial school for young children. A class was in session, and several of the children noticed Constance looking through her window. They started laughing and waving.

"Hello," Constance called out. She smiled and waved back. A nun in a black habit appeared, apparently the teacher; she was not at all happy at the distraction from her lesson for the day. She gave Constance a ferocious glare and shook her fist and then grabbed one of the children by the arm. Constance couldn't hear what she said to him. The other children, wanting to avoid the same fate as their classmate, turned away from the window and pretended not to have seen Constance.

Constance closed the blinds, feeling shocked at her first encounter with the Roman parochial educational system. She then emptied her suitcase, putting the contents into a very old wooden dresser. She had a hot shower and afterwards got in bed and fell into a deep, deep sleep.

Bam! Bam! Bam! "Constance! Are you in there?" someone yelled. Bam! Bam! Bam!

The yelling and pounding on her door woke Constance. She sat up, her heart was pounding, too. From the light, she could see that it was early in the morning.

Bam! Bam! Bam! "Constance!" the person at the door yelled again. Bam! Bam! "We need you, now!"

Constance got up quickly and put on her bathrobe. She went to the door and looked through the little peephole. A man who seemed like he could be Dr. Johnson Jones Johnson was on the other side of the door.

"I'm here," Not used to yelling, Constance raised her voice as best as she could. "Is that you, Dr. Johnson?"

"Yes, it's me. There's been a change in plans, and we need you urgently," he replied, not yelling this time.

"Okay, give me a minute to change."

"I'll be waiting for you in the lobby. Please hurry!"

Ms. Dalrymple didn't like being rushed. Yet, at the same time, she sensed something exciting was about to happen. She looked at the clock; it said 7:30 *LUNEDÌ*. "I thought the manager said they were going to pick me up at 9:00." She almost stuck her head out the window to see what the temperature was like but realized that it would be a bad idea. She didn't want to get the school children in trouble again. "I wonder why Dr. Johnson is here so early. They did say it might be a little before 9:00, but this is an hour and a half!"

Constance got dressed quickly, donning her sensible touring outfit, complete with her sensible shoes that she bought for the trip from REI. "Okay, no time to make the bed, just the teeth and hair." She was in the habit of giving herself instructions when she was tense and in a hurry. In a flash, she was out the door and heading down the marble stairs to the lobby and a waiting Dr. Johnson Jones Johnson. To her surprise, Constance felt the esteemed archeologist did indeed look a lot like Harrison Ford from the *Indiana Jones* series.

"Constance, so sorry for the rush, but like I said, we have had a change in plans." Dr. Johnson was already heading to the door. "My car's out front," he said, over his shoulder.

"I'm ready," Constance said, following close behind.

Constance and Dr. Johnson hopped into his tiny yellow four-door Fiat 500. The archaeologist started the car, stomped on the accelerator, and the two sped down the narrow road before them.

"You mentioned a change of plans," Constance asked.

"No catacomb tour today. I need you to go with me to the Rome registry office. I need a witness."

"I'm to be a witness?" Constance was confused.

"Yes, but first we have to pick up Priscilla."

"Priscilla, who's she?"

"That's a long story. Dr. Boson accidentally left the Quickener on last weekend, and she's alive now. We never thought that would happen." Dr. Johnson quickly looked at Constance. "Dr. Kirk, our historian, and Dr. Boson, our physicist, are with her as we speak."

"Dr. Kirk and Dr. Boson are with Priscilla?" Constance asked. She stopped talking for a moment as they made a very sharp turn, barely missing some café tables and nearly running over a German tour group who had to jump into a doorway to avoid a trip to the hospital. "Who is Dr. Kirk, and who is Dr. Boson?"

"Dr. Catherine Kirk is the historian, and Dr. Michael Boson is the physicist in my catacomb project. We need to interview Priscilla before she goes back."

"Why are we going to the municipal registry office?"

"Priscilla needs an identification card so they don't deport her."

"I'm so confused. Why do we need to interview Priscilla?"

"We have to record what she remembers; otherwise, it'll be lost again."

"And that's where Dr. Kirk and Dr. Boson come in?"

"No, just Dr. Kirk. We need you to take notes. Dr. Boson is the one who got her here."

Constance was feeling very confused. "Maybe this will all make sense soon," she thought to herself.

Having arrived at the Registry office in the Rome municipal building, Constance, Dr. Johnson, and Priscilla took their seats in the waiting room. Being third on the waiting list, they hoped to see a registry clerk quickly. With the completed forms, letters of reference from the *Journal of Bible and Church Archaeology*, and the results from a fingerprint criminal background check in hand, Dr. Johnson thought things should go quickly.

"I think we have enough documentation so they won't have to ask Priscilla a lot of questions," Dr. Johnson said, looking at Constance. "That might be bad for us if they do." Dr. Johnson turned to Priscilla. "Remember, don't say anything about your being kicked out of Rome," the archaeologist whispered to Priscilla. "That was long ago, and it happened to a whole bunch of people."

Constance was starting to feel nervous. "I hope they're not up to no good."

"Priscilla Apostoli," a clerk announced, signaling she was ready. Dr. Johnson didn't mention to Constance that he had made up a last name for Priscilla. Apostoli sounded good enough to him and to Dr. Kirk.

The trio followed the clerk to her spartan office and sat down in front of a worn metal desk.

"Your papers, please-a." Dr. Johnson handed the documents to the clerk, who took several minutes to read them.

"These-a look-a to be in order." The clerk looked at Constance. "You-a Priscilla?"

"No, she is," Constance said. She pointed at Priscilla.

"So, no one-a recorded your-a birth-a?"

Priscilla was very nervous, having never dealt with a modern government clerk. Dr. Johnson responded for her. "The town where she was born was abandoned years ago," Dr. Johnson said. "I'm trying to help her get settled here in Rome."

"Where has-a she been all these years?" the clerk asked Dr. Johnson.

"She lived in Greece for a while and then Turkey. She and her husband made tents."

"Where's her husband?"

"He's deceased."

"Has-a she been a widow long-a?"

"A very long time," Dr. Johnson said.

"I-a should-a be asking-a Priscilla to answer my-a questions directly, Dr. Johnson, not-a you-a." Looking at Priscilla, the clerk wanted more information. "You-a didn't complete-a your birth-a date on the form-a. What-a year born were you-a?"

"Nine, I think. It could have been eight. I'm pretty sure it was nine, though," Priscilla replied.

"Nine-a what?" the clerk asked.

"Just nine," Priscilla replied, getting a little irritated.

"I can't-a put-a just-a nine in the year box-a. What-a decade?"

"The first one," she replied. "The 36th year of Augustus."

"Augustus? Augustus who?" Getting frustrated, the clerk turned to Dr. Johnson. "What-a she-a talking about-a?"

"I told you she was from a small town that's since been abandoned. Just enter 69."

The clerk wrote 69 in the box. "Okay, what-a month?"

"Sextilis."

"She means August," Dr. Johnson clarified.

"Okay, I've-a got everything." Finally satisfied and wanting to move on to the next applicant, she stamped the form and officially approved an ID card for Priscilla. "You'll-a have an electronic card in-a six-a weeks," she said, handing a receipt to Priscilla.

"What's electronic?" Priscilla asked.

"I'll tell you later," Dr. Johnson said. "Let's get back to the lab." Constance had a lot of questions.

"Dr. Johnson, can you please tell me what's going on?" Constance started to think she should have stuck to her parents' approach to life. "I was supposed to get a tour of the catacombs, not go to a government office. Besides, I haven't even had breakfast yet," she thought. They were sitting in a small conference room at the Archaeological Museum of the Ancient Church, a few blocks from the Vatican.

"Okay, let me explain all of this to you, and then the five of us will go get something to eat. But before I forget, we have a big meeting tomorrow morning." Dr. Johnson Jones Johnson paused, took a deep breath, and continued. "Okay, here we go. Dr. Boson left the Quickener on for a whole weekend . . ."

"Quickener? What's that?" Constance cut him off mid-sentence.

"It's Dr. Boson's creation. We wanted to see what ancient artifacts looked like when they were first made, especially clothing, shoes, bits of food remains, things like that. So, after a lot of trial and error, Dr. Boson invented a device that beams photons combined with the God particle at ancient artifacts. After a few seconds, the objects return to their original appearance." Dr. Johnson paused again in order to gather his thoughts. "He named his invention 'The Molecular Protonization Quickener,' and everything went great until the weekend before last."

"That's the weekend you mentioned that the Quickener was left on?"

"Yes. It was pointed at mummified remains. When Dr. Boson went home for the weekend, he forgot to turn the machine off."

"Then what happened?"

"Before I tell you, you must keep all of this top secret. I called your pastor at St. Fillup yesterday, and she assured me that you could be trusted." Dr. Johnson seemed more like a spymaster than an archaeologist.

"I'm listening." Constance was sitting on the edge of her chair. "I will not say anything to anyone unless you tell me."

"Good. When Dr. Kirk and I got back to the site on Sunday, we saw that the Quickener was still on and it had been on for three days. And instead of a mummy, we found Priscilla. She was wrapped in new-looking cloth and was sitting on the edge of the sarcophagus, feeling very confused, very hungry, and most amazing of all, she could speak very good English."

Suddenly, everything made sense to Constance. "So, are you telling me that the Priscilla for whom we got the identification card approved is the same Priscilla from the New Testament?"

"Precisely."

"The one that was a friend of St. Paul?"

"Exactly."

"This is very hard for me to believe." Constance thought for a moment. "What about Aquila? Why is he not here?"

"The Quickener was not pointed at him. Besides, Priscilla wants to go back. She feels she was risen prematurely."

A horrifying thought came to Constance. "Are you planning on raising anyone else? I mean, they're people we wouldn't want to ever see again."

"Once Priscilla goes back, Dr. Boson will destroy the Quickener. We definitely don't want that machine falling into the hands of the wrong people." Dr. Johnson got even more serious. "Could you imagine if the CIA or MI6, or even worse, the Russians got their hands on that thing?"

"When is Priscilla going back?"

"She agreed to be interviewed by a super-secret select group of scholars tomorrow morning. Then, after lunch, she's going back to Aquila."

Dr. Kirk and Dr. Boson wandered into the room. "Let's go get something to eat," Dr. Boson said. "We're all hungry."

Constance, Dr. Johnson, Dr. Kirk, Dr. Boson, and Priscilla left the museum to look for a good place to eat. "I feel like Italian," Dr. Johnson said.

"We're in Italy," Dr. Kirk reminded him. "They don't have Italian restaurants here. I know of the perfect place; it's an intimate café around the corner that never gets any tourists."

Ristorante Emily Dickinson saw its first customers on December 2, 1945. It was opened by a thankful Italian chef, Matteo Grato; a restauranteur filled with gratitude for the American troops and their help getting rid of the fascists and for kicking the Nazis out of his beloved Rome. A soldier from Amherst had shared with Matteo the poem *I Died for Beauty*, which became the inspiration for his new café.

"Very few people know about this place," Dr. Kirk told Constance. "I find it so peaceful, and people come for its simple menu and gentle atmosphere."

"Gentle and peaceful is definitely not in vogue where I'm from," said Constance.

"And not where I came from, either," Priscilla added.

"And you're from Rome?" Constance asked Priscilla. She waited for the server to take their lunch order before continuing, "I guess Rome has changed a lot," she laughed.

"It doesn't stink like it did in my day. Oh, Lord, it was so foul back then. Corinth wasn't nearly as smelly. That's where the love of my life, Aquila, and I met Paul."

"How did you end up in Corinth?" The three project team scholars already knew the answer to the question. Since she didn't get her catacomb tour, Dr. Johnson thought it good for Constance to get better acquainted with Priscilla.

"We got kicked out of Rome when Claudius was emperor. There was a lot of tension in the Jewish quarter when we started evangelizing. So, everybody got kicked out."

"That's terrible."

"So, you met Paul in Corinth?"

"Yes, we had a tent-making business there, and we gave him a job."

"I remember reading that Paul was a tentmaker."

"Yes. But he wasn't very good at it; he sure thought he was, though." Priscilla laughed. "Paul was much better at evangelizing. Aquila always had to double-check Paul's work before it went to a customer; I was really glad when Paul spent more time preaching and teaching."

"What was Paul like?"

"Well, in all honesty, he wasn't good-looking like my Aquila."

"Really?"

"Paul was a lot shorter than Aquila, bald, and his legs were kind of crooked. His eyebrows met at his nose too; that gave him a sort of intense look, but he was an angel. He loved to laugh and tell jokes, too. He could be full of himself sometimes, though."

"He wrote about having a thorn in the flesh, I remember," Constance said. "Was it a physical disability? That's what a lot of scholars think."

"Heavens no, he stuck himself with a tent needle; it went in deep under his fingernail and got badly infected. He prayed three or four times for it to heal, but the infection lasted for several months. Aquila and I thought we'd have to amputate his finger. That's when Paul realized his tent-making skills left a lot to be desired."

"Didn't you follow Paul to Ephesus?"

"Well, sort of." Priscilla seemed peeved at the question. "Ephesus was a bigger city than Corinth, had a lower cost of living, cheaper housing, better schools for our kids, lower taxes, and all-in-all, it was a better place for tentmakers. So, Aquila and I decided to move there, and Paul came along with us." She paused for a moment when the server put lunch on the table. "That's when Paul shaved his head. It didn't help the way he looked one bit, and I never understood why he did it. All he would say was that it was for a vow."

"Maybe he was a Mason," Constance suggested. She whispered to Dr. Kirk, who was seated next to her, "It says in Acts that Priscilla and Aquila accompanied Paul." They both chuckled.

"I heard that," Priscilla said in a friendly tone. "Paul had a tendency to be a little on the alpha side, if you know what I mean. But we still loved him dearly."

When Constance, Dr. Johnson, Dr. Kirk, Dr. Boson, and Priscilla finished their meal, Dr. Johnson asked for the check. "My treat," Dr. Johnson said. Priscilla wondered about the small card that the archeologist had given to the server. She had expected him to hand over a bunch of bronze coins. "I'll explain how we pay for stuff later," he said to Priscilla.

"We're going back to our hotels for the evening," Dr. Kirk instructed everyone. "Constance, Dr. Johnson will pick you up tomorrow morning at 7:30, and we'll all be back at the museum for breakfast and to prepare for the morning's discussion and interview. And Constance, you'll need to take copious notes."

"Who will be there?" asked Dr. Boson.

"We have a super-secret select group of seven historians and New Testament scholars. They come from Sweden, the Philippines, Nigeria, Peru, Japan, India, and Canada. The scholars were chosen because they all share a common ancestor with Dr. Johnson and, according to their online DNA profile, they have the same genetic propensity towards discreetness as has our Dr. Johnson."

Dr. Johnson added two things to the instructions. "After the meeting, Priscilla will be going back and then, Dr. Boson, you will destroy the Quickener. Is that understood?" He was very serious.

"Yup," Dr. Boson replied. "It's a goner."

Constance, Dr. Johnson, Dr. Kirk, Dr. Boson, and Priscilla got up and headed out the door. They did not notice the cleanly shaven, shadowy man wearing a dark grey suit, starched white shirt, and a blue tie seated by himself at an adjacent table. He had been recording their conversation on his cell phone using a super-sensitive microphone. He followed them outside at a distance.

"First, let me welcome you to this super-secret meeting." Dr. Johnson Jones Johnson was at a lectern greeting the distinguished participants. Seated at a table behind him were Priscilla, Dr. Kirk, Dr. Boson, and Constance. "We have with us today seven Bible and church history scholars who are the most trustworthy and discreet teachers I know, and they have traveled from across the globe to be here with us today. Please stand when I call your name." Dr. Johnson paused after each person was announced. "Dr. Johanna Johansson from Malmö Theological Seminary; Dr. Jonamiento Joannadoro of Baliwag School of Theology; Dr. Johnadan Johnaporo at Osogbo School of Theology; Dr. Juana Juanalosa with Arequipa Institute of Religion; Dr. Yohanashida Johanokatou, Gamagōri University; Dr. Janya Sharmajon of Pimpri-Chinchwad University; and Dr. Jean Jeanadeu from Portage La Prairie School of Religion."

Dr. Kirk got up and walked to the lectern as Dr. Johnson took his seat at the table. "You all know about our super-secret guest, Priscilla, most recently of Corinth and Ephesus, by way of Rome. She will be returning to Aquila in several hours, so we do not have a lot of time to record her recollections of Paul and the first years of Christianity." She turned to Priscilla and smiled.

Priscilla smiled and waved at the audience. "Good morning," she said.

"I will take your questions, one at a time. There will be no interrupting, no challenges to the comments Priscilla makes; we are only here to record her recollections. Am I clear?" Dr. Kirk paused for a moment and looked at each of the seven distinguished guests. "Let me also introduce Constance B. Dalrymple from St. Fillup on the Bypass Episcopal Church. She is giving up an all-expense-paid exclusive tour of the Christian catacombs so she could be here with us to take notes of our conversation." The audience cheered and applauded Constance.

Constance stood up and waved at the group. "Good morning," she said with newfound pride and self-confidence.

"Thank you, Constance," Dr. Kirk said. "Okay, first question." Dr. Sharmajon was first to raise her hand. "Yes, Janya."

"Priscilla, Paul leaves me very confused about the role of women. At one point, he says that we're all one in Christ, suggesting a radical equality like he wrote in Galatians. But he writes in 1 Corinthians and 1 Timothy that women should keep their mouths shut in church. What did he really teach?"

Priscilla thought for a moment. "Paul's attitudes towards women changed quickly after he wrote to Timothy and to the church in Corinth." She smiled as she remembered dealing with Paul. "After he wrote those two letters, Paul received a very stern letter from me. Everybody called my letter *Priscilla the Apostle to Paul.* He also got two other letters, one called *Lydia the Apostle to Paul,* and another called *First Phoebe.*" She then started laughing. "After getting those three letters, he wrote Galatians. I think that should answer your question. I don't suppose any of you have ever read the letters Lydia, Phoebe, and I wrote to our dear friend." Everyone in the audience shook their heads.

"They must have been lost," Janya said. "They were never added to the canon."

"Johnadan, your question."

"Did Paul ever make it to Spain? Did he travel anywhere else that we do not know about?"

"No, Paul never did go to Spain," Priscilla replied. "He did, however, travel to Britannia the summer after he arrived in Rome for the last time." The scholars looked surprised and started whispering to each other.

"Where in Britannia did he go?"

"Londinium and Liverpolium; he established churches in both of those towns. In fact, the best and most authoritative letter he ever wrote was to the four Beedles of Liverpolium, to Ioannis, Paulus, Giorgius, and Anulius." The scholars looked confused.

"That epistle must have been lost, too," Janya said.

"Johanna, your hand is up." Dr. Kirk pointed to Dr. Johansson.

"Which of the letters attributed to Paul did he actually write?" Dr. Johanna asked.

"I don't think he wrote any of them." The room was suddenly silent. "He always dictated his epistles to somebody else, Tertius, Apollos, or Timothy, for example. He got into the habit of using a scribe after he stuck a tent needle into his finger, right under the fingernail. As I told Constance yesterday, it became an infected mess. Clearly, tent-making was not his calling. When he got better, sometimes he would add personal thoughts or a greeting at the end of the epistles."

"Oh heavens," Johanna said. "That must have hurt like hell."

"The famous thorn in the flesh," Priscilla said. "He was a proud man and did not like being dependent on anyone."

Dr. Kirk was about to call upon Jean when she noticed four ominous, shadowy-looking, clean-shaven men in dark gray suits standing in the back of the room. Dr. Johnson noticed them, too. He stepped to the lectern and whispered something to Dr. Kirk.

"We are going to take a five-minute break. Priscilla needs to use the facilities. She'll be right back," Dr. Kirk said.

At that moment, Dr. Johnson took Priscilla by the arm. "Follow me, now!" he said to Constance. The three of them hastily exited through the back door of the room, ran down the hallway, darted out of the museum, and hopped into Dr. Johnson's little Fiat.

"I guess several people needed a bathroom break," Dr. Kirk said to the scholars.

It took a few minutes for the four shadowy men to realize that Priscilla, Dr. Johnson, and Constance were not coming back. "Let's go," the one who had been at the restaurant said. They ran across the conference room, heading in the same direction as Dr. Johnson and his two companions.

"They won't get away," another of the ominous men said once they were outside. They got into a shiny black BMW SUV. Given the power of their vehicle, it didn't take long for them to catch up to Dr. Johnson, his companions, and his sputtering Fiat.

Dr. Johnson pushed harder on the gas pedal of his Fiat 500 than he ever had since purchasing his beloved little yellow car. They sped down the Via del Corso, crossed the Piazza Venezia, bouncing down steps and sending tourists and vendors fleeing for their lives. They veered onto the Via dei Fori Imperiali and went around the Colosseum, but the black BMW SUV was always right behind them. They made a sharp right turn onto the Via Delio Vibenna, knocking over a display of flowers and two metal stands holding postcards; the shadowy men in the BMW followed close behind. Dr. Johnson knew their only chance at escaping was by heading into the ancient neighborhoods of Rome and through its maze of streets too narrow for the big black BMW SUV. They made a very sharp left turn onto the Via Capo d'Africa, running through a flock of pigeons that were trying to enjoy a lunch of discarded trash left by some American tourists. Dr. Johnson didn't know that once they crossed the Via Celimontana, their street would become one-way, heading in the opposite direction. Dr. Johnson looked over his shoulder at the BMW SUV; it was only inches from touching his Fiat's bumper. When he turned around to look forward, they were heading straight for a Volvo delivery truck coming towards them; there was no time to avoid a collision. Priscilla and Constance screamed.

Zrp, zrp, zrp. . . Zrp, zrp, zrp. . . Zrp, zrp, zrp. The hotel telephone in room 2-12 was making an electronic noise that constituted a "ring." Zrp, zrp, zrp. . . Zrp, zrp, zrp.

"Hello?" a very groggy Constance said, answering the phone.

"Ms. Dalrymple, this is your-a wake-up-a call." The hotel manager was on the other end of the line. "It's-a 8:00 and it's-a beautiful day-a."

"Wake-up-a?" Constance mumbled.

"Yes-a, Signora, Dr. Johnson Jones Johnson will-a be in the lobby at-a 9:00, maybe-a little before-a and maybe-a little after-a."

"I'm alive?" she asked.

"Of course-a you are-a alive-a. And it's-a beautiful day for the tour-a," he replied and hung up. "What does-a she mean, I'm alive-a?" he wondered. "She must-a be sick."

Constance got up from the bed and wandered into the bathroom. She splashed cold water on her face and looked into the mirror. "What a dream," she said. "It was so real." She brushed her teeth and took a shower.

She found her sensible touring outfit and sensible walking shoes where she had left them the night before and got dressed. Heading down the marble stairs to the first floor, she saw Dr. Johnson Jones Johnson waiting for her. Wearing a New York Yankees baseball cap, shorts, a wrinkled, half-tucked-in white Oxford shirt, mismatched socks, and purple high-top Converse All Stars, he did not look anything like the Fedora-wearing Harrison Ford she had been expecting.

"Dr. Johnson?" asked Constance, walking up to the man in the Yankees cap.

"You must be Ms. Dalrymple," Dr. Johnson said. "It's a pleasure to meet you. Are you ready for your tour of the catacombs?"

"I am so ready," she replied. "I've been so looking forward to this!"

"I have a taxi waiting."

They headed out the door and got into a little Fiat Panda taxi. Constance noticed it was the same driver who had dropped her off the day before.

"*Buongiorno*." The driver suddenly realized who he was greeting—the same woman from yesterday and the famous Dr. Johnson, her tour guide.

"Hey, I remember you!" Constance said.

"Your-a ride yesterday, it shoulda been for free." The driver did not want to get on the bad side of the renowned archaeologist; he had come to depend upon the business that came with his equally renowned museum. "I-a have-a some money for-a you." Before Dr. Johnson could ask any questions, the driver handed Constance two one-hundred euro notes.

"Thank you for returning my money," Constance said, putting the cash back into her wallet. "And I appreciate the free ride."

"Our first stop is the Catacomb of Priscilla," Dr. Johnson said, enthusiastically.

"Is that where she and her husband Aquila are buried?"

"No," Dr. Johnson replied. "Tradition holds that a different, lesser-known Priscilla was buried there along with thousands of Christians from the second and third centuries." Dr. Johnson was quite excited.

"I can't wait to see it," Constance said. "Will Dr. Boson be there?"

"Who?"

One week later, Constance was back at her desk with a stack of business transactions, memos, documents, and mail to sort, enter, and process. Later that day at the monthly staff meeting, everyone noticed that Constance had a different attitude. She spoke up and looked people in the eye when speaking. She was not going to settle for being unnoticed again.

When asked about her adventure in the catacombs of Rome, she spoke of the frescos, artifacts, and wonders of the ancient city. At the same time, however, it was Priscilla that she thought most about. Though it was all in a dream, experiencing an adventure with the bold and outspoken first-century saint gave Constance a newfound desire to live a fuller and more spirit-filled life. That afternoon, she turned in her two-week notice to the Reverend Austen.

"What are you going to do without us?" the rector asked her.

"I am going to be a New Testament archeologist!" she replied enthusiastically. "That's what I'm going to do."

Ron took a bow as the other O'Postles applauded. That is, of course, with the exception of Ken, who was driving.

"Thank you, fellow clergy. I appreciate your applause."

"Well, that was a surprise ending," Ken said. "I never thought it would all be a dream."

"I don't buy that stuff about Paul changing his views towards women." Reverend Ed Steel jumped into the conversation. "There's no way Paul would have been pressured by Priscilla, Lydia, and Phoebe; it never would've happened."

"There's no way he would have traveled to Britain, either," Reverend Princeton Newport added. "Most scholars say he did go to Spain."

"Look, it's a story about a dream," Ron said. "Don't get so upset. I'm just making a point. Men dominated women back then; it's clear to me from Acts, however, that not all women allowed themselves to be dominated."

"I agree with Ron," Reverend Sue Moyers said. "Acts was written by a man and therefore probably overlooked a lot of the contributions by the women in the early church."

"And, who knows, maybe Paul's attitude towards women did improve over time," Reverend May Presley added. "I don't believe that anybody knows with absolute, total, complete certainty which of Paul's letters came first, anyway."

"Personally, I find it hard to reconcile Galatians with First Corinthians or First Timothy if I believe Galatians came first," Reverend Sarah Priestly said. "I appreciate your story."

"That's not what I learned in seminary," Princeton said. "But you have an interesting theory."

"Don't forget the story was about finding abundant life in the midst of a moribund existence. Constance was a downtrodden woman, pushed low by domineering parents and a community that overlooked her contribution."

"And I see you just had to slip in the Beatles, didn't you," Sally said. "I guess you're saying they're timeless," she laughed.

"I couldn't resist," Ron said. "And yes, they are timeless."

"Are those mountains to our left?" Sarah asked. "Shouldn't they be on our right?"

"I'm following the AI directives," Ken said. "I feel fine. So should you."

"Okay, who's next? Let's get moving with our stories," Dave asked.

"I'm next," Reverend Ben Boyle said. "My text is Luke 9:23 from Today's New International Version. My tale, called *By Invitation Only*, is a story of greed of the highest order. I hope y'all enjoy it!"

By Invitation Only

Whoever wants to be my disciple must deny themselves and take up their cross daily and follow me.

(Luke 9:23 TNIV)

"Holy smokes, Paul, where'd you get that fancy card?" Raymond Lee was watching his prayer partner pay for their breakfast at the Crisscross Diner in Alpharetta, Georgia. It was a beautiful October morning, and the shrimp and grits were terrific.

"It's my new credit card; I got it a few days ago." Paul was feeling slightly embarrassed about Raymond seeing his crème-de-la-crème of credit cards. "This's the first time I've used it." Paul felt good because life was good; his credit card was validation.

"It's incredible," Raymond said, taking the card from Paul after it was tapped on the payment terminal. "Wow, this thing's heavy. It's metal, huh?" Embossed across the top of the credit card in gold letters were the words, *The True Cross Indulgence Card*®. A smaller marketing motto was on the bottom, also in gold: *Indulge yourself!* Pictured in the middle of the card was an old rugged cross that, to the touch, felt a little bumpy; at the foot of the cross were thirty Double Eagle gold coins in three neat stacks. "I'd sure love to get me one," said Raymond.

"They're by invitation only." Paul took his card from Raymond and put it back in his Goyard wallet. "Maybe you'll get an invitation, too." Paul then thought to himself, "Fat chance, Raymond." If Paul felt a bit embarrassed over having a premiere financial instrument in his wallet, he still took great pride in the fact that he was worth more than any other member of their parish, St. John of the Cross.

The True Cross Indulgence Card® was the brainchild of Junius P. Morgan and the newest product from the Atlanta-based Carion Bank and Trust of America's Secret Banking Division. Recently promoted Division Executive Vice President, Morgan's success creating a new faith-based Christian Stable Coin called *The Manger Coin*® added a lot to Carion's profits, making CEO Andrew Mellon-Collie III, the board of directors, and the investors very happy. Sensing an opportunity to extract more fees from the ultra-wealthy Christians of all types, Morgan created an alternative to the invitation-only-anodized-titanium-black Atlantic Express *Poseidon Card*® and convinced Mr. Mellon-Collie that they could charge higher initiation and annual charges—currently only $10,000 and $5,000 respectively for the secretive Poseidon Card.

"My focus group of ultra-wealthy-conservative-Christian-businessmen-who-own-Panamanian-registered-yachts-with-heliports-docked-in-the-Cayman-Islands-who-pay-no-income-taxes says we could get away with charging an initiation fee of $100,000 and $25,000 for an annual fee," Morgan told his fellow executives at the January Secret Banking Group management meeting. It was an unusually cold and grey cloudy day when the card was formally announced to the team. "We'll make tons more money on each card than Atlantic Express does, a hell of a lot more. And, and this is a big *and,* our credit cards will be untouchably exclusive." Junius, like a peacock, pushed his chest forward and stiffened his back. He was proud beyond measure. It was but ten years ago that his recycled-plastic Atlantic Express Green Card got cancelled during a period of unemployment. Today, he felt on top of the world, pulling the rug out from under Atlantic's (and the world's) most prestigious credit card.

"How in heaven's name are we gonna justify a $100,000 initiation fee, let alone $25,000 each year thereafter?" a very skeptical Kendra Rheebar, Vice President and Senior Secret Client Manager, asked.

Excited and sitting on the edge of his chair, Carion CEO Mellon-Collie was attending the meeting at the request of Junius. He looked at the Secret Banking head, "Well, Mr. Morgan, tell everybody about your secret sauce!" CEO Mellon-Collie too had always wanted to outdo Atlantic Express, especially since he had not been able to get his own invitation-only-anodized-titanium-black *Poseidon Card*® and felt embarrassed at having to make do with a seventy-five percent stainless-steel Platinum Card. "I was poor in spirit because of Atlantic Express," Mellon-Collie thought, "but starting today the credit card kingdom is mine!"

"Like the *Poseidon Card*®, our premium credit card will be genuine titanium," Junius explained. "But embedded in each of our cards will be a tiny piece of the True Cross—the real thing, the one that Pilate hanged Jesus on."

CEO Mellon-Collie jumped in, "That's the secret sauce." With a huge smile of satisfaction, he slapped the table with his right hand. "Every time customers stick this card into their wallets, they are literally taking up the cross of Jesus! No bank can match that."

"I don't think that's what Jesus meant. . ." Kendra started to say.

Fortunately for Kendra, Bob Tuepher, Division Manager for Card Operations, interrupted her. "How on earth can we put a piece of the True Cross into a credit card?"

"It's easy," Junius replied. "It's all a part of the card manufacturing process. A machine sticks a tiny spec of the cross into the card as it's stamped."

"But where are you gonna get enough True Cross bits anyway?" Herbert Stickseller, Division Manager for Product Marketing, asked.

"Y'all are joking, right? Kendra asked. "We can't be serious about doing this, can we?"

"We're totally serious," Junius responded. "We now have a whole inventory of True Cross bits. They are literally in the head-office vault as we speak."

"I'm not sure I follow you, sir," By now Kendra was totally gobsmacked.

"Mr. Mellon-Collie and I put several dozen boxes containing pieces of the ancient wood relics in the head-office vault yesterday morning," Junius explained.

"I am afraid to ask, but how did we find the relics?" Kendra was afraid to ask, truly afraid. She could see that Mr. Mellon-Collie was getting tired of all the questions.

"Haven't you heard of eBay, Kendra?" Mr. Mellon-Collie thought the Secret Banking leadership team was a little slow and should be excited about the profits that would come from embedding bits of the True Cross in credit cards.

"For the past six months, we've had an army of straw buyers scooping up True Cross relics from eBay and other websites, some of them dark," Junius added.

"But Sir, how can we be certain they're real?" Bob asked.

"Does it really matter, Bob?" Junius responded. "As long as they look real and we say they're real, the customers will believe they're real. And if the customers believe they're real, they'll pay us $100,000 to have it in their credit card."

"The Bible does say, 'Faith is the substance of things hoped for,'" CEO Mellon-Collie added. Looking at each person on the team, CEO Mellon-Collie became very serious. "Junius and I need you to be on board with this, now." The room got very quiet while Andrew spoke. "Our Secret Banking Division is gonna dominate the ultra-wealthy Christian market with the most exclusive faith-based card in the world, bar none. Research indicates it is an untapped market for moneymaking and our most efficient path to a glorious future of massive dividends, exploding capital gains, and big fat bonuses. If you're not with Junius and me on this, you know which door to go through when you leave."

"I apologize, Sir. I didn't mean to imply that I wasn't supportive of our new credit card." Herbert was nodding as Bob spoke, "I was just surprised about the 'secret sauce.'"

Kendra had an uneasy feeling about the new card but decided to keep her thoughts to herself. And besides, both she and her husband were happy with their Atlantic Express green cards and didn't want a special invitation from Atlantic or any other bank for anything.

"I'm on board, boss, one hundred percent!" Herbert Stickseller said. "Watch Atlantic Express get downgraded by analysts when they see what we're sticking in rich folk's wallets." Like Junius and Andrew, Herbert hated Atlantic Express. A year ago, he applied for a Platinum Card, and they sent him a Gold Card instead. Apparently, Herbert's credit score was one point too low.

"Me too," Bob added enthusiastically. "We're gonna kill Atlantic by gettin' all the wealthy Christians." Bob couldn't wait to get started, especially since Atlantic Express didn't approve his Gold Card application last month. It was the third time he had tried to get one, and he too was mad at them.

"Mark my words," Junius said, wrapping up the conversation. "Christians with the most money are the ones who will pay the most money to have the most exclusive credit card. And now, the most exclusive card in the world today is the one that literally touched the hand of Jesus, although I'll be the first to admit it was while he was being crucified."

"That couldn't be helped," Herbert said. "What other relic did Jesus touch that would fit into a credit card?"

"Look into that for our next product, Herbert," CEO Mellon-Collie said. "Let Junius know what you come up with."

Standing up from the table and making eye contact with each person, Junius had another peacock moment. "The harvest is ripe for *The True Cross Indulgence Card*. This is the day that the invitations will go forth."

"I think that we should close with a brief prayer," CEO Andrew Mellon-Collie III said. As if on cue, everyone in the meeting stood up and held hands. "This moment is truly sacred, for this is the day the card has made. Let us rejoice and be glad in it." He continued, "Our product will go forth literally bearing the cross of Jesus." The staff closed their eyes and bowed their heads. "Father God, you have blessed Carion. Father God, you have blessed this product. And now Father God, bless the people worthy of indulging themselves with this credit card. Amen."

"I've got to get out of here," Kendra thought. She got up from the table and left the meeting while the others lingered.

"Thanks for taking care of dinner tonight, dear." Kendra gave her husband Mark a long hug. He had been waiting for her at the door. He could tell something was amiss when she called, letting him know she was on her way home.

"Tough day, huh?"

"Let me change. I sure could use a shower, too. We'll talk over dinner."

Mark finished setting the table. This night, he put together a collection of Kendra's favorite comfort foods—fresh macaroni and cheese, green beans with almonds, and a cupcake. He also used the placemats and cloth napkins they bought on their honeymoon and stemware that was a gift on their first anniversary from his wife's now-deceased parents.

When Kendra sat down at the dining table, she let out a loud sigh, looked at her husband, and shook her head. "This is so wrong," she said. "I can't go on like this."

Mark's heart stopped beating. "Is she going to leave me?" he thought to himself. "Good God, I thought we were happy together." Mark finally said something, "Tell me what's wrong, sweetie."

"I know I should be supportive, but my faith is pulling me away from this," she responded. "I don't think I can keep it up."

"This can't be happening," Mark kept thinking. "We go to Mass every week; we pray together. Maybe she's becoming Baptist like her sister." Mark got out of his chair and knelt in front of Kendra. "If you need me to become Baptist, I'll do it. I don't want you to leave me," he pleaded.

"What are you talking about?" Kendra asked. "Why would I want to leave you, and why would I need you to become Baptist?"

"You said you couldn't keep this up. I thought you were talking about us. And then your sister. . ."

"Mark, no, no, no. You've got it all wrong. I was talking about work."

"Oh." He got back into his chair. "So, tell me about work." Mark's heart was beating again.

"Honey, I don't know where to start. The place has become crazy. They're coming out with this new, extremely expensive credit card that they say will have a piece of Jesus's cross embedded in it."

Mark's jaw dropped, and his mouth was wide open. His lips couldn't formulate any words. If Kendra didn't know where to start, Mark didn't know how to respond. Then it dawned on him: "She's teasing me," he thought. He smiled at Kendra and started laughing. "You really had me," he said aloud.

"I'm not kidding. They're issuing credit cards with True Cross relics inside. They're calling it *The True Cross Indulgence Card*® and they're gonna charge a fortune for it."

"Is that even legal?"

"Yes. But I can't be a part of it. It's so wrong." She looked at Mark. "I can't quit because we need both our incomes. We'd lose our health insurance; we wouldn't be able to pay our mortgage and our car note—we could lose everything. I just feel trapped."

"Look, Carion is not worth getting sick over. If you need another job, you'll get work. In the meantime, we could make do." Mark was very supportive.

"Love, I'm having lunch with our priest tomorrow. Maybe he can offer some advice," Kendra said.

Father Toirdhealbhach Flanaganagan, a native of Graiguenamanagh, the small but long-named village on the east side of Ireland, was the much-loved priest of Roswell, Georgia's Holy Cross Catholic Church. Recruited from Ireland to be the senior pastor of the Atlanta suburban church, no parishioner could pronounce his name, so everyone affectionately called him Father Flan. It took a while to get used to his heavy Kilkenny accent, but once they did, they found his sermons and homilies quite moving—no priest before Father Flan had been able to communicate the practical side of Christian living with as much passion as he.

"Lord and Savior Jesus, Holy Mother of God, blessed Joseph, and all of the saints of yore!" Father Flan was in shock. He and Kendra were having lunch at the Crossroad's Café, a diner that sat along the perpetually clogged Roswell Road. The priest was about to take a bite of his sandwich at the moment when Kendra mentioned *The True Cross Indulgence Card*. He dropped his tuna sandwich into his lap, spreading mayonnaise, mustard, tuna, cheese, and tomato onto his newly washed cassock. His face grew redder than a Cardinal's skullcap. "No, no, no, no," the priest said repeatedly. "No, no, no, no."

"My boss at the bank says they've got dozens of boxes of True Cross relics in a vault, probably enough to last them several years. He and the CEO don't care if they're real or not. They said it was all a matter of faith—that if the bank says it's a genuine piece of the True Cross and the customer believes it, that's all that matters."

"Why are they doing this?" Father Flan asked.

"Money! Just so they can get an initiation fee of $100,000 and an annual membership fee of $25,000. They want to create the most expensive, exclusive credit card in the world, and they're targeting very wealthy Christians."

"It is hard to believe they would do this." Not even in his wildest dreams could Father Flan have imagined such a thing as *The True Cross Indulgence Card*.

"The guy who created the card said something I thought was kind of sick." Kendra was trying to recall how he put it. "Now I remember; 'they are selling a credit card that has literally touched the hand of Jesus.'"

In the twinkling of an eye, Father Flan's face went from Cardinal skullcap red to Pope skullcap white. For a moment, Kendra thought her priest was going to pass out. "Kendra, I need to speak to the archbishop about this, as soon as possible."

His Excellency Archbishop Gregory Fernández dropped his chicken salad sandwich into his lap, spreading mayonnaise, mustard, chicken, cheese, lettuce, and tomato onto his freshly washed and starched white cassock. His face turned rosy-red, much like the color of his amaranth skullcap. "Oh, blessed Savior," he cried, shaking his head. Tears rolled down his cheeks.

Father Flan was having a private lunch with the archbishop at his residence the day after he met with Kendra. At the moment his excellency was about to take a bite out of his sandwich, Father Flan told him about *The True Cross Indulgence Card®*.

"Never in my life have I heard of such a cynical and execrable use of Christian faith by a financial institution. It is an abomination, your excellency," Father Flan said.

"This is more than just an abomination; it's an abomination of desolation!" The archbishop understood the serious moral stench now emanating from Carion Bank.

"I hope we can stop this credit card in its tracks." Father Flan was concerned about an abomination of desolation spreading to other objects of devotion. Now that the bankers got their hands on pieces of the True Cross, next in line were bones, cloth, or other sacred relics from the saints of the church. "There would be no end to the bankers' profiteering," he thought.

"I am personally friends with his eminence Antonio Ghislieri," the archbishop told Father Flan. "We were in seminary together, and we've been friends for a long time."

"Should I know him?" asked Father Flan.

"He is the Cardinal Prefect of the Dicastery for the Doctrine of the Faith. I'll call him in Rome tomorrow morning to talk about this so-called *True Cross Indulgence Card®*. I think he'll want to bring an end to this abomination of desolation."

"What can he do?"

"Well, Father Flan, he can take it up with a tribunal; I believe the Dicastery has a meeting in a few weeks." The archbishop took a sip of water and thought for a moment. "What we have with this new credit card is either a doctrinal or a disciplinary abomination. With the help of their scholars and consulters, the Dicastery will make a moral judgement, decide upon a course of action, and send it to the Supreme Pontiff for review. His Holiness must approve their decision before they can make an announcement. He rarely goes against their recommendations."

"So, your excellency, do you truly think that His Holiness will judge *The True Cross Indulgence Card®* to be a great abomination of desolation?" Father Flan asked.

"Yes, Father Flan," Archbishop Fernández said. "And he'll be grateful that you brought it to everyone's attention."

Cardinal Prefect Antonio Ghislieri's tuna tramezzino slipped from his hands and fell into his lap, spreading mayonnaise, tuna, and olives on his clean white starched cassock. His jaw dropped, and his face became redder than his skullcap. With the Cardinal Prefect were his doctrinal and disciplinary secretaries, both of whom dropped their tramezzini into their laps, too. Seated in the Prefect's dark Renaissance-era office at an ancient wooden table, the very one where Galileo had his first grilling by the infamous Inquisition, the Dicastery Trio, as they called themselves, were in a virtual meeting with Archbishop Fernández, who had just described *The True Cross Indulgence Card®*.

"This is a very sad day in the life of the church." The Cardinal Prefect was the first to speak. "Brazen profiteering off one of the most venerated relics by a greedy bank looking to make a lot of money. This is the work of the devil."

"Not since the summer of AD 954 when Filippo Zamboni sold hundreds of bottles that he claimed contained the ink used by St. Paul has there been such a scandalous use of relics—Zamboni's 'Ink Hoodwink' scam sold hundreds of the bottles all over Europe." Disciplinary Secretary Monsignor Abbot Romano knew his history.

"That's not as bad as the time in the winter of AD 823 when Silvano Renzo peddled collections of twelve pairs of leather sandals that he guaranteed were worn by the Apostles at the Last Supper. The 'Sandal Scandal' sold enough to shod an entire Roman legion. That was worse." Doctrinal Secretary the Most Reverend Dr. Costello Galli knew his history too.

"No, no, no. What about the time in the spring of AD 722 when . . ."

"You've made your points, Monsignor Abbot and Reverend Dr. Costello." The Cardinal Prefect was ready to move on. "Your Excellency, Archbishop Fernández, we're thankful that you brought this to our attention. Your official notice of an abomination of desolation and supporting documentation you emailed to me will be before the College of Members next week. In light of the severity of this abomination of desolation, I will make certain you hear from us as soon as the Supreme Pontiff has added his signature."

Pope Sixtus VI was the first pope who had himself been a banker for a few years before God called him into the parish ministry. Even after the white smoke had signified his elevation to the position of Supreme Pontiff, leaving him with few places to shop and dine on his own, Sixtus VI insisted on keeping his own Atlantic Express Green Card. Every once in a while, he would put on his street clothes and sneak out of the Vatican to mingle with the regular people of Rome, oftentimes paying for their meals or food using his own Atlantic Express card. Many of his street friends, with great affection, called the very attractive pope "Sixy." It was on one of those escapades that Cardinal Prefect Ghislieri, using the secure Vatican messaging app, pinged the Supreme Pontiff with the following message, "Abominatio-Desolationis." His Holiness Pope Sixtus VI knew that something doctrinally was amiss and that waiting for him on his desk would be a wax-sealed leather folder containing the results of a very serious investigation.

"What's up, Sixy?" asked his friend and street vendor Marcus Aurelius. Marcus, the Pontiff, and several other vendors were sitting by a small brazier discussing St. John Chrysostom's Second Discourse on the Rich Man and Lazarus.

"I've gotta rush; a problem at the office," his holiness the Supreme Pontiff said. He bade farewell to his street friends and rushed back to the Vatican.

Pope Sixtus VI did not much like the official pontifical office space used by his predecessors. Designed by Michelangelo and decorated by Rafael back in 1520, it was cold; you couldn't get a strong cell signal; there were too many cardinals milling about with nothing to do; and the ancient furniture was very uncomfortable, especially the heavy marble desk chair that had hand-carved images of Adam and Eve on the back. Sixtus instead chose a plain, sunny room with a nice window that overlooked the Piazza San Pietro. He enjoyed watching the many pilgrims and tourists who came to visit the Vatican.

Sitting at his simple IKEA desk, Sixtus opened the wax-sealed leather folder that had awaited his arrival. Removing the stack of papers, he briefly read the cover sheet:

> From: Cardinal Prefect Antonio Ghislieri
> The Dicastery for the Doctrine of the Faith
>
> To: His Holiness Pope Sixtus VI
>
> At the most recent meeting of the Congress of the Dicastery for the Doctrine of the Faith, we examined the actions of Carion Bank and Trust of America violating canon 1190. The supporting documents, included with this summary, detail the bank's violation

> that constitutes an Abomination of Desolation that endangers the spiritual well-being of the faithful.

"Hmm, this seems very serious," Sixtus VI said to himself. With one hand, he picked up his egg salad panini, and with the other hand, he opened the report to the first page, which unfortunately was a facsimile of *The True Cross Indulgence Card®* along with the now infamous words of Junius P. Morgan: "The most exclusive card in the world today is the one that literally touched the hand of Jesus." Sixtus VI's panini slipped from his hands and fell into his lap, spreading mayonnaise, egg salad, and olives on his purple cassock. "Holy Mother of God."

"What the hell is this?" CEO Mellon-Collie was reading a letter to him from His Eminence, the Cardinal Prefect Antonio Ghislieri, the text of which stated:

> The Congress of the Dicastery for the Doctrine of the Faith met to conclude the extrajudicial penal process regarding canon 1190 and *The True Cross Indulgence Card®*. Carion Bank and Trust of America and its Chief Executive were found guilty of Abomination of Desolation, a finding subsequently submitted to the Supreme Pontiff, who concurs.
>
> Carion Bank and Trust of America, in its immoral appropriation of venerated relics, has created a perverse culture that favors greedy and unscrupulous business practices driven by selfish personal gain. Thus, Carion Bank and Trust of America and its Chief Executive have willfully violated canon 1190 and should immediately cease production of *The True Cross Indulgence Card®*.
>
> Clerics or laity engaging with Carion Bank and Trust of America by the use of its products or through employment with the institution are henceforth in rejection of communion with the church.

Mr. Mellon-Collie threw the letter across his office and rang Mr. Morgan. Without saying hello, he barked into the phone. "Junius! Do you know anything about a Congress of the Delicatesery?"

"Is that a restaurant? Are you thinking of eating there?" Junius asked.

"I don't know what the hell it is! I got an official letter from the Vatican, and some damn Perfect Cardinal says we're greedy and selfish and that we must stop issuing our new credit card. It talks about cannons and abominations of delusions." It was clear to Junius that Mellon-Collie was madder than a yellow jacket protecting its queen and he was making no sense. "Just get up here, Morgan. You need to read this!"

It took Junius less than two minutes to arrive at the CEO's office on the 24th floor of the bank's Peachtree Street office. "Hi Clio, the boss wants to see me."

"I've never seen him so mad," Clio, the CEO's Executive Assistant, told Junius. "Good luck." She buzzed CEO Mellon-Collie to let him know that Junius had arrived. "Mr. Morgan is here to see you, Sir."

"Send him in, Clio."

"Hello, Sir. What's this about a letter from the Vatican?" Junius stepped into Andrew Mellon-Collie's very formal office. One wall had bookshelves filled mostly with pictures of the CEO with various luminaries of the business and political worlds. Two sides of his office were glass windows overlooking Atlanta, and one wall was paneled, accentuated in faux brown leather with several trophy animal heads, all purchased over the internet.

"It's over there on the floor," Mr. Mellon-Collie pointed to a spot near the bookcase. "I am too pissed to read it. You look at it."

Junius walked across the room, stepping over a cease and desist letter from the Federal Reserve Bank of Atlanta president, two warning letters from the Federal Deposit Insurance Corporation, and one from the state banking commissioner that, from what Junius could see, mentioned *The Manger Coin®*. "Ah, here it is." Mr. Morgan picked up the letter and sat down next to the CEO's desk, hand-made out of Brazilian rosewood smuggled from the Amazonian Rainforest. "Hmmm," he muttered. Junius looked at his boss and said, "This is garbage."

"What do you mean?"

"First, I'm greedy, and I'm a firm believer in personal gain. So, if that's something to feel bad about, then guilty as charged. Second, in the Secret Banking Division, we created a culture in which our bankers are hungry for personal gain, too. Why else would they be in the industry? So again, guilty as charged."

"What about the issue of relics?"

"The church is the relic; our bank is the future. I say we keep up the momentum and make as much money as we can on this new card. Isn't that what our board and investors expect of us?"

"You're right, Junius. We can take this letter as a compliment. We wanted a groundbreaking, bold, and exclusive product. Judging from the cardinal's reaction, we did just that. I'm gonna nail it to my office door so everyone who comes will see it."

"Let those human relics try to stop us!" Junius said in a threatening tone. "Let's use the letter in our marketing, too."

"Okay. How?"

"Those socialist relics are really telling our ultra-wealthy Christian clients that they can't have a piece of the True Cross in their credit card if they want one. I'm gonna use parts of the letter to add a sense of urgency for people to respond to our application invitation."

"I like it!" said the CEO.

"The fact that the church doesn't want our customers to have *The True Cross Indulgence Card*® in their wallet will make more people want to get one while they can."

Junius started laughing. "That Cardinal actually accused us of being in it for the money. We're a big bank; why else would we be here?"

"That's ironic, isn't it," CEO Mellon-Collie said.

"Oh, I forgot to mention that Kendra Rheebar quit this morning."

"Did she say why?"

"Something about irreconcilable differences with her faith; it didn't make sense to me. Anyway, I don't think she was really one of us."

"I thought that, too," the CEO said. "In fact, I've thought that for a long time."

"Thanks for breakfast, Paul," Raymond said. They were standing in front of the Crisscross Diner talking for a few moments before going their separate ways.

"No problem. You can get the tab next time," Paul said.

"You never mentioned if there's anything I can be praying for you. I'm your prayer partner, after all."

"I can't think of anything. I'm in a great place, Raymond. Life's really good. I'm playing golf this morning, which I love. You could pray for my business; we're on a roll, and I think we can make even more money. My golf score could use improving, too. I guess I do have things you can pray for."

"Keep me in your prayers, Paul. I'm worried about what the future holds for me and my family. My wife lost her job, so we lost our health insurance. We're not gonna be able to pay both our rent and the COBRA insurance at the same time. I've gotta get my car fixed, and the kids—gosh, it's expensive to raise children these days."

"Will do," Paul said. His golfing start-time was in half an hour, and he was in a great hurry to get to his country club. "And don't get your hopes up for that credit card invitation. I doubt you'll get one." Paul slid into his red Ferrari Icona. The engine made a rumbling purr when he pushed the start button; Raymond stood on the sidewalk and watched Paul zip down Main Street.

Raymond let out a long sigh. He walked a little further down the sidewalk and got into his rusty yellow PT Cruiser. The engine made tired clanky noises when he turned the ignition, which cleared up after he hit the accelerator several times. "I wish I could afford to get this thing fixed." Raymond headed home, thinking to himself, "I wonder if I need an actual prayer partner. Paul is doing fine without me."

Meanwhile, back in Rome, the Dicastery Trio made an appearance at the Club Tivoli. In addition to their daytime work at the Dicastery for the Doctrine of the Faith, evenings were devoted to music. The three members of the Trio all shared a lifelong love of jazz, which they enjoyed sharing with the people of their ancient city.

"I wish it were not the case, but your story, Ed, is completely believable," Dave said.

"Y'all know that I once worked in mortgage banking," Reverend Steale said. "I based some of my characters on folks from my prior professional life."

"Real people?" Sarah asked.

"Yeah, Sarah," Ed responded. "And one of those real people was me. I know what it means to have a credit card be the definer of your self-worth."

"I've fallen into that trap, too," Princeton said. "It's not just the credit card but your car, your clothing, and more."

"When I took up the cross, or perhaps it's more accurate to say each day when I try to take up the cross, I have to set my mind on 'things above,'" Ed added.

"I'd like to point out that the threatening letter from Rome didn't stop Carion Bank from doing what they were doing," May said. "In fact, it encouraged them to work harder at it."

"And we can't forget about prayer partners Raymond and Paul," Ed said.

"Ed, do you think that in our churches, income and wealth create a barrier between believers?" Princeton asked. "Don't you think they can overlook their economic circumstances and be brothers and sisters?"

"That's a harder question," Ed replied. "Personally, I don't feel that The New Testament gives me much guidance there."

"It's hard to imagine a billionaire being an equal prayer partner with someone who is unemployed and close to bankruptcy," Sarah added.

"Acts never mentions prayer-partners. It does show believers sharing their possessions, though," May said.

"So, if you live in poverty and your prayer partner can afford a $100,000 credit card that sits in his $1,000 wallet, what should be shared?" Ed asked. "A meal out? A prayer for hope?"

"Let's leave that question for another time," Dave said. "Okay, who's next?"

"I'm next, Dave," Reverend Princeton Newport III said. "I am afraid that I'm only going to raise more questions for us, ones that we really can't answer for our congregations."

"I'm intrigued," Sue said. "Let's hear your story."

"I take as my text John 14:2–6, and I take them from the old 1901 American Standard Version of the Bible. As I share the story, my choice of this version should become self-evident." Princeton then took his place at the front of the bus. "My story, I call, *The Bird's Nest in the Belfry*."

The Bird's Nest in the Belfry

In my Father's house are many mansions; if it were not so, I would have told you; for I go to prepare a place for you. And if I go and prepare a place for you, I come again, and will receive you unto myself; that where I am, there ye may be also. And wither I go, ye know the way. Thomas saith unto him, "Lord, we know not whither thou goest; how know we the way? Jesus saith unto him, "I am the way, the truth, and the life . . ."

(John 14:2–5 ASV, 1901)

"I have something that I want to give to you," Miles said to his grandson, Robert. Miles, or Paps as he was known in the family, started laughing. "Your great-grandfather got it for perfect Sunday School attendance. I'll tell you in a minute why I'm laughing." Paps removed a small book from the top right drawer of his old leather-topped desk and handed it to Robert; it was a well-worn century-old pocket-sized, leather-bound American Standard New Testament. It had gilded page edges and a gold imprint on its cover. "His Sabbath School teacher gave it to him in 1907, I believe."

Robert, a high school junior, was spending the weekend with his beloved grandparents in the family home that had once belonged to his great-grandparents. It was a cool fall Saturday morning; he and Paps were in the quiet home office, talking about the family.

"Sabbath School, that's the same thing as Sunday School, right?" Robert asked.

"Yes, that's what they used to call Sunday School, long ago. You must promise me that you'll take good care of it," Paps handed the New Testament to Robert.

"Thank you, Paps. I'll keep it safe." No one had to tell Robert that the small New Testament was priceless; indeed, he would cherish it beyond measure for years to come.

"Your great-grandfather was the most honest and trustworthy man I ever knew. He truly believed that everyone was created equal, and he treated them that way, whoever they were and from wherever they came. And he and your great-grandmother lived a simple life; they were always happy with enough."

"I'd like to be the same way," Robert said. "In my youth group, we talk a lot about wealth, welcoming the stranger, and sharing with those in need."

"I wish everyone felt the same way," Paps said. "In our society, we don't talk about the causes of poverty; we don't welcome the stranger, especially those from another county; and we don't share with those in need."

"I wish it wasn't that way." Robert was somewhat sheltered from the harsher side of life, which concerned Paps.

"You're still young with much to learn. But we're getting ahead of ourselves." Paps smiled at his grandson. He knew the boy was perceptive and would better understand the world in short order. "I want to tell you why I laughed when I told you that your great-grandfather had perfect Sunday School, or should I say Sabbath School, attendance."

Robert looked at the New Testament and felt the softness of the worn leather cover. The old pages were becoming brittle. "So, why were you laughing?"

"I can think of only four times your great-grandfather was in a church during his adult life—my wedding, your great-aunt's wedding, your parents' wedding, and the Eldbrook Methodist Church Christmas Carol Singalong way back in 1951, or was it 52?" He thought for a moment, trying to remember.

"Wasn't he a Christian?" There was a tone of disappointment in Robert's voice. He looked at the New Testament again.

"You're getting ahead of the story, just wait," Paps replied. "Your great-aunt and your great-grandmother tried very hard to get him to go to church, but he wouldn't budge. He disliked church; he once told me that the only time the minister comes calling is during pledge week."

"I'm glad my pastor isn't like that."

"That's good," Paps smiled at his grandson. "Your great-grandfather also said that if he were ever to set foot in a church, the building would catch fire and burn down. Of course, he was joking." He paused for a moment to gather his thoughts. "Well, after years of badgering by the family and the minister, your great-grandfather finally agreed to attend a popular Christmas carol sing-along service that the family's church held every Christmas Eve. I remember that service as if it were yesterday! The candlelit sanctuary was packed, every pew filled, and folding chairs were added to the side aisles so they could squeeze in as many people as possible. They had a full choir with their special red and green Christmas season robes; the organist was there, and several members of the city orchestra brought trumpets and horns for when everyone sang *Hark! The Herald Angels Sing*. The altar was filled with poinsettias and garland, and the church's Christmas tree was so tall it seemed like it would touch the vaulted ceiling."

"It must have been amazing," Robert said.

"Yes, it was, but the one thing the minister thought was truly amazing was the fact that your great-grandfather was there. He was shocked. It was too bad your great-granddad had to leave early and quickly."

"He didn't stay for the whole service?"

"Nope, he didn't." Paps laughed so hard he started coughing.

"What's so funny about that?"

"No one at the church stayed for the whole service, either." Paps slapped his thigh and laughed harder.

"Why?"

"Well, long before the sing-along carol service began, early that spring, some birds decided that the church's bell tower made a good place to build a nest, right where the old wires for the Christmas lights were located. The church staff left the lights up there because that was a lot easier than having to take them down every year. So, after they turned on the bell tower Christmas lights just before the service began, the old wires heated up and ignited the dried-out bird's nest and started a fire. When the smell of smoke reached the narthex, the ushers yelled, 'Fire, fire!' and everyone rushed out of the building."

"Was anybody injured?"

"No, fortunately. The bell tower was made out of stone and though it created a lot of smoke, the fire was actually pretty small and easily contained."

"That was crazy." Robert started laughing with his grandfather. "They were lucky the fire wasn't worse."

"How true," Paps said. "It gets better—after being forced out of their warm and comfortable sanctuary, the pastor, the choir, and all of the church members had to stand outside in the freezing cold, waiting for the fire trucks to arrive. Folks fled the church, leaving their winter coats, scarves, gloves, purses, and if they bought them, their musical instruments, inside. Your great-grandfather looked at us and at the minister who was standing with us and said, 'I told you so.'"

"Was he angry with great-grandma or the minister?"

"Gosh no, he was laughing. He thought the whole thing was hilarious. The minister, however, wasn't laughing. He was angry. For that matter, so was your great-grandmother."

"What a great story, Paps. So, why didn't he like church?"

"I would rephrase your question, Robert. I wouldn't ask why he didn't like church; I would ask why he believed the church didn't like him."

"So, why'd he think that?" Robert asked. He was confused and feeling troubled now.

"I mentioned that your great-grandfather believed that all people were 'created equal' and had the right to 'life, liberty, and the pursuit of happiness.' It was the way he lived his life—I never knew him to cheat, lie, or hurt anyone, period. Yet, he was at his heart, an ordinary man who also had extraordinary questions."

"What questions did he have?"

"To answer that, I need to share with you some things about his life. You might not know this, but when your great-grandfather was a young boy, there were seven kids plus his parents living in a very small three-bedroom row house. He was only nine years old when his mother, your great-great-grandmother, got really sick with what they called consumption. Today it's called tuberculosis. They used to call it consumption because people who had it struggled to breathe, and they lost a lot of weight; it seemed like the body was consuming itself, hence the name. I cannot imagine how scary this would have been to your great-grandfather. A few days after his mother got sick, she passed away. I remember him telling me how they had the wake in their parlor; all the neighbors and many church members stopped by the house to pay their last respects and to see your great-great-grandmother one last time."

"How horrible that must have been."

"Yes, it was a horrible experience for him as it would be for any child."

"And for the person who died," Robert said.

"Well, yes, you're right." Paps smiled at his grandson. "In any event, his father, your great-great-grandfather, remarried three years later, and the family moved to a different part of town. I'll bet you didn't know it, but back then, most boys your age had to work full-time and didn't go to school much past the eighth grade. By the time he was your age, your great-grandfather had been working as a department store clerk for three years."

"It's hard to imagine not going to high school, let alone college."

"When your great-granddad was eighteen, he and his best friend decided to hitchhike all the way to Indiana to see the Indianapolis 500 race, which was in its early years. Can you imagine that?"

"What a crazy thing to do," Robert started laughing. "I cannot imagine doing that."

"Yes, it was a crazy thing to do. While there were a lot of roads back then, most of them weren't yet paved, never mind the fact that automobiles weren't as common as they are now."

"He had to have been pretty brave to do that," Robert said.

"Along the way, a newspaper article got their attention. You have to remember that back then, there was no radio, no TV, and no internet; everybody read the newspaper."

"I knew that, but it's still hard to imagine."

"Anyway, he read an article about the sinking of the Lusitania. Nearly 1,200 passengers—men, women, and children—drowned when the ship was torpedoed by a German submarine during World War I. It happened before the US got directly involved. The Germans said they sank the passenger ship because they believed it was carrying war ammunition. Everybody was furious at the Germans, and there was a lot of talk about the urgent need for more ships, especially ones that could be used for only cargo."

"I've never heard of the Lusitania," Robert said. "We didn't cover that in school."

"Well, you should know about it. 1,200 is a lot of people to kill. Your great-granddad and his buddy were angry at what happened and felt they had to do something. So instead of going to the races, they joined the Merchant Marines to help our country build ships and be ready in the event of war. They went to Duluth, Minnesota, for training and spent the next three years working on a ship that transported iron ore from Minnesota and Wisconsin to ports along Lake Erie, where there were a lot of new factories. When World War I was finally over, more than ten million people had died, civilians and soldiers."

"Did anyone else in his family fight in that war?"

"Your great-grandfather's brother ended up fighting in the trenches of France. He got mustard gassed during one of the fierce battles."

"Mustard gassed? What was that?"

"Robert, they sure do miss a lot of things in your history class." Paps looked at the wall for a moment and sighed. "Well, armies filled canisters with various chemicals; in the case of your great-grandfather's brother, it was sulfur mustard. Then they used cannons to fire them at their enemies. When the canisters hit the ground, they released poison gas that filled the air. The gas would burn the skin, eyes, and the inside of the lungs. While your great-grandfather's brother survived the war, his lungs were so damaged that he had to have an oxygen tank with him all the time—for the rest of his life! He spent his last years living with your great-grandparents because he got so weak that he needed a lot of help. In fact, he slept in this very room."

"I never knew about him," Robert said, looking around the room. "That was horrible."

"Mustard gas is banned now, as are the other kinds of military gas," Paps explained. "Most countries signed a treaty in 1925 called 'The Geneva Protocol' that banned those weapons."

"It's good they don't use that stuff anymore."

"After World War I, your great-grandfather came back home and got a job helping to manage a grocery store. A Jewish family that took him under their wing owned the store and got him started in the food business. He learned enough to eventually have his own store. But keep in mind, those were the days before Walmart and big national chain stores like Kroger and Publix. It was a lot easier to own your own business back then."

"There used to be individually owned grocery stores?"

"What do they teach you in school, Robert? Yes, individual people owned grocery stores, hardware stores, office supply stores, pharmacies, clothing, and more. Times were very different then."

"It's so different today. No matter where we go on vacation, you always see the exact same stores everywhere." A whole new world was opening for Robert.

"Let's continue the story." Paps looked at his grandson. "Are you ready for more?"

"Yeah, let's keep going."

"In January of 1922, there was a huge blizzard, the biggest one to ever hit the city. In fact, there was so much snow that the roof of the old

Knickerbocker theatre collapsed on the audience that was there watching a movie. The theatre was close to the grocery store where your great-grandfather worked. On the morning after the collapse, he walked by it on his way to work."

"How horrible. Were many people killed?" Robert asked.

"At least a hundred, if I remember correctly. And yes, it was horrible. Well, then as now, when there's a big blizzard, most people stayed home for several days until the streets were cleared, but your great-grandfather went to work anyway; he knew that people would need to eat, and he knew that the grocery store owner, Mr. Blumenthal, would need help running the store, even with everything buried under tons of snow."

"I can see why people felt he was so trustworthy."

"Ironically, the movie people were watching when the theatre roof collapsed was *Get-Rich-Quick Wallingford.*

"I wonder if you can stream that movie."

"It's an old silent film; I don't know about streaming it."

"A silent film?"

"Back then, movies didn't have sound; sound came later. But that's for another discussion."

"Really? I didn't know about silent movies."

"Let's keep going," Paps said. "Did you know about the Jewish refugees from Germany that our country turned away in January of 1939?"

"No, I never heard about it."

"Nine hundred women, men, and children were aboard a ship called the *Saint Louis.* The refugees were turned away once their ship reached the port of Miami; they were fleeing Germany because of persecution. We weren't the only country that refused them entry; they ultimately had to go back to Germany."

"Wow, that's terrible."

"Well, your great-grandfather and the Blumenthals were really angry; they knew that horrible things were gonna happen to the refugees, as you will learn in a minute."

"I think I know where this is going."

Paps continued the story. "By then, your great-grandfather had opened up his own grocery store, and he served his community all through World War II. He had a customer and close friend whose son, Ray, was a photographer in the Army Signal Corps. Towards the end of the war, Ray accompanied the US troops when they were liberating the German concentration camps where Jews were imprisoned and murdered. He took pictures of what the troops saw. Ray gave your great-grandfather several dozen photographs that included empty ovens with human bones, piles and piles of bodies on carts, and other things too horrific to describe." Paps paused for a moment to see how Robert was reacting to what he was saying. He seemed distressed but okay enough to continue the story. "Looking at just one of the photographs, there must have been at least a thousand emaciated dead bodies abandoned by the fleeing SS guards."

"This was the Holocaust, wasn't it?" Robert asked. "We didn't go into a lot of detail about it when we covered World War II in history class. I know that a lot of people died."

"Six million Jews died, Robert."

"Six million?" Robert asked. "That's so hard to imagine."

"It's hard to imagine until you look at Ray's photographs. Your great-grandfather kept those photographs in the same drawer with the Bible you're holding; a few pictures are of a camp where he and Mr. Blumenthal believed some of those refugees aboard the St. Louis ended up."

"I don't think I want to see them today. Is that okay, Paps?" Robert was a sensitive soul; his grandfather knew that the life he lived was sheltered in the peaceful suburbs.

"That's okay, Robert. You'll see them soon enough."

"Thanks, Paps." Robert looked at the worn New Testament and was very still and quiet.

"Robert, here's the point of these various stories. Your great-grandfather was an ordinary man who ran a grocery store, just like all of the thousands of other ordinary shopkeepers of his time. But with your great-granddad, there were things he witnessed during his life that left indelible impressions on his very being, on his soul." Paps paused for a moment to let his words sink in. "What he saw remained with him, always."

"I wish I had known him," Robert said.

"I wish you had, too, Robert. You're a lot like him." Paps continued, "And because of the things that he saw, I believe your great-grandfather had these extraordinary questions, deep and abiding questions to which he was always seeking some sort of explanation or way to understand why they had happened. Perhaps he knew that there was never going to be an explanation, I don't know. But I think this is why he held on to that New Testament you're holding for his entire life. It's also the reason why he couldn't see his way to being in church."

"I'm not sure what you mean, Paps."

"Your grandfather's soul was deeply troubled by what he had witnessed during his life." Paps looked at his grandson and thought for a moment. "And he also felt that his church didn't have a place for him or that he didn't fit into the congregation. I believe this was because his church never acknowledged or incorporated into its life the horrors that he encountered; no matter what was happening in the world around him, he knew his church would always be the same, that it would shut itself off from the people and things it didn't want to see. That's why he never attended worship services."

"That, I can understand, Paps," Robert said.

Paps paused before continuing. "Your great-grandfather knew that his minister didn't believe that he was a real Christian simply because he refused to come to the worship service on Sunday. But I think that minister was wrong. Do you remember when Jesus talked about the many mansions in God's house?"

"I do; we talked about that in youth group last week."

"I think the place in God's mansion that Jesus prepared for your great-grandfather was very different from the place that his church and his minister thought he had to have."

"I'm glad you told me about great-grandad." Robert looked at the New Testament again as a few tears formed in his eyes. "This Bible is really special."

"He held on to that New Testament, which clearly he read and cherished. I believe he found a path to that mansion. That's why the fire in the bell tower story was so funny to him, and to me. Your great-grandfather didn't find the path inside of a church, no matter how much his minister and family wanted him to. And the one time he agreed to go to church, and this is what really drove the minister crazy, the church caught fire and everybody had to flee the service; just as he had predicted."

"I like my church, Paps. It means a lot to me. But I understand why great-granddad wouldn't go."

"I'm glad. And I like mine, too."

"You've given me a lot to think about, Paps."

"You have your whole life to ponder such things. Attend your church, be a part of your faith community. But Robert, always keep your eyes open to life in this world and never be afraid of those extraordinary questions that will at some point arise."

"That's good to know. We usually want quick and simple answers."

"You're absolutely right, we do. But there aren't any, are there?" Paps said. "And there's one more thing to remember, Robert. Be ready for the bird's nest in the belfry."

"What do you mean?"

"What I mean is there will always be a day when something forces your church to go outside into a cold and dark world to face people and things it would rather not see," Paps said. "So be ready when that time comes."

"Wow, this tale wasn't so funny," Dave said.

"I'm sorry, my friends, but I've been reading a lot of history and have seen some things that have left me in a bad way," Princeton responded to Dave. "Six million Jews murdered in the Holocaust, two million in Cambodia in the 70s, and another million in Rwanda in the 90s. Now we're seeing the same thing in Sudan. For me, sometimes it's exceedingly difficult to see God's presence in history. Then I ask myself, 'Is God's action an enigma in my life, too?' That's what I've been thinking about."

"So, how do we, as church leaders, provide answers to those really difficult questions that have no simple answers?" Billy asked.

"Billy, do you mean individually or for the whole congregation?" Ben wanted to know for himself, too. "Quoting Bible verses can make things worse for people."

"Both, for people facing hard times and for people like the great-grandfather in the story who have witnessed or read about horrible things," Billy said.

"And for ourselves as well, I might add," May said. "I feel that genocide is the proverbial enormous elephant in the room that's always lurking in the background in my life of faith. Not once did we talk about it in seminary."

"It's always easier to ignore the world outside our individual churches and week after week only preach and pray about the things that are simple and easy to handle," Sue said. "Certainly, I'm guilty of that and I would wager that we all are."

"And then we brush aside those who, like the great-grandfather in the story, are true seekers," Jim said.

"To be honest with you," Ken said, "they scare me because I fear I can't help them."

"I wonder how many of our churches have classes called *Seekers* that are not really seeking anything," Dave added. "Sometimes we should call ourselves *Seaters*, believers who are not truly going anywhere." The ministers laughed a little.

"That was one of the points I was trying to make," Princeton said. "The congregation had to be forced out of Eldbrook Church to feel the cold, wintery world."

"Maybe it's when we're forced outside of our places of comfort that we can truly become seekers," May added. "It's a lifelong journey."

"Didn't Jesus actually say, 'Keep on seeking without stopping, and you will find?'" Princeton said. "And sometimes the seeking requires that we disrupt our ordinary routines."

"Then perhaps we shouldn't use the term, *Ordinary Time,* for the longest part of our liturgical calendar," May said. "It should be the *Seeking Time.*"

"There were other people who suffered—in the African slave trade, forced plantation labor, and later segregation and Jim Crow, plus the ethnic cleansing of our own indigenous people," Ed added.

"All supported by many in the church," Sue added.

"Well, I appreciate you and your tale, Princeton," Sarah said. "We're on our way to Santiago, and this is a really, really difficult conversation, a lifelong one at that. Let's continue this discussion, but later in the week."

"I appreciate you too, Sarah, and all of you," Princeton said. "I agree, let's continue the conversation. But now it's time for another tale."

"Who's got a turn at the storytelling now?" Dave asked. "Oh, wait, it's me!"

"Get up here, my friend," said Ken.

"I hope my tale doesn't upset any of you Presbyterians. I take as my text Luke 11:17. The title of my tale is, *Kirkin' o' the Columns.*"

Kirkin' o' the Columns

Jesus knew their thoughts and said to them: "Any kingdom divided against itself will be ruined, and a house divided against itself will fall."
(Luke 11:17 TNIV)

Founded on the seventeenth day of August 1760, two hundred years to the day when the Church of Scotland adopted the Scots Confession, the Great Highland Scottish Presbyterian Church of West Dairen, Georgia, has survived conflagrations, contagions, depressions, incursions, infestations, invasions, recessions, and many other manifestations of evil blight that the enemy could throw their way. Yet with each generation, the church always survived and looked forward to the Great Tribulation and the end of the world. "We're Scottish to the bone," the Reverend Hamish McKenzie said to Brenda Pierce, a religion reporter from New York City, when describing his congregation. They were in the minister's bare-bones office that, were it not for the fact that they entered the room from a hallway inside the church building, you'd think they were sitting in a colonial-era prison cell. He then sang to her a few verses from a hymn his great-great-grandfather had penned:

> In the fairest of days thy clouds of gloom dost fly,
> Our blessings of hearth and home are soon gone awry,
> At our heels a blow most foul is ever nigh.

Hamish smiled wistfully. "You can quote the hymn in your article if you like."

"What about the joy of salvation?" the reporter asked Reverend McKenzie. "Isn't that supposed to be a part of the walk of faith?"

"As God hath appointed some to glory, so hath God appointed others to destruction," Hamish explained, paraphrasing a text from the Westminster Confession. "My counsel is that you focus on confession and daily prayers for a sober hope that your appointment is to glory and not to destruction."

"Okay, Reverend McKenzie. I've got what I need," Brenda said. "Thank you for your time. I've got another interview to conduct." Feeling an urgent need for sunshine and fresh air, she left the pastor's dimly lit, dank office and called her editor in Manhattan. "You would not believe the conversation I just had. This guy makes a dour Puritan look downright Pentecostal."

Confessing is quite the tradition at Great Highland Church. Many, inside and outside of the faith, are familiar with Double Predestination, or Double P, a theological orientation typical of Scottish Presbyterians who are steeped in Calvinism. Many are not, however, aware of its related and uniquely Scottish Presbyterian practice called Dutiful-Diligent-Despondent Confession, or Triple D & C, a confessional practice model for believers who want a glory appointment at the by-and-by but who at the same time know their eternal fate might be, as Reverend McKenzie put it to the religion reporter, destruction anyway.

Following the Triple D & C model, even baptisms at Great Highland Scottish Presbyterian begin with a confession, as do confirmations, weddings, Sunday School classes, Bible studies, wedding anniversaries, potluck suppers, birthday parties, funerals, and gala events.

"We are diligent with the confession of our sins," Reverend McKenzie said to a group of new elders. "The only time we don't bow our heads is while we are driving."

A local Baptist preacher once jokingly told his members that all of the churches in West Darien had subcontracted the confession of sins to the gloomy folks at Great Highland Scottish Presbyterian, even the Roman Catholics. Shaking his head in wonder, he recently noted that, "Reverend McKenzie has stitched his church together with the twin feelings of pending doom and an ever-present need to apologize."

A native of Scotland and the sixteenth pastor of Great Highland Scottish Presbyterian, the lean, tall, long-necked, and wiry-haired Reverend Hamish McKenzie is certified in Double P and Triple D & C and is a strong proponent of the structure they provide to the practice of faith, as was his father, grandfather, and great-grandfather before him. And, like his forbears, Hamish hails from Dull, a small village in the Highlands of north Scotland. In fact, fourteen of the previous fifteen clergymen called to the congregation over its 260-year history were either born in or were the child of someone from the Dull area and were in some fashion related to the McKenzie clan; a requirement set forth in the founding 1760 charter of the church.

The historic Great Highland Scottish Presbyterian Church sanctuary has a high vaulted ceiling with seven rows of two-hundred-and-sixty-year-old loblolly pine beams that meet at the center peak; the fourteen beams are supported by columns, seven on one side of the church and seven on the other. Each column is dedicated to one of the fourteen clans whose ancestors founded the congregation. On the left side, starting near the pulpit, in the place of honor for the largest clan, is the MacMurkey column, followed by the related clans of MacGray, MacCheerless, MacDimly, MacDismal, MacSomber, and MacDrabie. On the right side, starting near the lectern, in the place of honor for the second largest clan, is the McDownface column, followed by its related clans: McGlumly, McDoleful, McDownsy, McCloudy, McBleakly, and McWoeful. Below each column name is a small plaque with the tartan colors of its clan. And from its steeple, Highlands Presbyterian proudly flies an enormous Church of Scotland flag; a banner with the white cross of St. Andrew against a blue background and a centered image of the bush that Moses saw, the one that burned but was not consumed. The flag is so large that big rig truck drivers can see it while driving over the Cathead Creek bridge on Interstate 95.

Every year, on the seventeenth day of August, Great Highlands holds its "1560 Scots Confession Anniversary Memorial Games and Potluck Picnic Celebration Gala," or simply the "1560 Day." There not being any other sporting events or fetes in West Darien, the church's annual summer gala, as Scots call such events, was the highlight of the summer.

"Don't you think it odd to include the words confession, memorial, and celebration all in the same title," Mayor Sam Pike said to reporter Brenda Pierce. He was a Baptist, and she was a New Yorker in town to cover this year's 1560 Day Event.

"I certainly wouldn't do that," Brenda said. "The day will be interesting; that's for sure."

"You're just in time to hear the opening sermon," the mayor said.

"Sermon?"

"Don't fret; he'll keep it short."

Even since the first 1560 Day Event one hundred years ago, the pastor of the Great Highland Scottish Presbyterian Church, following a lengthy

Triple D & C model prayer of confession, would offer a brief sermon celebrating the adoption of the Scots Confession in 1560. Fortunately, preparing the sermon was a simple task; Hamish and those before him merely chose an appropriate text from the *McKenzie Book of Sermons*, a compilation of homilies published by the family in 1859, the year Reverend McKenzie's great-great-great-great grandfather retired. This year, however, Hamish had to prepare a new text as the family book had gone missing.

Unbeknownst to the pastor, his eighteen-year-old son, Clydesdale, and a friend took the book to Jacksonville and sold it to an antique dealer for $25. Clydesdale told his father that he and his friend were going to check out some college campuses. Expecting to get upwards of $25,000 for the family book of sermons, the buyer explained to the boys that sometimes an object that is rare and priceless means that no one wants to buy it, and its value is so low it can't be determined. Over a barrel because they needed the $25 for gas to get back to West Darien, Clydesdale took the cash anyway.

"I thought I'd get a lot for that old book," Clydesdale told his friend. "So much for getting a new car."

"At least you won't have to explain to your folks where you got the money," Clydesdale's friend said as they headed home.

Meanwhile, back in West Darien, 1560 Day was getting underway.

"Let us bow our heads in prayerful confession." Revered McKenzie was holding the microphone close to his mouth. He got down on his knees and began, "Our heavenly creator, we ask your blessings on this day. . ." Ninety-nine minutes later, he ended the prayer, "In the name of your Son we pray, Amen."

"Why didn't you tell me the prayer of confession was going to be so long?" Brenda asked the Mayor. "I could have said my own prayer, had a nice lunch in Brunswick, and been back in West Darien in the same amount of time."

"It's the cost of having access to our event, that's why." The mayor explained. "If we're gonna let you cover the games, then you have to pay the price."

"And the price is kneeling in the hot sun through the longest prayer I have ever heard?"

"You got it, my friend. And each year they get longer."

"Thank heavens, there won't be a next year for me."

Standing next to Brenda was Calvin Knox McCloudy, a private at the nearby Army base and a member of the Great Highland church. "Is the world coming to an end next year?" he asked the mayor. "Are you thinkin' this could be my last competition?"

"Don't think so, Cal," the mayor said. "The government's still selling long-term savings bonds, and I'm still gonna buy me some."

"So you and the people-in-the-know think they'll still be a next year?"

"You got it, Cal," Mayor Sam Pike said. "I don't think you need to worry."

"Cal, when I told the mayor that there wouldn't be a next year for me, I wasn't saying I thought the world was coming to an end," Brenda told Cal. "I simply meant that I wouldn't be coming to the event next year."

"Thank God! I'm not ready for the rapture; I still wanna become a second-class private," Cal said. "Its gonna take at least another year or three. They keep sticking me with different sergeants, so I'm never sure."

Brenda pulled out her reporter's notebook and a pencil. "Anyway, Cal, what events are you competing in?"

"I'm doin' the Lolloby Loll . . . I mean the Loblolly Lob," he replied. "Thanks for asking."

"That's a tongue twister," Brenda laughed.

"He did pretty well last year," the mayor mentioned to Brenda.

"Thank you, sir."

"I have to ask, what exactly is a Loblolly Lob?" Brenda was looking at Cal.

"That's when you lob a loblolly log."

"What's a loblolly?"

"Look, there's one," Cal said, pointing to a very tall, very straight pine tree.

"So that's a Loblolly. I'll have to see your event! Are you doing anything else?"

"Yeah, the Banger Gobble."

"That's when you gobble a banger, I take it."

"A whole bag of bangers," Cal replied. "Whoever gobbles a big bag of bangers first wins."

"So, what's a banger?"

"It's kinda like a hot dog, only a lot thicker."

"What's the prize if you win?" Brenda asked Cal, taking notes.

"A free bag of assorted bangers and a box of instant mashed potatoes."

"I think I'll pass on that event," Brenda said.

"I'm also doing the tug-of-war; that's the last event. It's the MacMurkey clans versus the McDownface clans; we do it every year."

"You must come, Brenda," the mayor said.

"I wouldn't miss it for the world."

"After the tug-of-war, we have our picnic, too," Cal added.

"Scottish food, right?"

"Not necessarily. It's potluck. Lots of casseroles, salads, deviled eggs, fried chicken, you know, traditional church fare," the mayor said.

"You forgot Mr. MacDrabie's haggis," Cal said. "He always has two types, meat lovers and vegan."

"Vegan haggis? I've never heard of such a thing," Brenda said.

"It's mostly oatmeal and onions and pretty good. It's served with Mrs. McDownsy's neeps," the mayor replied.

"Did you say peeps, those yellow candy things?" The thought of a dish made with the sugary yellow Easter treat almost made Brenda get sick.

"No, neeps, it's mashed turnips," the mayor explained. "All that Scottish stuff gives me . . . well, I'd better not say."

"I've gotta get to my event," Cal said. "Hope to see you there!" He darted to the other side of the park where people were gathering around some long logs.

"I'll be there," Brenda yelled.

Meanwhile, Reverend McKenzie, having just finished a short sermon that no one could hear, wandered over to see Brenda and Sam. "Hello, Ms. Pierce and Mayor Pike."

"Is the day gloomy enough for ya," Brenda said, teasing the minister. In her ten years working as a religion reporter for a major New York City newspaper, she had never encountered a man of the cloth as dour as Reverend McKenzie. "I'm sorry, I should have been more respectful."

"As I was praying to the Lord a few minutes ago, he told me about your final predestination destination," Hamish said in a very serious tone. The faces of the reporter and the mayor turned white.

"You can't be serious," Brenda said, not a little angry at the minister.

"My dear, I am not . . . at all serious." Reverend McKenzie smiled at the reporter. "I've been waiting all morning to say that."

"So, you're not all doom and gloom, I see."

"Only most of the time."

"What are the other events for the day?" the reporter asked the Reverend McKenzie.

"Loblolly Lob's on in five minutes. Then there's the Table Toss, the Stone Put, the Carry-a-Sheep Run, the Posthole Dig, the Old Cow Race, the Banger Gobble, and finally, the Tug-of-War. Then we eat."

"I take it the titles are self-explanatory?" Brenda asked as they started walking towards the Loblolly Lob event.

"You could say that," the mayor said.

After the Loblolly Lob event, Mayor Sam Pike went back to his house to help his wife Gwendolyn, or Gwen as she was called, prepare their casserole contribution for the 1560 Day Potluck. Once finished, they returned to the event and noticed something was seriously amiss.

"What's all that noise?" Gwen asked, getting out of the car.

"It sounds like it's coming from the picnic area," Mayor Pike said.

They could see a state trooper's patrol car with its emergency lights flashing parked near the picnic tables. Reverend McKenzie and the reporter were speaking with several officers.

"Mayor, come here, quick!" Hamish was waving at the mayor. "We've got a big blow today!" Sam and Gwen dashed over to where Hamish and Brenda were.

"What's going on?" Sam could see fourteen handcuffed members of The Great Highland Scottish Presbyterian Church sitting on the ground; some even had bruises.

"Why were they arrested, Reverend?" Gwen asked. In all her life, she had never witnessed such a thing at any 1560 Day Event.

Now closer, Sam and Gwen could see that the involuntarily seated parishioners were covered in coleslaw, potato salad, tuna salad, bits and pieces of deviled egg, Mrs. McDownsy's neeps, and both varieties of Mr. MacDrabie's haggis. One arrestee had a smashed peep stuck on his head.

"What happened?" Sam asked, shocked at the turn of events. "You'd better hold on to your casserole," he told Gwen.

"From what I understand, there were accusations of cheating at the tug-of-war. At first, it seemed that the contest went okay. When the teams were heading to the potluck, everybody was talking like they were all friends. But once they got to the picnic tables and started eating, Calvin McCloudy stood up and accused the MacMurkey-related clans of cheating," Brenda said, reading from her notes about the fracas.

"Cal is related to the McDownface clan," Hamish added. The minister turned around to look at the picnic area again to see if there was anything left of the food. Gwen noticed something that looked like a cat hairball stuck to the back of his pants.

"Hamish, I hope that's not . . ."

"No, I think it's a banger, Gwen," Sam said. "You've got one of Mr. MacDrabie's bangers stuck to your backside, Hamish." As Hamish tried to brush the banger off of his pants, Sam noticed the heels of his socks had holes in them.

"Reverend McKenzie, now I can see why you're always feeling like a big blow is always nigh. Your members are wound pretty tight." As she was speaking, Brenda also noticed something stuck to the side of the minister's head. "What's that stuck in your hair?"

"It's neep. I got some in my ear, too. I thought I got it all out," Hamish said as he was picking neep out of his hair. "There was food flying everywhere."

"Hopefully, a few nights in jail and $500 fines will turn these fools away from another big blow," the mayor said.

"I'm very disappointed in them," Hamish said. "Behavior that's most uncharitable."

"But what a great story," Brenda was laughing. "My editors in Manhattan will love it—*Banged up and trashed after bangers and mash!*"

Sunday came not soon enough for Reverend McKenzie. He worked hard on his Triple D & C confession and the sermon that followed. But once in the pulpit, he noticed something strange. "That's odd," Hamish thought to himself. He was about to begin the time of confession when he noticed one of the columns was missing. He went ahead with the Triple D & C, deciding to investigate the problem after worship.

Following the benediction, Hamish waited for the last members to depart. He then walked to the McDownface side of the sanctuary and could see that somebody had removed the McCloudy column from its place. "That's odd," he muttered again.

Bob Richmond, the church's building engineer, wandered over to Reverend McKenzie. "Yeah, somebody stole the column last night," Bob said. "Whoever swiped the column left this here note." He handed a small white envelope to Reverend McKenzie.

Hamish read the note aloud. "Calvin Knox McCloudy falsely accused us of cheating. Excommunicate him for lying (read Exodus 20:16!) or your column is never coming back." It was signed, "Clan MacMurkey." Hamish looked at Bob with an angry look on his face. "This is ridiculous. I'm gonna get to the bottom of this."

The next day, Reverend McKenzie made several dozen calls to the members of the congregation but could not make any headway into finding out who stole the McCloudy column. "I really don't wanna call Mayor Pike about this," he said to himself. "I'll say something next Sunday at worship."

The following Sunday, again in the pulpit and just about to mention the missing column, Hamish noticed that another column was gone; this time it was on the MacMurkey side of the sanctuary. He stepped out of the pulpit and walked to the place where there once had been a MacDismal column. Taped to the nearest pew was another note. He took the note, walked back to the pulpit, opened the envelope, and read its contents to the congregation. "Someone of the clan MacMurkey stole our McCloudy column (read Exodus 20:15!). We will not return the MacDismal column until such time as the McCloudy column is returned to its rightful place, herewith and forthwith." Reverend McKenzie looked at the congregation. "This behavior is sinful and unacceptable to our Lord. I expect both columns to be in their rightful places by noontime tomorrow. This worship service is now over!" With those words, Hamish left the pulpit, walked out of the sanctuary, and headed to the manse.

The worshipers were shocked. To the best of anyone's recollection, no minister had ever ended a worship service prematurely at any time in the church's 260-year history.

"Stealing church columns is a sin against Almighty God!" Senior Elder Alistair MacMurkey said loudly. He then stood up from his pew and addressed the congregation in a very serious and stern voice. "I expect the guilty sinners to return the columns tomorrow morning, just as our Reverend McKenzie said. May God have mercy on their souls if they do not." Alistair, his wife, children, and grandchildren then exited the sanctuary and went home.

One-by-one and family-by-family, the members of Great Highland Scottish Presbyterian Church quietly left the sanctuary and went home, too.

Monday was the traditional Sabbath rest day for ministers. At noon on this particular Monday, however, Reverend McKenzie was at the church with Alistair. Entering the sanctuary, Hamish flipped on the lights; both men hoped to see that the two columns had been returned to their rightful places.

"Oh dear Lord," Reverend McKenzie said. Instead of the two columns being returned, two more columns were missing, one from each side of the sanctuary. Taped to the end of each pew nearest to the space where a column once stood were two similar notes calling for the excommunication and banishment of a church member. One quoted Exodus 20:14 and made a salacious accusation against Alistair, accusing him of having an affair. "They want you excommunicated, otherwise they will not return the MacDrabie nor the MacDismal columns."

"What?" Alistair said. "Why would I need to be excommunicated?"

"Well, Exodus 20:14 refers to adultery, so they must think you're cheating on Fiona."

"Hamish, never in my life have I been unfaithful to my beloved Fiona."

"I believe you, Alistair. Let's look at the other note. It's quoting Exodus 20:13 and the author wants Rowan arrested for murder before they will return the McCloudy and the McGlumly columns."

"Rowan, murder? Oh how ridiculous," Alistair said. "Rowan is three years old!"

"I'm going to call Mayor Pike right now. We've got to get to the bottom of this."

"Did you hear that?" Sam asked Hamish. The mayor, Alistair, and the minister were meeting at the manse when they heard loud creaking noises. "There it is again!"

Hamish walked over to the window and looked outside. Parked in front of the church were two Ford Transit vans, one was white and the other blue. "Sam, Alistair, come here!" Hamish yelled. "It looks like they're finally returning the columns."

Sam and Alistair were both at the window peering outside. "Why do you think those men are arguing?" Alistair asked.

"I don't know, and right now I don't care. I just want them to put the columns back," Hamish said.

"Wait, Hamish. Something's wrong." Alistair turned to look at Reverend McKenzie. "Get me your binoculars, quick. The minister darted to the coat closet and retrieved his beloved pair of Opticron binoculars.

"What's wrong?" Sam asked Alistair.

"Wait a second." Using the Opticron binoculars, Alistair surveyed the columns lying next to the vans in order to see which ones were being returned, as there were only two and not four. Two church members were in a heated argument as well. "The tartan colors are all wrong," Alistair said. "These aren't two columns coming back, they're two more being . . ." Before Alistair could finish his sentence, there was one more final creaking noise, then the sound of breaking glass and cracking wood. Seconds later, there was one, very loud, final crash. ". . . stolen." Alistair finished his sentence, which was now pointless.

"It's gone, Hamish," Sam said. "Your church is gone."

Reverend McKenzie ran back to the window. "I don't believe it; it's all gone." In the place where The Great Highland Scottish Presbyterian Church of West Darien stood for 260 years was a pile of bricks, beams, wire, and glass. The only things left standing were a half dozen pews and the old lectern that once stood on the right side of the former sanctuary. The men who had been arguing were now covered in dust and debris, staring at the mess before them.

Several weeks later, on a beautiful Sunday morning, the Reverend Hamish McKenzie was standing at the now wobbly and damaged lectern reading the lectionary text for the day, Ezekiel 37:5–6 from the King James version:

> Thus saith the Lord God unto these bones; Behold, I will cause breath to enter into you, and ye shall live: And I will lay sinews upon you, and will bring up flesh upon you, and cover you with skin, and put breath in you, and ye shall live; and ye shall know that I am the Lord.

Squeezed in the half dozen remaining pews, a majority of the members of The Great Highland Scottish Presbyterian Church were listening intently. Hamish closed his Bible and surveyed the congregation participating in a worship service in the midst of piles and piles of rubble.

"A pile of bones, dry bones, this is what is left of our once beautiful home, our place of worship for sixteen generations. We will salvage our bones; the bricks of our building and the sinews of mortar that bind them together will rise from the rubble. Plaster will then cover the walls much like the skin that covers our bodies. And then, when the rubble you see is reassembled into a new sanctuary, the spirit of the Lord will breathe new life into this congregation." Hamish could see tears in the eyes of many. Alistair had a look of hope that warmed Hamish's somber heart. "There will be no named columns, no tartan colors, no big flag, and no allegiances to anything other than our common life as a part of the body of Christ."

Following Reverend McKenzie's sermon, the congregation stood and sang the hymn penned by the minister's great-great-grandfather, including the fourth verse:

> In the fairest of days thy clouds of gloom dost fly,
> Our blessings of hearth and home are soon gone awry,
> At our heels a blow most foul is ever nigh.
> With our hearts knitted together we will trust in the Lord on high.

Brenda Pierce and Mayor Pike were seated several yards back on a pile of bricks that once formed the narthex wall. "These people are predestined for glory," Brenda said to Sam. "I misjudged Reverend McKenzie. He's calm, patient, gentle, and a strong pillar that remained in place when everything collapsed around him."

"What he lacks in charisma, he's got in character, and then some," Sam said. "And that goes a long way."

"Who's that woman at the lectern now?" Brenda asked Sam.

"Oh, that's the Reverend Maria Alianza; Hamish is retiring soon, and Maria will be the next pastor for Great Highland."

"She's not a man, she's not Scottish, and I doubt she's from a village called Dull," Brenda said. "What happened?"

"Hamish mentioned to me that the elders are changing their charter. So, no more Dull ministers," Sam explained. "And Maria is from Puerto Rico. The elders felt it would be safer if their new preacher had no possible connection to any Scottish clan whatsoever."

"I guess the menu at the next 1560 Day celebration will expand a bit, too."

"I sure hope so. I'm tired of haggis and casseroles. Wouldn't you be?"

"Oh, don't you know it. You should visit Manhattan sometime and see what church member diversity can add to a great potluck picnic."

"I forgot to mention that the gala won't be called 1560 Day next year. Hamish tells me it will be 1967 Day in honor of the Confession of 1967," Sam said.

"It's good to update your program every once in a while, I guess," Brenda added, laughing.

"Pretty much well-nigh, for this group."

"We stopped that Kirkin' stuff long ago," May said. "We couldn't find anyone who could play the bagpipes."

"We go all out," Princeton said. "Bagpipes, drums, tartans; it's quite spectacular."

"Your clans don't get clannish, do they?" Sarah asked. "Kirkin' o' the Tartan is all new to me."

"We've got an elderly member who's a Campbell. That's about it as far as clans go at my church," Princeton responded.

"So, why do you still do it?"

"Honestly, I don't know. I guess we do it because it's a Presbyterian tradition."

"That could be one more thing y'all need to confess about," Ben said, laughing. "Tell me you don't wear a kilt for the service."

"No, I don't, but Mr. Campbell still does. He's ninety-six and manages to lead the procession, though he uses a walker now."

"I can't deal with kilts," Billy said, pretending to shiver. "As a Baptist, they just seem wrong to me."

"They'd defrock me if I wore one," Ben laughed. "No doubt about it. Besides, no Baptist preacher would dare sit in the big pastor's chair in front of the whole congregation wearing one of those things."

"There's no churchgoer on this planet who'd want to be looking at your skinny legs while sitting in a pew, believe you me," Sarah said, laughing very hard.

"If you're a Baptist preacher, that frock could get you defrocked," Ken added with a snicker. "A Presbyterian preacher wearing the same thing would be celebrated as a great Scotsman."

"That's so funny," Sarah said. "One denomination's cultural deviant is another's cultural devotee."

"I, for one, would never wear a kilt," Jim said. "I think they look silly."

"Well, if I wore a kilt in any Baptist church, everybody would notice," Billy said. "If a member says to me, 'Hey Pastor Billy, why you wearing a dress?' and I say, 'No, it's not a dress; it's a kilt,' that member will think, 'Lordy, lordy, lordy, I wish he wouldn't wear that thing.' But if Princeton wore a kilt to his Presbyterian church, as long as he's wearing knee socks with tasseled garters, no one's gonna ask, 'Hey Pastor Princeton, why you wearing a dress?'"

"I agree," Bob said. "Baptists see things for what they are. Knee socks or no knee socks, if it looks like a dress and it's worn like a dress, it's a dress."

"That's why you'd never catch any Baptist preacher ever wearing one of those things," Billy added. "Especially one from South Georgia."

"We're missing the point of the very funny story," Dave said. "We can have disagreements, but we can't tear each other apart."

"That's a lesson lost on the church today," Ron said. "We're here to make disciples of Jesus, not fight amongst ourselves."

"On that note, let's have our next story," Dave said. "Who's next to go?"

"I'm up," Billy said. "My story is about forgiveness in a world gone to the cats and dogs. My text is Matthew 18:21–22 from the TNIV Bible. I call my story, *Petrina and Polycarp*."

Petrina and Polycarp

Then Peter came to Jesus and asked, "Lord, how many times shall I forgive someone who sins against me? Up to seven times?" Jesus answered, "I tell you, not seven times, but seventy-seven times."

(Matthew 18:21–22 TNIV)

Most cats, when satisfied with a session of under-the-neck stroking, typically stop purring and walk away without expressing gratitude to their human companion. The tortoiseshell cat, however, will oftentimes bite and scratch her companion to signal she is ready to move on to another activity. Within a very short span of time, she'll return to the same person expecting more petting and neck rubbing. This attitude, and its associated behavior, is what is called tortitude. Simply put, a cat with a tortoiseshell coat will often attack you after an intentional act of kindness. Furthermore, you cannot train it to stop this pain-inflicting behavior, and neither can you take it personally; it's in their genes.

Joan Habersham always wears leather gloves when she pets her cat, Petrina. Neither her husband, James, nor her son, Jimmy, will get close to the family pet that models tortitude better than most of her peers. Five years ago, the tabby cat of Joan's sister, June, had a litter of kittens that included one tortie, one calico, and two grey tabbies. Joan thought the cat with the tortoiseshell coat was the prettiest and best option for her family, unaware of the obnoxious personality traits that would come with the fur that she found so attractive.

Since the day Petrina arrived at the red-brick, split-level Habersham home in Doraville, Georgia, the family adjusted its lifestyle to accommodate the eccentricities of their tortoiseshell cat. If Petrina wanted to spend the night with Joan, James would sleep on the couch. If Petrina was resting on the couch and James and Jimmy wanted to watch a ball game on TV, they would sit on the floor. If Joan wanted to close the window blinds, she would wait for Petrina to finish looking out the window. And, if Mr. and Mrs. Habersham were away from the home, they would be sure to return before dinnertime. The family cat was so replete with tortitude that her electronic patient file at the vet's office had a "WATCH OUT!" pop-up notice in bold red letters to ensure that employees knew to be extremely cautious when touching her.

"Mom, can we get a dog?" Jimmy asked his mom at breakfast one morning before school. "Petrina's your cat. She doesn't like me."

"She loves you in her own way, Jimmy."

"Then why did she scratch me?" Jimmy made sure his mom and dad could see the large Band-Aid on his arm. "I was only cleaning out her litter box like you asked me to."

"She's a cat; they do that sometimes," Joan said. She had thought about a dog for the family and now that Jimmy was twelve, she was more amenable to the idea. "What do you think, honey?" she asked her husband.

"I had a dog growing up, and I think it's a great idea," James said. "You know what I think about Petrina; she's really your cat."

"I wonder how Petrina will react to a dog in the house," Joan thought. Looking at her husband, she said, "There'll be a long period of adjustment for the cat, you know."

"Boy, I'll say," James replied. He shook his head. "And for the dog, too. Where's that cat, anyway?"

"Last time I saw her, she was on your desk chair cushion; she was sound asleep."

"I wish she wouldn't do that. Last week, she left a hairball on it. Do you know what it's like sitting on a wet hairball?" James started laughing. "I didn't know it stuck to my pants until someone at work pointed it out."

"Oh, gross!" Joan said. "How long were you there before someone said something?"

Before James could respond, Jimmy interrupted the hairball discussion. "Can we get a dog, can we?" Jimmy was excited about the prospect. "I promise I'll take good care of it!"

"Why don't we go to the animal shelter on Saturday?" James said. "Maybe they'll have a dog that will do okay with your cat."

"You two go," Joan said. "I've got a bunch of work I have to do. Besides, I'd better be here with Petrina if y'all come back with a dog."

"Dog? Come back with a dog?" Unbeknownst to Joan, James, and Jimmy, Petrina overheard the conversation about the possibility of a new pet for the family. "This will not do," the tortie thought to herself. "No, not at all!"

"This is Polycarp," Julie, an enthusiastic shelter staff person, said to James and Jimmy. "I hope he gets a home," she thought. Sitting in a back corner of a fenced cage with a concrete floor was a sad-looking puppy with huge paws that looked like they belonged on a full-grown Saint Bernard. "He arrived a couple of weeks ago, but so far no one has taken him."

"He's a cute pup," James said. Jimmy was standing next to James with his fingers holding onto the chain-link fencing. "What kind of dog is he?"

"Your guess is as good as mine. Obviously, he's part Lab. His previous owner said that there was some Saint Bernard in him; you can tell that by the size of his feet." Julie searched for the key to the cage amongst a large collection on her key ring. "He's also part Beagle, and there may even be some Border Collie in him, too. Do you want me to let him out?"

"Well?" James asked Jimmy, looking down at his son. "It's your call."

Jimmy turned towards Polycarp, and the two looked at each other for a minute. Polycarp's tail started wagging slowly. "Okay. Can I hold him?" Jimmy asked Julie. As she unlocked the door, the dog's tail started wagging faster, though he remained seated in the back of the cage. "Why's he just sitting there?"

"He's a little nervous. But he'll perk up." Julie entered the cage, avoiding the soiled newspapers on the floor. She attached a leash to his collar and led him out. "Here's Polycarp," she said, handing the leash to Jimmy.

Jimmy got down on his knees and began petting Polycarp. Now the dog's tail was wagging so fast that his back side moved back and forth too. "Hi boy," Jimmy said. With that, Polycarp started licking Jimmy's face. "He sure is goofy looking."

Indeed, Polycarp looked goofy. In addition to big Saint Bernard paws, he had the nose and coat of a black Labrador, the long-haired tail of a Border Collie, and the eyes and ears that were clearly from a Beagle.

"Why don't we take Polycarp outside to one of the runs? That way, you can see what he's like." Julie led James, Jimmy, and the dog to a grassy, rectangular-shaped, fenced enclosure.

Once off the leash, Polycarp made three full-speed galloping laps around the enclosure before stopping in front of James and Jimmy. He sat down and wagged his tail. The look on his face seemed to be saying, "Got a stick? I'll go get it."

"Can we keep him, Dad?"

Polycarp's expression read, "Can I go home with you?"

James smiled at Polycarp and Jimmy. "Let me call Mom."

Meanwhile, back at the Habersham home, Petrina had pushed her way through the cat slot on the back door. She walked across the yard, jumped the fence, and passed through several of the neighbors' yards on her way to see Jehoshaphat, an old Siamese cat known as the Don of Doraville.

"Indeed, this is bad news," Jehoshaphat said in a quiet tone. "But there are ways to greatly shorten the residency of a new dog in your home," he said to Petrina. "I think we can have him gone within the month." The tortie and the Don were meeting in a secret place five doors down from the Habersham home in what its homeowners thought was an unused portion of their backyard shed. Jehoshaphat made his meeting spot quite comfortable with carpet scraps and a few pillows he had neighborhood cats steal from nearby deck chairs.

"Are you sure? I don't want to share my house with another pet, especially a dog. They demand so much attention."

"You're going to have to control your tortitude, Petrina." The Don of Doraville was very, very serious. "No more biting or scratching the hand that pets you. You can't draw blood when you're ready for them to stop doing something nice to you."

"It'll be hard. It'll be really hard. I can't help myself."

"But you have to understand you will be competing with a creature that exudes excessive appreciation for even the most meager amount of attention."

"I got it; I got it. But isn't there something else that can be done?"

"Yes, Petrina. There is." The Don paused for a few moments, deep in thought.

"Then tell me." Impatient, Petrina could feel her tortitude rising.

"Every human has what we experts call an infraction limit, both in number and in severity. Our goal will be to help your family reach its infraction limit with respect to the dog."

"Okay, I'll do whatever it is you think I should do."

"The fact that you are a tortoiseshell and are still living with the same family tells me that they have an exceptionally high cat infraction limit. Now, if you are able to control your tortitude, we may be able to lower their dog infraction limit."

"And this is a good thing?" Petrina asked. She knew that this would be difficult.

"It will be difficult, especially for you. Here's your infraction limit mantra: "Mine must increase; his must decrease."

"I got it. Mine must increase; his must decrease."

"And we must be prepared to go all out."

Petrina paid Jehoshaphat with the customary amount of catnip she took from her supply kept in a kitchen cabinet. "I'll let you know how it goes."

"We're home, dear!" James said loudly. The "we" included Polycarp, and all three entered the house through the kitchen door.

"Mom! Wait 'till you meet Polycarp!" Jimmy was very excited.

"I'm coming." Joan was in the den and had Petrina on her lap. She stopped petting her cat and was about to take her leather gloves off. For a second, the cat started to bite and scratch the gloves, but she stopped herself. "Are you okay?" Joan asked, looking at Petrina.

"Mine must increase; his must decrease," the cat said to herself. Petrina jumped from Joan's lap, and she and her owner headed to the kitchen to meet Polycarp.

"Hsss. Thhhh. Hsss." Petrina arched her back and spit. "Increase. . .decrease," she reminded herself. "Mine must increase; his must decrease." She stopped the instinctive threat movements and walked over to Polycarp, rubbing her side on his left front leg. "Increase . . . decrease."

"Oh, look," Joan said. "She loves him."

"Mine must increase, his must decrease." Petrina then darted into the living room.

"Stop," James yelled at Polycarp, who ran after the cat. Seconds later, there was a loud crash and the sound of something breaking. James, Jimmy, and Joan went into the living room to see what had happened.

"Increase . . . decrease." Petrina was sitting in the middle of the living room. Polycarp was looking at the remains of two very expensive Lladro ceramic figurines of dancing ballerinas that James had given to Joan on their fifth anniversary. Looking at everyone's facial expression, Polycarp realized that his tail should be between his legs and not wagging.

"He needs training!" Joan said. "Jimmy, you'll need to take Polycarp to a dog training class. The shelter probably has one."

"I'll do it, Mom. You're not going to send him back to the pound, then?"

"He's a young dog; he needs to be trained." She looked at James, "I hope you're planning on replacing the Lladros. I'm not happy!"

Petrina couldn't believe what she was hearing. "That mutt breaks valuable ceramics, and the only thing that happens is a training class. That's not right." The cat could feel her tortitude rising. "Mine must increase; his must decrease. Mine must increase; his must decrease." She kept repeating Jehoshaphat's mantra.

Polycarp returned to the kitchen. He was so nervous that he piddled on the floor along the way. He sat in the corner with his tail tightly tucked between his legs. "I can't do this again; I won't do this again. I can't do this again; I won't do this again." The dog was repeating the mantra he learned from another dog at the shelter.

Cats have a way of directing people to a particular place without their human companions being aware that it is happening. Petrina had guided Joan to the main bedroom as she wanted her to see the chewed-up jewelry case lying on the floor next to her dressing table.

"What on earth," Joan said to herself. She bent down and picked up the shredded remains of a felt-lined leather container. "James!" she yelled. "James!"

James came running to the bedroom. "What's wrong?"

Holding the container remains for James to see, she said, "Who do you think did this?"

"His just decreased." Seated on the bedroom floor, Petrina felt proud of what she had orchestrated. She was sure Polycarp would get sent back to the shelter.

"And where are my pearls?"

Petrina speculated that if she snuck some kibble into the container with the pearls, an excitable doggie would consume everything in sight, not waiting to determine which was edible food and which was inedible jewelry. "I knew he'd do that," she thought to herself.

At that moment, Polycarp trotted into the room, wondering what all of the ruckus was about. "Uh, oh," he thought when he saw the angry faces. James forced the dog's mouth open to see if there were any pearls. Piddling on the carpet, a scared Polycarp realized that he shouldn't have trusted the cat's explanation of why the jewelry container was on the floor and why it had kibble in it.

"He ate my pearls!" Joan said. "I can't believe it."

"Maybe the vet can get them out," James said.

A wave of nerve-driven nausea swept over Polycarp, and within seconds, Joan's pearls were on the bedroom carpet within a mass of partially digested kibble and other matter that Polycarp had eaten on the morning walk through the neighborhood.

"I am not picking up those pearls," Joan said sternly. "And you have to get them professionally cleaned today!"

"How did Polycarp get them in the first place?" James asked. "There's no way he could have reached them." He and his wife then looked at Petrina.

"I think we have two problems here," Joan said. "We have to keep the bedroom door closed, and we need more chew toys for Polycarp, especially since he might be teething."

"Wait a minute," Petrina thought. "The dog eats the pearls and chews up the box, I get banned from the bedroom, and he gets new toys?"

"I can't do that again; I won't do that again." Polycarp repeated to himself. "I can't do that again; I won't do that again. I can't do that again; I won't do that again." He made sure his tail was between his legs and not wagging, which happens sometimes when a dog gets nervous.

"We also need to make sure he knows what are chew toys and what are not!" Joan said.

Petrina sighed. Looking at the dog, she decided that further consultation with the Don of Doraville was needed.

"He's not decreasing," Petrina said to Jehoshaphat. "That dog broke expensive ceramics and ate a set of pearls. I got banned from the bedroom, and he got new toys!"

"Don't you see your logic model failed," the Don explained. "You should have known the humans would wonder how the dog got ahold of the pearls that were kept out of his reach."

"Hmm." Petrina hadn't realized this. Tortitude frequently gets in the way of building a thoughtful logic model.

"Somebody pushed the jewelry case onto the floor and added the kibble bits. Who would the humans have thought did this?"

"Me?"

"Obviously," Jehoshaphat said. "Tortitude isn't only about biting and scratching. Your planning must not be reactive, either."

"Oh, I see."

"Your next plan must ensure that your paw prints are nowhere to be found, literally or figuratively."

Petrina paid Jehoshaphat's fee with more of her catnip. "I'll let you know how it goes."

"Please do."

"Oh no," James yelled. He was looking out the living room window, watching the family golf cart roll down the long driveway, heading straight for the side door of Mr. Johnson's brand-new Cadillac CT-5 Blackwing, his new pride and joy that cost him almost $120,000—he had just returned from the dealership and was in the driver's seat waiting for his family to join him on a maiden drive around Doraville. James ran out of the house towards the rolling cart.

Seated in the golf cart with his tail between his legs was a petrified Polycarp. "I hope I don't piddle on the seat," he worried, keeping his eyes closed. The new pet dog mantra ran through his mind, "I can't do this again; I won't do this again. I can't do this again; I won't do this again."

"No, no, no!" Jimmy screamed. Jimmy, in the driveway behind the golf cart, was about to start the lawnmower when he noticed that it started rolling down the hill. He had not seen the cat dart from the golf cart and climb up into the old oak tree. "Stop, stop, stop," he yelled, running down the driveway.

Petrina, meanwhile, was hiding on a large tree limb just above the driveway, watching the event unfold with glee. "They'll never suspect I was behind this," she thought. "Mine will increase; his will decrease, guaranteed." Petrina was filled with great tortitude.

Looking out the driver's side window, Mr. Johnson saw the golf cart heading straight towards him. "Ahhhhhh!" he screamed. Losing precious seconds, he tried to find the car key in his pocket until he remembered that his new Cadillac had a start button. Panicking, he struggled to get his hand out of his jean pocket.

Mrs. Johnson and their twins, looking through the living room picture window at the new car and at the free-rolling golf cart, were yelling in unison, "S-t-o-p!"

Fortune smiled upon Polycarp that day. The golf cart rolled over the big weed-whacker, rake, and hose that Jimmy had left in the driveway, causing the cart to shake and wobble quite a bit. Polycarp lost his balance and fell into the footwell, landing on the brake. The golf cart quickly slowed and came to a complete stop about three inches from the Cadillac's shiny custom metallic blue door.

Returning from a trip to the hardware store, Mrs. Habersham parked her car along the street. She noticed her husband, son, dog, cat, Mr. and Mrs. Johnson, and their twins standing in the street next to the golf cart and a new Cadillac. "I wonder what's going on," Joan thought as she walked over to her husband to see what was up.

"Honey, you won't believe this," James said. His heart was racing, and his legs were still shaking from his Olympic dash out of their front door and across the yard. "Polycarp averted a huge disaster!"

"He what?"

"Our golf cart almost rammed into the Johnsons' new Cadillac Blackwing. But somehow Polycarp managed to push the brake and stop the cart just before it crashed into their car!"

"Doggonit!" Petrina thought to herself. "I can't believe this."

"Think of the insurance claim," James said. "Our rates would have skyrocketed!"

"Good boy, good boy," Jimmy said, petting Polycarp on his head. "I knew you were a good doggie." Polycarp looked up at Jimmy and wagged his tail.

"I don't believe it," Joan said.

"It's true; I saw it for myself," Mr. Johnson said. "I was sitting in my new Cadillac, and I saw your dog hop into the footwell to hit the brake."

"We saw it too," Mrs. Johnson added. "The twins and I were watching everything from our front window."

"It's true!" her twins said in unison.

"We're getting rid of that golf cart," Joan said. "There must be something wrong with it. And besides, we don't need it anyway."

"Great. I almost got the dog to ram the cart into a new Cadillac, and they keep the dog and get rid of the cart!" The Habersham family's tortie was not happy with the day's outcome.

"I'm out of catnip, and the dog is more popular than ever." Petrina turned her tortitude towards Jehoshaphat, the Don of Doraville.

"You should have had more forethought in your planning."

"I'm done with the Don," she thought to herself. "I am gonna stop fighting and learn to live with that dog," she told Jehoshaphat. "Maybe there is a way I can find him useful."

"That's always an option."

"Why didn't you suggest that in the first place?"

"You wanted to get rid of him, remember?"

"But you could've talked me out of it."

"That's not my job."

"What is your job, then?"

"My job is to help you and other cats get what is wanted, whether or not what is wanted is what should be wanted."

"Who decides what should be wanted?"

"That's not my problem," Jehoshaphat said, wanting to end the conversation.

Petrina was feeling foolish. "Can I have my catnip back?"

"I'm done with you, Petrina," he said. "Now go away."

The tortie left the Don's den and headed back to the Habersham's home, temporarily feeling angry with herself and with Jehoshaphat. "I guess I can learn to live with Polycarp," she thought. "But if he licks me, I'm still gonna scratch and bite him."

"A surprise tale of three tails," Dave said. "Let's hear it for something enjoyable."

"Hear, hear," Princeton said, clapping. "Billy, are you a Petrina or a Polycarp?" he asked.

"When I first get up in the morning, definitely a Petrina, but after coffee and breakfast, a Polycarp."

"I wonder if the church can be a tortie?" May posited a strange question for her colleagues. "Our history's not so glorious sometimes."

"Sometimes?" Billy said.

"Okay, oftentimes."

"If the church is the tortie, who's Jehoshaphat?" Ben asked.

"Anyone or anything we follow who is not the 'Author and finisher of our faith,' don't you think?" Princeton asked. "How many times over the last 2,000 years have Christians jumped on board with kings and political leaders who have not been true to our faith?"

"Yes, it's easy to turn a blind eye to evil intent," May added. "Isn't that what the antichrist is all about?"

"So, Jehoshaphat was a sort of antichrist?" Ben asked. "That seems a bit much for a simple story about a cat and a dog."

"Remember, Ben; it's a parable," Billy said. "It's a simple story to illustrate something deep."

"You know, I wouldn't want to be a Polycarp, either," Jim said. "While he's good-natured, he's a hapless creature, doing good accidentally."

"Perhaps then the church can be either a Petrina or a Polycarp," May said.

"I had a dog like Polycarp once." Sue thought about her Labrador retriever fondly. "He was a goofy dog that was always taking things from the bathroom trash can and dropping them on the living room floor whenever I had friends over. The stuff that goes in those trash cans you'd prefer not being plopped in front of guests. But he'd do it anyway."

"How embarrassing," May said. "I had a dog who would do the same thing; once she dropped off some unmentionable bathroom trash in the middle of my pastor/parish relations committee meeting!"

"Stop the trash talk," Dave said with a chuckle.

"Let's get to the point of the story," Billy said. "Jesus said to forgive someone 'seventy-seven times.' But like Petrina, we sometimes want to destroy people we don't like."

"Is another way of saying it, Jesus wants us to be people of forgiveness?" May asked.

"I'm not sure what you mean," Jim said.

"Forgiveness is a way of life. It's part of our daily walk of faith and not an individual moment of forced inspiration," May said.

"I think that's well put, May," Billy said. "It's something we should always do naturally, without ever giving it a second thought; otherwise, we run the risk of harboring bitterness and our own kind of tortitude."

"Well, I hate to stop the conversation," Ken said, "but it looks like we're heading in a different direction."

"What do you mean?" Princeton asked.

"We were heading towards Santiago, but it was Santiago de la Espada in Jaén. According to the AI program, we were sent there because there were too many tourists in Santiago de Compostela. But now the Jaén province is overrun with visitors."

"What?" Princeton asked. "I knew we were heading in the wrong direction."

"Everything's okay now," Ken said, trying to keep everyone calm. "Now it's directing us to the right Santiago because fewer tourists are there at the moment."

"I did notice we're heading northwest, finally," Princeton said, feeling more relaxed. "We passed some place called Segovia, and that sign over there says we're near Valladolid."

"Don't worry, the Cargado AI will get us there. I'm as certain as I am that there were ninety-four theses nailed to the door of that church. Oh shoot, what was its name? It keeps slipping my mind," Ken said.

"Wittenberg, and it was ninety-five," Sarah said. "You of all people should know this, Reverend Lutheran."

"Well, I disagree with one of them, number nine, I think it is," Ken responded. "That's why I go with ninety-four."

"You can't do that," Princeton said. "It doesn't change the fact that Luther nailed ninety-five on that door."

"So Ken, are we going in the right direction? Is everything fine now?" Dave asked.

"Yup, we're heading in the right direction. Everything is a-okay."

"Good, next story—the last one before we stop for lunch! Who's got it?"

"It's me, Dave," May said. "My text is from John 15:16–17. It's a modern take on an old story, the tale of the decommissioned St. Wilgefortis. I hope it's meaningful for you."

"Decommissioned?" Dave asked.

"That means the Pope knocked her off the list of Saints back in 1969. There are a lot of marginalized folks who miss her."

"Did she pass away?" Ed asked.

"Oh Ed, there's too much for me to explain to help you understand why that was not the brightest question to ask."

For a Peck of Oats

Do not suppose that I have come to bring peace to the earth. I did not come to bring peace, but a sword. For I have come to turn a man against his father, a daughter against her mother, a daughter-in-law against her mother-in-law—your enemies will be the members of your own household.

(Matthew 10:34–36 TNIV)

Reverend John Stiffer, senior pastor and founder of The Penultimater's Dispensational Tabernacular Church of God's Holy Kingdom, liked his coffee, oatmeal, and toast with jam at precisely 6:30 a.m. every day of the week without exception. If his breakfast arrived at 6:31, all hell broke loose; after 6:35, there would be hell to pay. As a widower, Reverend Stiffer depended upon his youngest and only unmarried daughter, Wilga Fortis Stiffer, to have the meal served at the right temperature and on the table at the appointed time.

The unyielding, unbending, independent-minded fundamentalist preacher named his fourth daughter after the ultra-reliable Polish Wilga, the airplane he flew while spreading his Penultimater Dispensationalism to the remote villages of eastern Portugal just after he graduated from the Inerrent Bible Institute of Quigley, Georgia. He believed that his youngest daughter, like his wife, older daughters, and any truly Christian woman, needed to be wholly reliable just like his trusted Polish Wilga.

"Mom, why did you name me after an airplane?" Wilga asked her mother shortly before her mother's death and right after her father told her about Wilga airplanes. Wilga remembers the conversation as if it were yesterday.

"Your father chose your first name, and I had no say-so whatsoever, Wilga. I didn't with your sisters' or your brother's names either, their first or middle. But with you, however, I insisted on picking your middle name myself." Weak and bed-bound, she held Wilga's hand and smiled. Speaking softly, she continued, "When I was still pregnant with you, I saw the word fortified on the box of your father's oatmeal. You know how I always loved words and their origins. So, when your father wasn't around, I looked it up in the dictionary; it said fortified came from the Latin word *fortis*, which means courageous and strong. I knew that had to be your middle name. Your older sisters have all followed the same path that I did, but I believe God has chosen a different one for you," she told Wilga. "I got tired and bored with life, and I so much want things to be better for you."

A young teenager at the time, Wilga didn't fully understand what her mother meant. Now a young woman, she did. Her older sisters, Defenda (named after the trusty Land Rover *Defender,* the model Reverend Stiffer used while a missionary), Darba (named for the nineteenth-century theologian John Nelson Darby, the father of Dispensationalism within whose writings Reverend Stiffer derived the Penultimater principles of masculinity), and Diorama (named for the display John used when raising money for his mission work in Portugal) all hated their first names. Unlike Wilga, all three got stuck with the same middle name which they hated even more: Weaker, a reference to the text from 1 Peter 3:7. Now, under the authority of their own husbands, Wilga's three older sisters, like her mother, were fast becoming tired and bored of life.

Their brother, Cyrus Scofield Stiffer, named after the famed creator of the Oxford University-published dispensationalist Scofield Reference Bible, did not understand why his three older sisters seemed so unhappy all of the time. Since they were mothers, he thought, they were free of the temptations that men faced and could more easily be assured of salvation, at least that's what Paul wrote in 1 Timothy, his father told him. Still, a perceptive and caring young soul, he worried about all four of his sisters.

"God made men to be real mighty manly men, men who are genuinely male, who are proud of their manhood and who are not afraid of being masculine male men," Reverend Stiffer began his presentation to the monthly meeting of the Loyal Order of the Pure Mallard.

The Loyal Order of the Pure Mallard Society split from the Loyal Order of the Mallard on account of the growing presence of women and immigrants in their ranks. Tall, bearded, and wearing an ill-fitting brown suit and tight shirt, the top button of which long ago stopped reaching its companion buttonhole, making his green clip-on bow tie look like a broken airplane propeller, Reverend Stiffer was receiving an award for his *Penultimater Mighty Manly Male Men* program. Every one of the manly Pure Mallard members, all seven of them, believed the program would reduce crime and promote economic growth in South Georgia.

"Biblically . . ." he paused for a second to adjust his old and worn horned-rimmed glasses and then continued, "Biblically, way back at the first dispensation, the man was made to be male and that means being a male man with mighty masculinity. It's when mighty men stray from being manly men and do many unmanly things like wearing clogs and shirts with flowers or driving electric cars, or playing dulcimers that they lose their mighty manly masculinity and become unmasculated, unmale, and unmanly. In God's kingdom, there is no such thing as mostly male!"

"Hear, hear," several Pure Mallards yelled. "Honk, honk, honk."

"No doubt about it, that's when men stop going to church and takin' care of their young'uns. When that happens, crime goes up and businesses leave our towns." Reverend Stiffer looked around the room and took a sip of water from a delicate flowered glass left behind accidentally by the Early County Women's Breakfast Club. Stiff and straight, and placing his hands firmly on the creaky portable lectern, he said at the top of his voice, "If our towns are to grow and prosper once again, the unmasculated, unmale, and unmanly should all be sent to Savannah or Atlanta!" The audience rose to their feet, clapped, and made their secret mallard wing flapping motions and honk sounds.

"Thank you, Reverend Stiffer, for your inspiring speech." Wearing the generation's old, upturned duck beak and feathered headdress, Pure Mallard Supreme Sultan Crocker Manie handed the award plaque to John and enthusiastically shook his hand. He and John returned to their seats. (Neither noticed the Reverend's name was misspelled—instead of Stiffer, it read Reverend Sniffer.) After a few other speeches and announcements, a prayer, and a benediction, the meeting was adjourned, and the Pure Mallards flew their separate ways.

Meanwhile, the Stiffer siblings were having lunch together at the Celery Patch Café, a popular diner a few miles off the highway. After a period of eating in silence, Wilga finally said something. "Good God, what a fool our father is. I'm really starting to dislike him. I can see why Mom was so unhappy." The siblings remained quiet until Cecil said something.

"I'm beginning to see your point, Wilga," Cecil said. "I think Dad's getting wacko."

It was Darba who spoke next. "I am tired, I am bored, and I am sad all of the time." She looked at Wilga. "Now you're gonna be married and end up just like me."

"Wait a minute," Diorama said, "I'm not sad all of the time. I love my kids, and I love my . . ." She stopped before completing her sentence. "Well, I wish Frank wasn't so much like Dad, but underneath he's a really nice man, and he treats me well."

"Why did you marry him, anyway?" Cecil asked.

"He was a member of our church, and Dad picked him out for me. I like him, and he works hard."

"Dad picked all of our husbands," Defenda said. "We didn't have a choice." She chuckled for a moment. "Dad told me, 'Better to marry than to burn.' Now I'm burned out."

Cecil looked at Wilga. "How come Dad didn't get you a husband?"

"Yes, he did," Defenda said. She blushed. "Oops, I wasn't supposed to say anything."

"What do you mean, he did?" Wilga looked at Defenda. "You better tell me!"

"Dad wants him to join the Loyal Order of the Pure Mallard and learn how to be a good duck," Defenda started laughing. "Dad's showing him how to be a Biblical Penultimater husband, too." Defenda knew she shouldn't be saying anything more.

"Who is he?"

Darba jumped in. "Billy Gunnerson. They call him 'The Spits,' and he used to be a professional wrestler. He had to stop because of an injury."

"He drooled on somebody, and then that person punched him, knocked him clean out," Cecil explained.

"You knew about this, too?" Wilga was shocked.

"So did I," Diorama said. "He's not bad-looking; he just drools a lot."

"That's why they called him 'The Spits.' If not for that, he'd be quite attractive." Darba laughed, followed by Defenda and Diorama.

"He's a stud that wants to be a duck," Darba said. The sisters all honked and made wing-flapping motions. They started laughing again. "Gosh, we haven't laughed this hard since we were kids."

"How did you know about the flapping and honking?" Cecil asked. "I thought they were super-secret."

"Oh, come on, Cecil, what other kind of sound does a duck make?" Diorama said.

"Don't any of you tell my husband! He'd get so angry if he knew I knew about the flap and quack thing," Darba said.

"And what about you, Cecil?" Wilga wasn't laughing. "Did you know I was getting married?"

"I knew nothing about any of this. Don't you get mad at me."

"Well, I have a surprise for you all." Wilga had her own secret to share. "I was accepted into Oxford University. I'm gonna study Biblical languages in England and learn to worship God with my mind, too! One day I'm going to be a New Testament scholar."

"How'd you manage that," Defenda asked.

"My guidance counselor, English teacher, and my history teacher all encouraged me to apply. They said I was smart enough and did well enough in school to have a chance at getting in. So last fall I applied. I got my acceptance letter two weeks ago."

"So what did Father say?" Darba knew he wouldn't let her go.

"I haven't told him yet. I've prayed a lot about how to tell him."

"Father will never let you do something crazy like that!" Defenda warned her. "He wants you to marry Billy, and he will not take no for an answer."

"I wish I had done something like you're doing," Diorama said. "Now it's too late for me."

"I think we should help Wilga." Cecil didn't want to see his youngest sister become weary and heavy-laden, too. He also didn't want to see Wilga with Billy Gunnerson. "Spits Gunnerson drools all the time," Cecil said. "He once drooled on my Bible, right on top of John 9:6, if you can believe it."

"Yeesh. He's more yuck than duck." Darba got everyone laughing again, Wilga too.

"We need a plan," Defenda said. "A grand plan. And Wilga, you're gonna go to Oxford for all of us, including Mom."

Before heading home, Defenda, Darba, Diorama, Cecil, and Wilga prayed together. Feeling hopeful, Wilga left the restaurant humming the hymn, *I Will Sing of My Redeemer.*

"Hi Spits. I'm glad you could make it." Cecil was having lunch with Billy "The Spits" Gunnerson at the Celery Patch Café. "How's the Pure Mallard prep goin'?"

"Oh, pretty good. I hate all the reading and studying, but I can't wait to become a full member of the society. I think wrestling really prepared me for that."

"How so?"

"You build your muscles and learn to focus on vanquishing your opponent, just like in the Old Testament. That's why I don't ever want to be a New Testament Christian."

"How's that?"

"By the time you get to the New Testament, men were getting a lot less manly and male. I much prefer the Old Testament. That's why I'll be a good Mallard, too. Oh, how's Wilga? I can't wait to meet her. Her dad tells me she's real cute."

"Spits," Cecil said in a somber tone. "I need you to keep her in your prayers."

"Is something wrong?" Billy was deeply concerned.

"No one knows this and I shouldn't be telling you, but . . ." Cecil looked around to make sure no one was listening. "You must promise me that you'll never, ever tell my father or anyone else that I told you this, okay?"

"Tell me what?" Now Billy became very worried about his unofficial fiancé. "I won't tell anyone, as God is my witness."

"She's got this hormonal disease that's really serious and no one has a cure."

"Oh my God," Billy said to Cecil. "Will she be okay?"

"No one knows. It might last for her whole life."

"What does it do to her?"

"Well, for one, it makes hair grow all over her body. You won't believe this, but she's got a full beard now." From his shirt pocket, Cecil took out a photoshopped picture of Wilga in her sick bed; Diorama had made it the night before. "Here's a photo of Wilga that I took this morning," Cecil said, handing the picture to Billy. "Look, she's got a beard, and there's hair all over her hands." Cecil paused for a moment. "It's all in God's hands now."

He let Billy take a long time with the picture, all the while thinking, "Wow, Diorama did a great job adding the hair."

"Man oh man, she looks horrible, really horrible," Billy said. "I, I, I mean, she must feel horrible." Suddenly, Billy felt very thankful that the engagement was not yet announced. He still had the chance to get out of marrying a girl who had a beard and hairy knuckles.

"She won't go out of the house anymore; she's so embarrassed."

"I wonder if people will think I'm marrying a man?" Spits thought to himself. He was horrified. "Did father say anything to you about Wilga getting hitched to anybody?" he asked Cecil.

"No, he hasn't said one word to me about that."

"She's gonna need to wait until she gets better, I'd say." Billy tried to sound sympathetic, but he was too horrified to do so. "I can't imagine her walking down the aisle looking like that."

"She could always wear a burka, you know, like the women in Afghanistan wear. It would definitely be a first for the Penultimater Church." Cecil wanted to implant an indelible image in Billy's already panicked mind. "Imagine standing at the altar with your best man and all your groomsmen and then you, your parents and their friends, and all of your relatives and their friends, plus your buds watch a woman with a beard and hairy hands walking towards the altar. Can you picture that?" Cecil paused for a moment. "I can't imagine how the groom would feel. Can you, Billy?"

"Oh, gosh, no." Billy's mouth hung open, and a little drool rolled down his chin.

"Are you okay, Spits?"

"I'm okay," Billy said, using his sleeve to wipe the drool from his chin.

"And then imagine slipping a ring on a hairy finger and then . . ."

"And then?" Spits asked. Focused on the imaginary wedding, his heart was now racing, and his eyes bugged out.

"And then . . ." Cecil paused for a few seconds. Billy turned pale and was sweating. "And then my father says, 'You may kiss the bride.'" With that, Billy "The Spits" fainted and fell out of his chair.

"Do you really think Father's gonna eat this oatmeal concoction?" Darba asked her sister Defenda. Defenda was adding a mixture of ground-up melatonin tablets, chamomile buds, lemon balm, passionflower, bits of boiled turkey, and magnolia bark into the morning's batch of oatmeal.

"I'll add a little more sugar and cinnamon," Defenda said. "I think he'll like it."

"Here's the coffee," Diorama had dropped a Benadryl tablet into the carafe that on this particular morning contained decaffeinated coffee.

Wilga added some ground chamomile buds into the jar of jam and onto her father's toast. "Here's to you, Mom," she said quietly. Cecil was outside loading Wilga's and his luggage into the trunk of his car.

Reverend Stiffer, seated at the table, was hungry and ready for his breakfast. "Spits Gunnerson's not interested in joining the Loyal Order of the Pure Mallard anymore. I was real disappointed," he said as Wilga brought out the food and coffee and put it on the table. Defenda, Darba, and Diorama were hiding in the kitchen.

"I don't know Spits very well, Father." Wilga was a little nervous hearing that name brought up.

"Well, I thought he'd be good for the Society, that's all. Do you know Butch Sudor? They call him 'The Sweats' because he and his dad make a lot of money in the sweat scraper business. You're gonna meet him."

"Sweat scrapers?"

"They use them on horses a lot. You'll like Sweats."

"Not today, Father. I have a lot to do," she said, returning to the kitchen.

"You're right, daughter. You do have a lot to do. The house is looking pretty dusty and cluttered." In a few minutes, Reverend Stiffer finished his breakfast. "Wilga," he yelled, "what did you do to the oatmeal?"

"Did you finish it?" Wilga was very nervous; nothing could go wrong with the plan.

"It was great! I loved it. Is there more?"

"I'm coming. There's a little more, Father." Wilga took his bowl back to the kitchen, filled it up with what remained in the pot, and then took it to her father. "I really like what you've done to the oatmeal."

"The toast was different too, daughter," he said to Wilga. "Wow, I'm feeling a little s-s-s-s-s-l-l-e-e-e." A second later, the pastor's face was in his oatmeal bowl. He was fast asleep.

Wilga rushed outside and got into the car and pulled the passenger door closed very, very quietly. Cecil backed out of the driveway, and he and Wilga were on their way to the county airport for their short flight to Atlanta's Hartsfield-Jackson Airport and then on to London. The sisters were ready for part two of the Stiffer siblings' grand plan they named *Project Duck, Duck, Scram.*

When Reverend John Stiffer woke up, Defenda, Darba, and Diorama were seated around the table staring at their father, who did not have a clue what was going on. When he sat up, his horn-rimmed glasses slid from his face as they were glued into the now solidified oatmeal that remained in his bowl.

"Father," Defenda opened the discussion. "Wilga's gone to the University of Oxford, and Cecil's gone with her, too."

"What, where, huh?" He was still groggy; bits of oatmeal were stuck to his face and formed an outline of the area where his glasses once rested.

"She's gone to the University of Oxford in England; she's gonna become a New Testament scholar. She's not gonna get married until she wants to, and she's not coming back until she's finished school. And Cecil's gone with her too."

"They'll be damned." He shook his head in anger. "And they'll go to perdition." He looked around the dining room and the adjacent living room and rubbed his eyes. "And who's gonna clean this mess?" He noticed that his glasses were still in the bowl. When he picked them up, the bowl came with them.

"You do it, Dad. We don't care," Diorama said. "Wilga has gone to a place where she can learn to love God with the beautiful mind she was given, and Cecil wanted to help her."

"We've pooled our money, and the three of us and the children are heading to Oxford tomorrow to help her get settled," Darba said. "We and the children will be coming back next week."

"I will not allow. . .," Reverend Stiffer started to say. When he yanked his glasses out of the bowl, the frames came free, but the lenses remained still stuck in the dried gruel. "Damn," he growled.

"Things are gonna change 'round here," Diorama said. "When we come back, we and the children will be attending a Methodist church. We've met with the pastor and the other elders, and we've already become members. You're welcome to join us. Our husbands can join us, too, if they want. And Father, this is something we have to do."

Defenda was next to speak. "I've got a job now. I'm not going to tell you what it is, where it is, nor what I'll be doing." She looked directly at her father. "I told my husband that I'm tired of being unhappy and that I want some fulfillment in my life."

Defenda unfolded a piece of paper that had been in her pocket. "I'm gonna read this to you, Father. You can choose to listen or not." Darba and Diorama smiled at Defenda. She smiled back and read the document. "Jesus chose us to be his disciples. You didn't choose us." She looked at her father and said, "Dad, we're not weaker vessels." She continued reading, "And Jesus appointed us so that we, as he said, 'might bear fruit, fruit that will last.'" Defenda paused for a moment to wipe the tears from her eyes. "Jesus also said that whatever you ask in his name, God will give you. I have asked God to give me my heart, mind, and soul back as have Darba and Diorama. Why have we asked for this and not something else? Because of what Jesus said next." Defenda handed the document to Darba. "Here, please finish reading it."

"After that amazing promise, Jesus gave this simple command: 'Love each other.'" Darba looked at her father and spoke from her heart. "If I can't have my heart, my mind, and my soul, I can't honor Jesus's command. I can't truly love you or my husband."

"Humph," Reverend Stiffer said. Not wanting to make eye contact with his daughters, he was focused on picking away at the dried oatmeal, trying to free his lenses.

After a few uncomfortable silent moments, Defenda, Darba, and Diorama got up from the table and headed to the kitchen. A group hug followed. As they then went out the door, they heard their father yelling.

"I need someone to take me to the optometrist now; do you hear me? Right now! I need new glasses before Wilga makes my lunch!"

They hopped into the car and drove to a hotel where their cousin was with their waiting children. The next day, they would be heading to England.

Wilga and Cecil remained in Oxford for five years, returning to the United States after she completed her graduate degree. Cecil wanted both to support his sister's transition from her father's clutches and to find his own calling away from the Pure Mallards. He did this by working for Oxford's refugee community. Wilga would eventually teach New Testament Greek at Good God Almighty Theological Seminary, and Cecil would find work in its development department.

Defenda, Darba, and Diorama returned home following Wilga's first week in England. Diorama's husband loved his wife and children more than a bunch of male Mallards and joined their church, too. Though still legally married, Defenda, Darba, and their children share a house together, across the street from where Diorama, her husband, and their children live. They all attend church together and are learning what it means to be a disciple of Jesus (and not a duck).

No one was surprised, however, when Reverend Stiffer and his other two sons-in-law chose to remain with the Penultimater Tabernacular Church and valued being loyal Mighty Manly Male Men and Pure Mallards over devotion to their own families. Perhaps one day, they will learn to let go of the God they created and come to embrace the living God, the source of faith, hope, and love.

And Billy "The Spits" Gunnerson decided to wait for Wilga to graduate and to become a scholar. "If somebody's brother and sisters could love their sister so much, then she must be something mighty special," he told Diorama when she got back from Oxford. "I'll be true to Wilga until she returns."

"She might not be interested in you, Spits," Diorama said. "But hear me, try to get a handle on your drooling!"

"I will. I've got an appointment with my doc next week," Spits replied. "I know I'm not the catch she deserves. But who knows, right? I simply want her to be happy, and it wouldn't surprise me if that don't include me."

"And no more duck calls and wing flapping imitations, Spits." Diorama started laughing.

"I did look like an idiot, didn't I?" Spits asked.

"You're the one who said it," Diorama replied. "By the way, Darba told me you're gonna go to the Community College. That's great."

"I'm taking classes in film production."

"Wow, Spits. What are you gonna do?"

"It's my plan B if Wilga turns me down. I'll head to Hollywood and become a famous movie director. I'm gonna do a movie about a scientist who lives with mallards—sort of like Jane Goodall and the chimpanzees only with ducks."

"Most of the men don't come out very well in your story, May," Ben said. "We're not all Neanderthal mallards like Reverend Stiffer and those two sons-in-law. Then there's Billy the 'Spits.' I don't know what to say about him."

"I never said you were," May replied. "And besides, why is it that whenever women criticize particular types of men or male behavior, we're accused of hating all men?"

"Yeah, that's so true." Sarah agreed with May.

"What's with the story title, 'For a Peck of Oats?'" Jim asked.

"It comes from Sir Thomas More's 1530 *Dialogue*. He mentions that for a peck of oats the saint, actually her English counterpart, will free women from evil husbands. 'Peck of oats' refers to a cheap payment."

"It reminds me of Jacob stealing Esau's birthright for a cup of lentil stew," Dave said.

"Sort of," May said. "In my story it was oatmeal."

"And what on earth is a Penultimater?" Bob asked.

"As a Baptist, shouldn't you be familiar with Dispensationalism? What's the sixth dispensation?"

"Grace," Billy replied.

"Don't you see the irony?" May asked. "A misogynist, judgement-focused fundamentalist pastor names his church after the sixth or penultimate dispensation," May explained. She started laughing.

"It wasn't that long ago women were not allowed to get a theological education," Sue said. "When my aunt went to seminary, she was the only female student."

"And women have added so much to the field of theology and biblical studies," Princeton said. "But I fear some Christian groups are going backwards and beginning to exclude women once again."

"What makes you say that, Princeton?" Billy asked.

"Just read the news, my brother," Princeton responded. "I read about a network of churches that want to repeal the Nineteenth Amendment."

"I wish more people would read the story of St. Wilgefortis," May added. "Back in the Middle Ages, she was very popular among women, especially those who were encumbered with husbands who were just like Reverend Stiffer."

"Until today I'd never heard of her," Ken said.

"According to the legend, Wilgefortis' father was the king of Portugal. He arranged a marriage for her, but she wanted to join a convent," May explained.

"Then what happened?" Jim asked.

"She prayed for deliverance from her father's grasp. When she awoke one morning she had grown a full beard. Her fiancé then split, never to come back."

"I'd like to learn more about her," Princeton said. "I'll read about her when we get back to Georgia."

"In some of the legends about Wilgefortis, her father had her crucified," May added. "I didn't want a violent ending for my story. There are people who want to see her feast day returned to the Catholic calendar. To them, she represents people who are marginalized."

Reverend Sue Moyers jumped into the conversation. "I can't wait to share my story; you'll see some similar themes."

"Great, I can't wait to be kicked again. There must be something in the water," Billy said.

"Or in the atmosphere," Sue countered. "It's not about you, but I do think it's getting bad out there for women."

"Is anyone hungry?" Dave asked. "Ken tells me we're close to Santiago. I can't wait to try some Spanish food."

"I'd like to try something local, something I've never had before," Jim said.

"Me, too," Ed added. "We don't get much variety back in Early County."

"Variety back home is often the choice between McDonald's and Burger King," Dave was not a regular consumer of fast food.

"We do have a bunch of southern cookin' restaurants," May said. "Six or seven, I think."

"That's true," Ben added. "But I do miss those local drugstore fountains we used to have."

"And what did they serve?" Dave asked. "Burgers, fries, and mac and cheese."

"At least you could get a blue plate special," Sue said. "I loved them."

"Meatloaf, slices of ham, or Salisbury steak, those were your choices," Ben said.

"We could go on and on, but we're not in Georgia; we're in Spain, and I can't wait to see what we'll be eating," Dave said.

Middlelogue

"THE CARGADO AI SAYS we're here. It wants me to park the bus right over there." Ken was pointing to a castle that had been abandoned about 500 years ago. Next to the ruins was an empty parking lot, and next to the parking lot was a small village. Ken pulled into the AI-chosen space and stopped the bus. "It says this is our preferred destination."

"This can't be Santiago de Compostela," Princeton said. Something's fishy with that AI.

"There's a sign, see it?" May was pointing to a small sign a few yards away. "It says, Santiago de Compostelita."

"This is where the Cargado AI wants us to be," Ken said.

"But this is not where we want to be," Dave said. "You were supposed to drive the bus to Santiago de Compostela."

"Well, I'm sorry," Ken felt offended. "The rental company told me to follow the AI box directives; that's what I did. They guaranteed that if we followed it, everything would go well."

"What did they mean, 'everything would go well?'" Dave asked.

"Well, the rental agent did mention that if we didn't follow the AI directives, we'd end up in a place where we were among hundreds of thousands of tourists with thousands of locals who weren't happy we were there."

"I've heard that Spaniards are sick of having so many tourists," Princeton said.

"Hey, everyone!" Sue was looking out the side window at a dozen people from the village who were approaching the bus. "I wonder what they want?" Suddenly, one of them was knocking on the bus door.

Ken got out of the driver's seat and opened the door. "Can I help you?" he asked. The other eleven O'Postles were nervous and remained in their seats, not saying a word. They feared these might be angry Spaniards ready to chase them away.

"Welcome to Santiago de Compostelita. I am Mayor Francisco Fernández, and this is Father Alcuin. We're glad you have chosen to visit our village, aren't we, Father Alcuin?" The priest smiled and gave the thumbs-up signal with his right hand. "We have lunch prepared for you if you would be so kind as to follow me."

"And we have rooms for you in the rectory that you will find quite comfortable," Father Alcuin said. "We have nice bathrooms at the end of the hallway; both are working. We also have internet Wi-Fi at the end of the block, near the big fountain. You are welcome to stay as long as you like."

"What are they saying?" Dave asked. "I can't hear what's going on."

"This is Mayor Francisco Fernández and Father Alcuin. They are saying they have lunch ready and that they have rooms for us in the church's rectory."

"How did they know we were coming?" Dave asked.

"How did you know we were coming?" Ken asked Mayor Fernández.

"How did we know they were coming?" Mayor Fernández asked restaurant owner Juana Garcia, one of the twelve from the village greeting committee.

"How did we know they were coming?" Juana asked Fernando Sanchez, head of the village visitor's center.

"The Cargado AI program sent me a message saying that they would be here."

"It was the Cargado AI program that told us they'd be here," Juana said to the mayor.

"The AI program from Cargado told Fernando you'd be here." The mayor pointed to the tourist bureau leader who had a bright smile and was giving them the thumbs-up message.

"It was the AI program," Ken told Dave.

"So, we're in this rinky-dink town and not Santiago de Compostela because of AI?" Princeton had a frown on his face. Unlike Fernando, he was not at all happy.

"That about sums it up," Ken said.

"Everybody, I'm really hungry, so we're having lunch here, period." Dave told his fellow pilgrims.

"That sounds absolutely perfect. I'll bet we'll get some wonderful Spanish food." May was happy. She winked at Princeton and gave him a thumbs up. "Smile, my friend!"

One by one, the twelve O'Postles got off the bus and introduced themselves to the greeting committee, known locally as the *Doce Saludadores*, who in turn provided much-needed information.

"Lunch will be fifteen Euros each, thank you," Juana said.

"Rooms at the rectory are twenty-five Euros and include dinner after vespers and breakfast after lauds, and they come with unlimited use of the hall *baños*," Alcuin added.

"What are lauds and vespers?" Ben whispered to May. "Some kind of exercise routines? I hope they don't make us jog; my knees are getting pretty bad."

"Prayers, not workouts; they won't hurt your knees unless you can't get down on them."

"And use of the town's Wi-Fi near the fountain," Francisco said. "It's free unless you are not in the town anymore."

"Francisco, you can't use it if you're not in the town," Juana reminded him. "You'd be too far away."

"But if you can't use it, it is not free because you are not receiving something for nothing," Francisco countered. "See, I am always right about the *tecnología*."

The Twelve led by *Los Doce* walked the half-mile stretch from the pink bus to Juana's restaurant along an ancient narrow street paved with stones quarried a thousand years ago.

Nestled deep in the middle of Santiago de Compostelita, Casa Garcia had been in continuous operation and owned by the same family for over four hundred years. On one side of the restaurant was a fireplace big enough to stand in; a roaring fire awaited the guests. Carved into the stone mantle were the numbers 1620 and 12, marking the year and month the restaurant was founded. Hundreds of autographed drawings and pictures of the not-very-famous people who had dined at Casa Garcia filled the walls. A large table in the middle of the dining area was set and waiting for the wary O'Postles of deepest South Georgia.

"Please have a seat," Juana said. "We are very glad *Señor* AI brought you here. Have you met him?"

"I think he works for the government in Madrid," shopkeeper, cobbler, and welcome committee member Julio Marcos said. "It's all very hush-hush."

Everyone looked at Ken, who shook his head. Not knowing what to say, he shrugged his shoulders. The Twelve O'Postles then sat down at the table.

"AI is an *it* on the bus and not a *señor* in the Capitol," Fernando explained to Juana and Julio. Speaking to the O'Postles, he said, "You see, in *España* we have so many Santiagos, we have them south, we have them north, we have them east, and we even have them on islands. But all of the tourists go to the one in the west. So, Cargado AI brought you to this one, the one in the middle."

"Is the one in the west Santiago de Compostela?" Princeton asked.

"Yes, my friend, you have it correct." Fernando was hoping this tour group would find value in their little Santiago and not leave. "Weeee," he said, opening his arms wide towards the *Doce Saludadores* committee, "we think you will see that our Santiago is best. We have everything you could want in a Santiago."

"We came all the way to Spain to see the pilgrimage site for Saint James," Dave said. "I don't see how this town compares."

Father Alcuin spoke up. "We too have a Santiago relic here," he said. "Our church, dedicated to the one and the same Santiago, has one of his fingers."

"That's true," Mayor Fernández said. "And those funcionarios from that hugely big Santiago want it, still."

Alcuin added, "They say that because they have the blessed saint's remains, they should have our little finger, too."

"That's not fair," Billy said. "What gives them the right to take your finger?"

"Their bishop, an important man in all of *España*, he sent an emissary to us with an official demand for our relic. But we refused to give him the finger."

"He had no right to do that," Dave said.

"No, he did not," Father Alcuin responded. "Then their town fathers sent two thieves to steal it. I caught them red-handed."

"No way," Dave said, shocked that something like this would happen.

"That's what they said when I caught them. The thieves told me that everybody knows that *The Way* goes to their cathedral and that there was *no way* pilgrims would ever find our little church with its finger of the blessed saint, which you will see later."

May, who was seated next to Dave, whispered in his ear, "We cannot in good conscience leave these folks and go to Santiago de Compostela. I feel so sorry for them."

"Look, we're small-town folks, just like they are," Ken added. "We're always losing out to Atlanta and Savannah when it comes to tourists." He was seated on Dave's other side.

"We'll talk about it over lunch," Dave said. "We have to see what the group says, but I will say I think you're right." At that moment, their meal was brought to the table, several kinds of dishes common to the people of Castilla y León.

"I hope we'll all agree," May said. She turned back to the table and froze. "That pig is staring at me. I cannot eat with him looking at me," she said to Dave.

"That's *tostón*," Juana explained. "You will like, I promise."

"How can I like *tostón* if he's dead?"

"May, *tostón* is the name of the dish, not the name of the pig while he was still alive," Ken said. "If you like barbecue, you'll like it."

"I still don't want him staring at me." She looked across the table. "Bob, can we switch seats?"

"I don't think so," Bob said. "I don't want him looking at me, either."

"I'll switch with you," Sarah said. She got up and took a seat next to Dave; May sat down next to Ben.

"Oh great, now I have to look at Toto's backside," May said, a little too loudly. "Good Lord, I am not in Kansas anymore."

"Shush, May," Princeton said. "Switch places with me." He got up and sat down where May had been sitting. May sat down at Princeton's former seat.

In addition to the *tostón,* on the table were plates of trout *escabeche*, white bean stew, two styles of green beans, and freshly baked bread. "Enjoy," Juana said.

As the O'Postles were enjoying lunch, Dave raised the idea of staying in Little Compostela, as he called the town. "Look, I like it here. The people are warm, the town is not overrun with tourists, and I feel we can find our spiritual journey here more than we ever could in Big Compostela."

"That's true. There are no tourists here. Maybe there's a reason why," Jim said.

"What if we share the rest of our stories seated by the fire," Sara suggested.

"And maybe then Father Alcuin can give us a tour of his church."

"What does everyone think?" Dave asked.

"I, for one, think it's a great idea," Ken said. "Maybe it was God who led us here and not the AI."

"You're just making an excuse for taking us to the wrong Santiago," Princeton said, laughing. "Actually, I agree with Ken, really I do. There's something special about this place."

"Well, I guess I could go along with staying here," Jim said.

"If no one objects, May and Ben, can you go speak with Juana to see if it's okay?" Looking around the table, the consensus was clear to Dave. May and Ben then went to the front of the restaurant where Juana was reviewing some documents.

"*Hola,*" Juana said to May and Dave. "When you're done eating, please spend afternoon around nice fire, yes? I'm sure you will have great discussion. Father Alcuin told me he can give your group a tour of the church and our relic after Compline. That's the best time to see our old church. After that, he can check you into the rectory. You like?"

"Yes, very much. *Gracias,*" May said. Whispering to Ben, she added, "Compline is a prayer time like Lauds and Vespers. We won't be jogging."

"*Grathias,*" Ben added. "We'll do that." They went back to the table to share the news with their colleagues.

"It's *gracias,* not *grathias,*" May told Ben. "I know my Spanish pretty well."

"Oops," he replied.

"Okay, everyone, let's all retire to the lounge area by the fireplace. That's where we will continue our storytelling," Dave said. Everyone found a seat in the comfortable chairs and couches around the fire, then Dave addressed the group. "Who's got the next story?"

"It's me," Reverend Sue Moyers said with great enthusiasm. "My text is Luke 10:41–42. I'm using Today's New International Version, and my tale is about how we sometimes get things Jesus said backwards. The title of my tale is, *In Heaven As It Is on Earth*. I hope you find it meaningful." Sue stood next to the fireplace and began her story.

In Heaven As It Is On Earth?

"Martha, Martha," the Lord answered, "you are worried about many things, but few things are needed—or indeed only one. Mary has chosen what is better, and it will not be taken away from her."

(Luke 10:41–42 TNIV)

"That woman must stop trying to lead the Bible study," Rev. Harding Stone said, feeling a wellspring of righteous rage. "If she doesn't stop, I'm gonna make sure no one attends." Reverend Stone was the pastor of Hard Rock Reformed Chapel, an independent church founded by members of the 1970s Christian rock group, Hard Rock for Jesus.

Originally a moderately progressive congregation, in recent years the new elders of the church were feeling increasingly paternalistic. Its pastor was, too. There was a rumor going around that Reverend Stone and Chief Elder J. Malus Mustard, a gold dealer who specializes in buying jewelry and coins from down-on-their-luck widows and orphans, were reaching out to the Restored Orthodox Protestant Reformed Church, a schismatic denomination that separated from the Orthodox Protestant Reformed Church in 2023 over doctrinal disagreements regarding whether the priesthood of all believers included women.

"Oh, come on Harding, what on earth's eatin' at you?" His sister, Allie asked. "Why are you so angry?"

"Lizzie should be there to learn from a male leader as should all the other women in the Bible study. She should not be the teacher," Harding explained. "It's as simple as that, and I shall say no more!"

"You wanted a women's Bible study, and now you've got one. They're not meeting at Hard Rock Church. They're not using any of the church's resources. And not everyone who attends is a member of Hard Rock," Allie shot back. "I'm glad you shall say no more because there's nothin' you can do about it, no matter what your silly ecclesiastical constitutions say. Period, end of story!"

"Humph," Harding muttered. "They're not silly. It's about Headship!"

"I knew you couldn't 'say no more,' Harding! The fact of the matter is, I'm gonna go too, 'cause I think Lizzie's great, and she's very insightful." Allie looked her brother in the eye. "And there isn't anything you can do about that, either! So, go forth, take a bath, and get ready for dinner."

Ever since Reverend Stone's wife Sandy left him for a woman she met on a Hard Rock mission trip to Yazoo City, and, in no particular order, underwent gender-affirming care, became a Unitarian, and filed for a divorce, Harding had been living with his sister, Allie Stone, a successful Cairo, Georgia real estate agent. Harding worried that if the church elders knew what his ex-wife had done, they would have serious doubts about his capacity to model godly Headship; they might even have him defrocked.

"I'm this far from kicking him out of my house!" Allie said to her mother, Blanche Stone. Allie was holding two fingers very close together. She had stopped by her parents' house for a visit after church one Sunday afternoon. "He's so heavy-handed, but he's my brother." Blanche and Allie were in the den, a room in which the decorations greatly offended Allie's real estate sales sensibilities. With old yellow paneling, space-age orange and white plastic furniture, and maroon shag carpeting, it reflected the bygone era of the Mercury and Gemini launches from Cape Canaveral. "He's getting more domineering, and he's getting more obnoxious about it, too!"

"You're the one who took him in, not me."

"I know, Mom. But if he's not careful, I'm gonna take him out!"

"That's a nice idea, Allie. A restaurant is a less threatening environment if the two of you need to talk."

"That's not the kind of take him out I was talking about." Allie never learned that the last person to speak to about a sibling conflict was one's parents. Jesus sort of hinted at that in the Parable of the Prodigal Son.

"Think Michael Corleone in *The Godfather*, Mom."

"Oh, I never saw that movie, it was too violent for me." She stopped cross-stitching and looked at Allie. "And it had nudity in it. Your dad wanted to rent it, but I wouldn't let him."

"Okay, Mom, what about *Scarface*?"

"Scarface? That one was too violent, too."

"*Goodfellas*?"

"Not that one, either. Didn't it have nudity, too?"

Allie was getting frustrated. "Do you at least get the picture?"

"What picture? Is there another movie you want to ask me about?"

"Oh, Mother, you're not paying attention!" Allie realized her mom's attention was focused on the cross-stitch pillowcase she was making, a representation of the planet Saturn and its 274 moons. When Blanche started the *Planets and Their Moons* cross-stitch pillow series upon which she was diligently working, she didn't realize that the gas giant planets had so many moons. She feared the project wouldn't be finished for the Hard Rock Reformed Chapel building renovation fundraiser.

"How about TV shows?" Blanche asked, looking up at her daughter, smiling.

"TV shows, Mom?" Allie wasn't sure if her mother manipulated the conversation in a different direction or if she truly wasn't paying attention.

"You know, dear, I really like the new *Masterpiece Theatre* show on PBS. Have you seen it yet?"

"The new *Masterpiece*? No, I've never seen the program. I stopped watching TV completely."

"Well, you'd like *Masterpiece*." Blanche was feeling more relaxed since Harding was no longer the topic of discussion. "You know, I read that *Masterpiece's* been on for more than fifty seasons. The first series I remember watching was *Shoulder to Shoulder*. Wow, that was the year I met your father."

"Really?" Allie knew the conversation had meandered away from her brother, so she decided to go along for the ride. "I'll give it a try for sure."

"Speaking about meeting your father, he took me to a nice restaurant on our first date, just like you wanna do with your brother, though it'd be weird to call dinner with your brother a date." Blanche smiled at her daughter. "He took me to a Hawaiian restaurant; Lord how I miss those pu-pu platters with the little volcanos in the middle; and they'd put little paper umbrellas in your drink, remember? You didn't tell me where you were gonna take him. He really likes Vietnamese food."

"Yes, I remember the pu-pu platters, but not the little umbrellas. Mom, I'm not so sure I'm gonna take. . ."

"No wait, not Vietnamese. It's Thai that he likes. Massaman curry's his favorite, I think. Gosh, I almost forgot the fake leis they'd give you. I wish Hawaiian restaurants could make a comeback, don't you?"

"Yes, Mom, but I. . ."

"He can't use chopsticks." Blanche stopped her stitching and looked at her daughter over her half-circle reading glasses. "Make sure he gets a knife and fork. Sometimes you gotta ask for 'em. They'd give you both at Hawaiian restaurants, and you didn't have to ask."

"Wait, Mom. . ."

"Not too spicy, either. Your brother gets acid reflux very easily."

"M-o-t-h-e-r, wait! I didn't say I was gonna take him out to eat."

"I distinctly remember hearing you say you were. If you don't want to, don't."

"Well, maybe I should. I hate it when he and I are angry with each other."

Ashe Stone suddenly wandered into the room. "Hi Allie," he said. He was up from his nap and glad to see his daughter. "How's my sunshine?"

"Allie was talking about going out to eat," Blanche said to her husband.

"Anything but Thai," Ashe said. "And not with Harding if he's still on that wacko Headship track. If you need to get him outta your house, Hard Rock Reformed has a basement apartment where he could stay, at least temporarily. I'll be glad when he's back to normal."

"Dear, don't you remember when you joined the Marxist Mennonites? You got that big scar on your hand from when you burned your draft card at one of their peace demonstrations," Blanche reminded Ashe. "I'm sure Harding will come around just like you did."

"Dad, you never told me you burned your draft card," Allie was laughing. "I'm shocked."

"Your mother was the one who was gonna hitchhike to Maine and become a simple-living, pacifist-Shaker. Your grandparents threw a fit and locked her in her room for two weeks." Ashe was laughing now.

"Is that true, Mom?"

"Yes, but don't feel so smug, Allie. You drove me nuts when you became a vegan Quaker. We'd be at the store, and you'd keep using thees and thous with everyone. It was so embarrassing. Your dad and I also had to throw out a lot of meat, eggs, and butter because of you."

"You guys could have eaten that stuff."

"We didn't want to offend you," Blanche said. "Remember what Paul said, 'If what I eat causes my brother or sister to fall into sin, I will never eat meat again?'"

"I guess we all had our wanderings. I will say that Harding's Headship kick is more than just a personal journey; he thinks he's got authority over people and he's forcing his beliefs on everyone. We just looked and acted weird," Allie said. "Were you aware that he hasn't told the congregation that Sandy left him and has filed for a divorce?"

"From what I hear, they already know about everything, including the sex change, I might add. I think most of them will be understanding; at least they would have been when I was pastor at Hard Rock," Ashe said.

Ashe, a retired minister, played a Hofner bass with Hard Rock for Jesus and later was the first pastor of Hard Rock Reformed Chapel when the band and its followers started the church.

"So, you think they'll understand?" Allie asked.

"Maybe. I also heard all about the women's Bible study. They better not let Harding stop it," he chuckled. "That Lizzie is a force to be reckoned with, don't you think so, Mother?"

"Yes, she can be. Don't you remember when Elder Mustard called her Missy?"

Ashe and Allie were laughing. "I thought she was gonna punch him," Allie said.

"She didn't punch him; she poured the pitcher of punch on him," Ashe said. "It was at a Wednesday potluck."

Allie got herself out of the old bean bag chair and gave her parents a hug. "Well, I best be goin'. I love y'all." Allie stopped at the door to say one last thing. "You know, I might take Harding to the Thai place this evening. Maybe I can reason with him."

That evening Allie did take her brother out for dinner at Hot Woks, a small family-run Thai restaurant within walking distance of Allie's house.

"No, I don't like massaman curry. Who said that I did?" He seemed a little testy. "Pad Thai is what I like, especially with shrimp." He looked up from the menu and smiled at his sister. "Look, Sis, I really appreciate you letting me stay with you. Sorry if I'm so edgy."

"There are some things I need to say to you, Harding." Allie was very serious. "Your ex, Sandy, was my friend when she was a she and will be my friend now that she's a he." She paused when the waiter came to the table. "I'll take the pork Pad Thai and water, no ice. Thank you."

"I'll take the chicken Pad Thai." Harding looked at Allie. "Do you mind if I have a beer?"

"Go ahead, my treat."

"And I'd like that Thai beer you serve here." He thanked the waiter and continued the conversation. "What Sandy is doing is. . ." Harding started to say, but Allie interrupted him.

"What Sandy has done, while it's upsetting to you, is not your concern anymore. You can't control her, and even more importantly, you can't take your anger out on everyone around you because of that. That's the first thing. The second thing is about Lizzie. I don't care what you think St. Paul says about a woman leading a Bible study. You need to accept the fact that a woman of your church is leading a Bible study, period. You're the pastor, not the dictator."

"But, in First Timothy. . ."

"It's not up for discussion, Harding. Look, are you gonna tell parents that when they have a rebellious teenager, they should have him or her stoned to death?"

"What?"

"Yes, that's what it says in Deuteronomy. Harding, I love you, but you gotta realize that just because you think there's a rule in the Bible that must be followed, it doesn't mean you're the one called upon to enforce it. So listen to me, the Women's Bible Study is none of your business. Period. If you're not going to be supportive, then keep your mouth shut and let it happen."

"You're right," Harding said. He was getting tired of being in charge of Headship enforcement and keeping track of the behavior of everybody in the congregation and whether or not their behavior fit within a divinely instituted order that was established before Adam and Eve ate the forbidden fruit. It was exhausting. Besides, like ninety-nine point nine percent of Christendom, he hadn't read Deuteronomy in a long time; it just now dawned on him that there were hundreds of other rules that needed oversight.

"I also want you to know that I'll be joining the Women's Bible Study." Allie stopped and looked at her brother. "Okay, I've said my peace." At that moment, their food was delivered to the table.

"Are you going to stay being friends with Sandy after all that she has done?" Harding asked.

"Let's enjoy our dinner, Harding. I've already said what I'm gonna say. Can you do that?"

He let out a long sigh. "I'll try, Sis."

"And lay off your rigid creeds and confessions for a while and listen to some of the sermons by folks like Fred Craddock or Barbara Brown Taylor. You might get inspiration from some people who found another way to look at a divine order in the world."

The first Hard Rock Reformed Chapel Women's Bible Study met in Lizzie's parlor, a good-sized sun-drenched room with bright green and blue speckled carpeting. Lizzie and Allie, expecting ten or twelve women, arranged the overstuffed couch and comfortable chairs so that folks could sit in a circle. On a sideboard were two coffee machines, a box of assorted bagels, and three containers of cream cheese, fat-free, low-fat, and full-fat.

"I'm glad you sent the announcement out a month ago," Allie told Lizzie. "That gave everyone time to get ready for some serious discussions."

"I want it to go well; I really do. By the way, is your mom coming?" Lizzie asked.

"She's got a very complicated cross-stitch project going for the fall fundraiser, and she's worried about getting it done on time."

"That's too bad; I was hoping she'd come."

"Hi Betty!" Lizzie turned and welcomed a very enthusiastic Betty Stanton, who had just walked into the parlor.

"Good morning!" Betty responded, taking a seat in one of the armchairs. "Wow, great chair. I can't wait to get started."

Within ten minutes, seven others arrived—Sarah Anthony; the Grimke sisters, Sandy and Anne; Lucy Mott; Mary Catt; Jenny Tubman; and Lydia Wells—everyone was eager to be a part of the Bible study group, especially with all of the changes going on at the Hard Rock Reformed Chapel and some other area churches, too.

"Good morning, sisters." Lizzie got the meeting started. "Before we begin, I wanna establish three rules. One, no foot washing. I dislike that ceremony, intensely. Two, no men. They already run everything at Hard Rock. And three, the conversations have to be respectful, unless of course they're not." She looked at everyone. "You can laugh, you know."

"It's the times in which we live, Lizzie," Betty said. "It's hard to laugh."

"I hear ya, but we must try," Lizzie said before continuing the introduction. "One or two of you don't know me; I'm Lizzie Stone, your facilitator. I use that word because our pastor told me that God won't allow me to lead the Bible Study. If God does let us know that it's okay for me to be the leader, then I'll be the leader." Lizzie looked around the room and realized no one was laughing. "I was kidding." Everyone started snickering.

"Look, we laughed a little," Sarah said. "That's a start."

"Let's go around the room and introduce ourselves and leave your shoes and socks on!" Again, no one laughed. "Another joke. Foot washing, removing shoes, get it? Goodness, y'all are one serious bunch. Allie, you're first—just your name and one sentence, whatever you want to say."

"Hi everyone, I'm Allie Stone. My brother is Harding Stone. I am glad to be here, and I am glad that he's not here."

"Good morning, Betty Stanton here. I don't like how anti-woman our church has become."

"Hi, Sarah Anthony, I sue people for doin' bad things to women and children."

"Sandy Grimke. I'm not grim, but my sister is."

"Hello, I'm Anne Grimke. Sandy's the grim one, and we both don't like the way things are changing at Hard Rock; we might move to Philadelphia and become Quakers."

"Lucy Mott's my name. I don't make applesauce, and I'm thinking about becoming a 'Quaker, too."

"Good morning, my name's Mary Catt. I'm glad to be here provided no one says meow; I'm a Baptist and don't attend Hard Rock church."

"I'm Jenny Tubman. I don't wanna lose the freedoms we've fought so hard to get. I want to learn from other women, and I need something to laugh about."

"Lydia Wells. Can I get a bagel and coffee?"

"Welcome everybody. Yes, Lydia, get your bagel and coffee. Now, I'd like somebody to open up our discussion with a question, a Bible verse, or anything to get a conversation going. I'll wait a few minutes, and if no one wants to start, I'll do the honors."

"Why don't you just get us started," Lydia said while she was pouring her coffee. "I think you've got a better idea of how this group will go."

"Yes, I think you should," Lucy added. The other women quickly agreed.

"As long as the room's not bugged," Lizzie said. Several people were concerned and started looking around. "Another joke. It's okay to laugh now."

"Thank you, Lizzie," Jenny said. "You'll get me smiling if not laughin' one of these days."

Lizzie looked around the circle with a serious expression on her face. "I once had a Bible with the most unfortunate of names," she said. "It was called *The Weaker Vessel Study Bible.* It had an essay inserted at the end of Genesis chapter two by some seminary professor. It was all about a so-called divinely instituted role for women, and it made me very angry. My ex gave me that Bible as a wedding gift. So picture this, here we are on our honeymoon, and he pulls that thing from his suitcase and hands it to me. It was pink, too! And I hate pink. Talk about a mood killer."

"What'd you do?"

"I was nineteen years old, and I didn't know what a vessel was. I did know that weaker applied to me and all the other women on this planet. Maybe even every female in the animal and plant kingdoms, for that matter." Lizzie felt a little embarrassed telling the story and didn't like talking about her very unpleasant first marriage. "I told 'im thank you and that I looked forward to reading it."

"*Weaker Vessel*—now that's a really grim title," Lydia said. "That's no reference to the Grimke sisters," she added quickly.

"Thank you," Anne added. "I'm sure Sandy thanks you too."

"I threw that Bible at my husband when I found out he was havin' an affair, and it sure was one big thick hardbound Bible."

"Yeah, from what I've heard, for being a weaker vessel, Lizzie, you sure got one powerful right arm. You almost knocked him out," Betty said.

"Clearly, having only one weaker vessel wasn't enough for that jerk, so I sent him and that Bible packing. It felt really good to hand it to him and to say, 'I'm not your vessel anymore' when he walked out my door."

"Good for you!" Jenny said while everyone was clapping.

"Let me summarize what the professor wrote in that inglorious essay I just mentioned. God gave Adam and all men something called Headship. God created Eve and all women to be men's helper, kind of like an amorous executive assistant. Because Adam came first and then Eve, a woman can never have a leadership role in which she has authority over a man."

"That's ridiculous," Sarah Grimke said.

"That professor wrote that because Adam named all of the animals and named the first woman, Eve, this reflects the man's position of authority over everything. Also, since God gave the command to not eat the fruit from the tree of the knowledge of good and evil to Adam, and then Adam told Eve about the command, this set in motion a divinely established order for communication between men and women for all time. Thus, a woman should never instruct a man about faith or the Bible, and in some people's thinking, a woman should never have any leadership role in business or government, and should not have a right to vote."

"I'm stunned," Lydia said. So was everyone else; Lizzie's parlor got very quiet.

"And, according to this scholar, Paul in 1 Corinthians made this the rule for the new church, too."

"When was that Bible published?" Jennie asked. "It must've been in the 1800s."

"Nope, not the 1800s."

"Then, the 1700s?"

"Nope."

"How about the 1400s?"

"No, you're going in the wrong direction, Jenny. Try again."

"The 1950s, that seems about right."

"Nope." Lizzie smiled as she shook her head.

"Really?" Jenny looked confused.

"The 1920s?" Anne suggested. "I bet it was in response to women getting the vote."

"Nope."

"Just tell us, then," Jenny said.

"2012." The room got very quiet again.

"Oh, for heaven's sake," Anne said. "That's crazy."

"Yes, it's crazy," Betty said.

"Let me get this straight, just because Adam named all the animals and because God gave the commandment about eating the fruit from the tree of knowledge to him, all men on this planet have Headship?" Anne asked.

"What is 'Headship,' anyway?" Sandy asked. It sounds ridiculous.

"It's all about who has authority and who doesn't. In that scholar's world, men have authority and women don't. All women are expected to happily affirm the authority of men in everything, the family, the church, the voting booth, or in any other place," Lizzie explained. "In fact, one Headship aficionado forbids women from being on a church council, being a minister, or leading adult Bible studies. He says sin inclines women to resist the divinely instituted limitations that come with their subordinate roles."

"So if Malus and Harding have their way, the female elders in our church will have to resign, is that what they're saying?" Sarah asked.

"Yup," Lizzie said.

"Lizzie, I just bought a study Bible for women online," Mary said. "It basically says the woman was supposed to have been the learner and the man the teacher, and that when Eve took on the role of the teacher, everything went to hell in a handbasket."

"So the fall of man and sin was all Eve's fault?" Jenny asked. "Now you see why I can't laugh anymore."

"Have any of you heard about that Bible for sexually active single women?" Mary asked.

"What? I've never heard of such a thing," Lizzie said. She was shocked.

"I haven't, either," Lucy added. The other women all shook their heads, signaling they hadn't either.

"It's called *Woman, Thou Art Loose*," Mary said. "The title's really bad."

"No, no, no, Mary. *It's Woman, Thou Art Loosed*," Lizzie corrected her. "It's another study Bible for women that's supposed to be focused on empowerment."

"It was done by a male TV preacher," Jenny said. "Now you've got me laughing."

"Oh. I wish I hadn't sent that vicious complaint letter to the publishers."

"I've got another Bible here; let me read what it says in the notes," Lizzie said. "Ready?"

"As ready as we'll ever be," Betty said. All of the Bible Study participants were quiet, waiting for more inglorious scripture annotations.

"But first, I have a question for y'all. In Genesis, what was the order of creation for animals, including humans?" Lizzie asked.

"Fish, land creatures, and then Adam, then Eve," Anne said.

"Now, listen to this note from Genesis chapter two that's in this book called *The Woman's Bible.* It comes from volume 1, page 19:

> It cannot be maintained that woman was inferior to man even if, as asserted in chapter ii, she was created after him without at once

> admitting that man is inferior to the creeping things, because he was created after them.

"What do you think of it?" Lizzie asked, laughing a little.

"When was that Bible published?" Betty asked. "And please don't make us guess."

"1895," Lizzie said. The parlor erupted in laughter.

"1895? I guess we've come a long way, baby," Sarah added.

"Let me read something else from the notes on Genesis. It also comes from volume 1, page 22:

> The assertion of the supremacy of the woman in the marriage is contained in 2:24: 'Therefore shall a man leave his father and his mother and cleave unto his wife.' Nothing is said of the headship of man, but he is commanded to make her the head of the household . . .

"Well, what do y'all think?" Lizzie asked.

"Let me see that Bible," Betty said. Lizzie handed her the book.

"It's sure different," Jenny said.

"*The Woman's Bible* is not really a study Bible, and it's not the complete text of Scripture either," Lizzie said. Instead, the authors, all women, focused on the parts that they felt pertained to women. A lot of church leaders then and now don't like it one bit."

"It's not hard to see why," Betty said, flipping through the book.

"I've got an idea," Lucy said. "Why don't we do a study on Genesis and compare what different study Bibles say about women?"

"Now that would be interesting," Betty said.

"I've another idea, why don't we just read *The Woman's Bible* from 1895," Lucy proposed. "For me, and I'm speaking only for myself, I'm tired of talking about what men have stuck in study Bibles about women. I'm more curious about what those women had to say back in 1895."

Looking around the room, Lizzie said, "It seems that this idea resonates with everyone. But I must warn you, *The Woman's Bible* was radical then and it still is today. We're not gonna agree with everything in it."

"I still think it'd be good for us to read it; that's what we should do next," Sarah Grimke said. The Bible study group members all nodded their heads in agreement.

"With *The Woman's Bible,* it's clear that it was reactive—activist women reacting to abuse and oppression by authoritarian men," Anne added, "Men who were steeped in that Headship junk."

"Then, let's do it," Anne said. She looked at Jenny and added, "Let's be loosed!"

"My brother's gonna throw a fit."

"I hope he does. And we'll be ready for 'im," Lizzie said.

The following Sunday, Allie was visiting her parents at their home. She wanted to give them an update about the Women's Bible Study.

"Hi Dad," Allie said when Ashe greeted her at the door. "Where's Mom?"

"I'd leave her alone right now."

"Why? Is she not feeling well?"

"Well, when she finished the cross-stitch Saturn pillow, I noticed that there were only 270 moons on it and not 274. I didn't want her to get upset, so I tried to add 'em myself. I think I messed it up."

"Oh no. Was she upset with you?"

"If she can fix it, she won't be. She's been at it for several hours."

"Sometimes it's best not to fix things for people, Dad."

"Ain't that the truth. You usually end up ruining the whole planet." Ashe shook his head. Clearly, he was frustrated with himself. "Tell me about the Bible study."

"The group decided to read Elizabeth Cady Stanton's *The Woman's Bible.*"

"Now that's very interesting," Ashe said. "Why'd y'all choose that?"

"We had a discussion about the new women's study Bibles out there and how many of them were focused on a supposed divine order for men and women."

"One of the Bibles had something called 'Headship' in it, right?"

"Yes, it's an awful term for an awful theology, unless you want to hitch yourself to a Neanderthal. How'd you hear about it?" Allie asked her dad.

"I'll give you one guess." Ashe smiled at his daughter.

"Mr. Neanderthal himself, right?"

"If you're talking about Harding, you're correct. But I wouldn't call him Mr. Neanderthal."

"Okay, how about Mr. Australopithecus? He's really gotten Headship into his head."

"A bunch of Hard Rock's elders have, too," Ashe added.

"Maybe they should change the name of the church from Hard Rock to Stone Age," Allie said sarcastically.

"One of the older elders mentioned to me that those younger firebrands want the women to sit on one side of the sanctuary and the men on the other. You know, like the Puritan churches did back in the 1700s."

"You're kidding me!"

"I kid you not, Allie."

"What's with those young elders? Why have they gotten so anti-women?"

"They've gotten mixed up with that splinter denomination called the Restored Orthodox Protestant Reformed Churches of America. It's misogyny to its core, if you ask me."

"How so?"

"That denomination split from the already very conservative Orthodox Protestant Reformed Churches of America because they didn't think women were part of the priesthood of all believers."

Allie stared at her dad for a minute; her face was easy for anyone to read—extreme shock from ear to ear and forehead to chin. "I don't think our Bible study group knows anything about that."

"And that's why your brother tried so hard to stop Lizzie from leading it. My older elder friend said they're gonna have a special meeting to vote on joining the splinter denomination. She said they'll schedule the meeting for some weird hour and time, like 11:12 p.m. on a Friday night."

"That's not right," Allie said.

"She also saw the announcement design—dark grey paper flyers with light grey, small font, hard-to-read typeface. These will be thumbtacked backwards on the nearest tree to the home of each church member."

"Why would they do that?"

"The church bylaws say notices of special called meetings have to be delivered to the home of each member. The rules don't say the notice can't be illegible and hung backwards."

They can't do that, can they? Allie shook her head. "I can't believe Harding is mixed up in this."

"Allie, I think he's afraid of those firebrand elders. They know all about Sandy and her sex change and her becoming a Unitarian." Ashe stopped for a moment to gather his thoughts. "This is what these men do. Instead of saying to the congregation, 'we don't believe that the priesthood of all believers applies to women,' they'll say, 'look, Sandy Stone dumped her husband, is getting gender-affirming care, and is becoming an atheist Unitarian, and we need to stop this from happening to our children.'"

"That's despicable."

"Yes, it is," Ashe said. "They'll scare the members with a trifecta of bugaboos—atheism, sex change, and divorce when what they really want to do is to stop women from participating in the life of the congregation in any meaningful way, whether it's as a minister, elder, adult teacher, lay leader, or even as a full voting member."

"Wow."

"It's a great strategy. If you're afraid of your child being harmed by one or more of the bugaboos, you'll think they're being reasonable."

"Dad, I don't know what to say."

"Fulfilling the Great Commission is not their objective," Ashe said. "Achieving control and purity is. In other words, they don't want to make disciples of Jesus, they want to make followers of their ideology."

"Now I really don't know what to say."

"Work with Lizzie. Get the Bible study group going and use *The Woman's Bible* as a starting point. No doubt the book is controversial, but it'll help the women in the group understand their role as leaders in our congregation."

Suddenly, a smiling Blanche walked into the room. "You're a lucky man, Ashe." Blanche exclaimed. "I fixed it. I'm on to Uranus, and thank the Lord it has only twenty-eight moons!"

"Oh, that's good news," Ashe said.

"And don't you ever try to fix things for me again."

"I promise," Ashe replied. "I know I shouldn't have done that."

"Allie, now that Saturn is fixed, I wanna be a part of that Bible study group. I heard you and your father talking about *The Woman's Bible,* and I think that's a great place to start; I read it when I was in college, and I'd like to read it again."

"Lizzie was hoping you'd join."

Two months after the Women's Bible Study's first meeting, a majority of the elders, being young men and into the Headship movement, managed to schedule a congregational meeting for a vote on joining the Restored Orthodox Protestant Reformed Churches of America denomination. Thanks to Reverend Ashe Stone's older elder friend, the Women's Bible Study members caught wind of the upcoming meeting and were able to spread the word to the whole congregation.

"If those who organized the meeting thought their sneaky efforts would succeed," Lizzie said upon hearing about the meeting, "it was only because they didn't anticipate the power of women focused on preserving their full membership in their church."

"We'll make sure the word is spread far and wide," Allie told Lizzie. "With Dad's help, we'll get just about every member at the meeting."

It was the Monday afternoon of the Labor Day weekend that Reverend Harding Stone and the young elders entered the fellowship hall at 2:12 p.m., five minutes before the congregational meeting was set to begin.

"Oh hell," Chief Elder J. Malus Mustard said to Reverend Stone. "Look at all of those women!" Malus was as aggressive on the church council as he was buying gold jewelry from people who couldn't pay their bills and had nowhere else to turn.

"How'd they find out about this meeting?" Harding was very surprised to see so many men and women. "I thought there'd only be a few folks here."

So confident were they at a successful vote that they printed only 10 copies of the agenda. Given the number of members who came to the meeting, they should have printed at least 40 or 50 copies.

Chief elder, J. Malus Mustard, whacked his gavel on the table. He was seated with the treasurer, payday lender Maxwell Edison, and the recorder/secretary, barber Comer Flattop, at one of the folding tables used for church potluck suppers. "I call this congregation meeting to order. First on the agenda . . ."

"You didn't print enough agendas," Lizzie said.

"First on the agenda is . . ."

"I guess you didn't hear me; you didn't print enough agendas," Lizzie repeated.

Malus whacked his gavel on the table again. "I'm not taking statements from the congregation at this time. The meeting is called to order, and the first item is a vote on the motion to join the Reformed Orthodox Restored

Churches of America; all in favor say aye." Malus waited for a few moments. "The ayes have it."

"No, they don't have it," Allie said. "You never asked for a motion or a second."

"I don't need to," Malus responded.

"Yes, you do," Recorder Comer Flattop said. "It says so in our bylaws."

"Oh, alright, have it your way! Is there a motion to have Hard Rock Reformed Chapel join the Reformed Orthodox Protestant Restored Churches of America?"

"I so move," Earl Doopster, internet influencer, a new member and an elder said.

"I second the motion," Maxwell added.

"All in favor say aye." Malus waited for ten seconds before saying. "The ayes have it." He whacked his gavel on the table and gave a long, smug look at Lizzie.

"We just voted to join the Reformed Orthodox Protestant Restored Churches of America and not the Restored Orthodox Protestant Reformed Churches of America," Lizzie said, challenging the chair.

"No, we didn't," Malus said.

"Well, yes, we did," Recorder Comer Flattop said. "I have it right here in my notes."

"I told you so," Lizzie said.

"Now, we have to vote to disengage from the Reformed Orthodox Protestant Restored Churches of America," Comer explained.

"But there's no such organization." Malus was getting flustered. He thought this would have been a quick and easy vote.

"There is now. We created the organization when we voted to join it. We're the only member."

"Well, just fix the minutes to reflect the correct name."

"That would officially withdraw us from the Reformed Orthodox Protestant Restored Churches of America, and you can't do that legally in Early County without a vote."

"Okay, I call a vote to officially withdraw from the Reformed Orthodox Restored Churches of America."

"It's not on the agenda. You have to amend the agenda first," Comer explained. "Or you might could schedule a new meeting with a new agenda."

"This is ridiculous!" Malus said angrily. "Is there a motion to amend the agenda?"

"Come to think of it, I kind of like being a member of our own denomination," Maxwell said. "I'd like to chew on it for a while before we close down the new denomination."

"Oh, for heaven's sake, Maxwell," Malus said. "Don't be an idiot. Is there a motion to set the date for a new meeting of the congregation of Hard Rock Reformed Chapel just so the pea-brained Mr. Edison can make a decision?"

Lizzie stood up and said, "Is there a motion that we close this meeting?"

"I so move," Allie said.

"I second the motion," Betty said.

"All those in favor, say aye; opposed, say nay," Lizzie waited for about fifteen seconds. "The motion to close the meeting has carried."

"You can't do that," Malus said.

"Yes, she can," Comer responded. "It says so in the bylaws we revised last month."

"I move that we open a new meeting of Hard Rock Reformed Chapel," Malus said.

"I second the motion," Maxwell said.

"Those in favor, aye; opposed, nay." He waited for ten seconds. "The motion carries."

"I move that this new meeting be adjourned and that we hold our next meeting of the Hard Rock Reformed Chapel on the first Sunday of October immediately following worship and that lunch be provided," Allie said.

"Wait!" Maxwell said. "Lunch sounds terrific, but can we add to the motion that Ashe brings some of his great barbecue?"

"And don't forget Mrs. Cobb's cornbread," Earl added. "We could put the cornbread and the barbecue into a single motion that would be an addendum to the motion for the adjournment of this meeting and the approval of the next."

"And Mr. Saul's tater tots," Sarah added.

"Okay," Allie said, "I move that this new meeting be adjourned and that we hold our next meeting of the Hard Rock Reformed Chapel on the first Sunday of October immediately following worship, and that lunch be provided, and that Ashe provides barbecue, Mrs. Cobb brings her cornbread, and Mr. Saul brings his tater tots."

"I second the motion," Lucy said.

"All those in favor, say aye."

After eight seconds, Allie said, "Sounds like the ayes have it. The meeting is adjourned, and our next meeting will be the first Sunday in October immediately after worship, with lunch provided, including the added stuff about the barbecue, cornbread, and tater tots." With the exception of Malus and a few of the new elders, cheers spread through the congregation.

"Would everyone shut up!" Malus was angry and could sense that support for the merger dissipated because of the barbecue, cornbread, and tater tot addendum. He stood up and said, "I move that we open another congregational meeting. All in favor say aye, opposed say nay."

"You can't do that," Comer said. "We've already scheduled our next meeting. You need a motion to move that we cancel the next meeting, and the barbecue, cornbread, and tater tots, and have someone second that motion and then have another motion with a second that proposes we open a new meeting." Several members of the congregation started booing.

"I move everyone leave the building and go home," Lizzie said.

"I second the motion," Allie said.

"All those in favor say aye, those opposed say nay." Lizzie waited seven seconds. "The motion carries. Have a great evening, everyone."

The meeting room cleared quickly as most members wanted to go home to watch Monday Night Football.

Malus and Harding sat motionless; they were stunned. It was supposed to have been a simple meeting with a simple vote with a simple outcome.

"I'm sending out a social media post telling everybody about Sandy as soon as I get home," Malus said to Harding. "Then they'll know how evil a woman can be!"

"I wish you wouldn't do that," Reverend Harding said.

"Do you want me to create a new partnership file for the Reformed Orthodox Protestant Restored Churches of America?" Comer asked. "I could do that before I leave."

"Do what you want, Comer," Malus said. He then glared at Harding and said, "The next meeting should be about you and your ex., Harding. We'll talk while I drive you home."

Unbeknownst to Malus and Harding, earlier that afternoon Allie and Lizzie had borrowed the license plate from J. Malus Mustard's BMW.

"We didn't steal Malus' tag, we borrowed it," Allie said to her brother. She and Lizzie were at the Sheriff's office to pick up her brother. Harding was riding with Malus after the meeting when they were pulled over by a sheriff's deputy. Malus' BMW, having no license plate, was immediately impounded.

"Too bad Malus has to stay in jail," Allie said when Harding got into the car.

"So, what did you do with the Malus license plate?"

"We lent it to the sheriff," Lizzie said. "We knew she was going to need it."

"And why would she need it?" Harding asked.

"She needed to put the tag back on the car after her deputy impounded it."

"Wait, you're telling me that you borrowed the tag from Malus's car so you could lend it to the sheriff so she could put it onto the car her deputy impounded, because it had no tag?" Harding asked. "I think I'm too tired to follow your logic model, Lizzie."

"It's all very simple. One of our Bible study group members, Sarah Anthony, has a friend in Little Rock who works with battered women. When we found out that J. Malus Mustard was from Little Rock, we figured it was worth checking him out," Allie explained. "You remember Hamlet saying, 'The lady doth protest too much, methinks?' Well, we-thoughts Mr. Malus protests too much, too."

"Mr. Mustard had an outstanding warrant on an assault and battery charge. He beat his wife several times," Lizzie said. "We knew our sheriff would want to send Mr. J. Malus Mustard back to Little Rock, so it made sense to provide a quick reason for Malus to get arrested."

"And tomorrow morning, he will be on his way back to Little Rock," Allie said.

"What made Sarah think to call her friend about Mr. Mustard?"

"Malus dislikes women for some reason," Lizzie said. "Why else would he be so adamant about taking away our participation in the life of the church?"

"And don't you go telling me about Headship in Genesis and about what St. Paul says," Allie warned her brother. "Jesus didn't treat women that way."

"But Paul was an Apostle and . . ."

"And when given the choice of cleaning or talking theology with Jesus, Martha's sister Mary chose Jesus," Lizzie said.

"And Martha got mad and complained," Allie added. "It's not in the Bible, but perhaps someone else helped Martha."

"Maybe Jesus said, 'Hey, one of you Apostles, you're not doing anything, go help Martha with the cleaning so I can talk with Mary.'" Lizzie thought this was entirely plausible. "And Luke, being a man, didn't think it important to include that in his gospel."

They pulled into the Stone's driveway and stopped the car. Allie looked at her brother and spoke to him in a calm voice, "We've more to talk about. Dad's made his barbecue, and we're all gonna have a conversation over dinner."

"That means the three of us plus Mom and Dad?"

"And the Women's Bible Study members, too," Allie said. "This Headship stuff has gone far enough."

Blanche greeted Harding, Allie, and Lizzie at the door and led them into the Stone's living room. Like the den, the living room was decorated in a 1960s Cape Canaveral style—space-age round tables with thin chrome-tipped legs and a low-backed plastic-sided couch. One chair looked a bit like an inverted helmet and another like an orbital satellite that had been cut in half.

"Wow," Lizzie said. "I love this room."

"It's my favorite," Blanche said. "I find space technology fascinating. When I was a kid, I wanted to be an astronaut."

"I didn't know that Mom," Harding said. "What stopped you?"

"Your grandfather," she replied. "He didn't think the space age was for women."

"That wasn't fair," Harding said. "So, what did you do?"

"Once I finished high school, I left home and put myself through college and got a degree in Astronomy. And that's where I met your father."

The doorbell rang, and Blanche headed to the front door, leaving Harding alone with his sister and Lizzie.

"Let me tell you why we're all here, Harding," Allie said. "Tonight, we're gonna enjoy our dad's barbecue and smoked veggies. He's also made your favorite dessert, pawpaw cheesecake. And then you're gonna to hear the testimony of each member of the Women's Bible Study. After that, you'll have the opportunity to explain Headship theology and what it would mean to them personally and not only to them, but to their daughters, too."

Lizzie smiled at Harding. "Don't worry, we won't bite. We'll all just leave Hard Rock for a more conventional congregation. It does amaze me, though, how food was enough to push a close vote away from those young elders."

"Harding, we'll all stay if you value our contribution to the life and funding of our church with the same enthusiasm and inspiration that you do with the men," Allie added.

"It's all quite simple, Harding," Lizzie said. "Partnership or vesselship, that's the way we see it. You're the pastor; tonight, you get to pick which one."

"And then we decide where we'll go," Allie added.

"Come to the table," Ashe said, stepping into the living room. He was wearing his trademark apron decorated with rockets and space capsules, with its wide belt that had slots for spatulas, tongs, and sauce squirters. "The feast is ready. Harding, I need your help serving the food."

Allie and Lizzie went to the dining room and took their seats with Blanche and the other members of the Women's Bible Study at a long steel table that was once used at the Cape Canaveral mess hall.

Later that evening, Harding and Allie were back at home following a long fellowship dinner at their parents' house. "I'm exhausted, Sis," Harding said. "It never occurred to me that for many women, the flip side to Headship is oppression."

"In our Bible study, we read Elizabeth Cady Stanton's *The Woman's Bible* and learned more about the suffrage movement. We didn't realize how closely tied they were to Frederick Douglass, the Abolitionists, and the work to abolish slavery."

"I didn't know that," Harding said. "That's really interesting."

"It's more than interesting," Allie said with passion. "When you talk about Headship, a lot of us women do hear oppression."

"And the more a woman pushes back against Headship, the more oppressive men become?"

"Exactly, Harding. Think about Mom's story. Granddad locked her up for two weeks. And then there's Malus. He beat his wife. And Malus was going to use Sandy's story to influence the vote on that Restored Orthodox denomination."

"And get me defrocked, too. Why do men feel they need to control women?" He asked rhetorically. "We get so focused on a bunch of Bible texts that support a particular ideology and then use every tool at our disposal, from manipulation to scare tactics, so that people acquiesce."

"That's what was happening when you and the elders were trying to keep members from attending the special called meeting," Allie said. "You wanted a positive vote, and you knew the only way to get one was to keep as many women as possible from attending the meeting."

"I wonder if I should resign."

"No, Harding. Just be honest with the congregation. Those young elders decided that on earth women should be controlled, unworthy of being among the priesthood of all believers. Y'all used lots of Bible verses to justify this and created an image of heaven to be forced upon Hard Rock Chapel. There's no way to sugarcoat what you and those elders did."

"For our next congregational meeting, I'm gonna have a lot of preparation to do. What a creep I've been."

"Look, Harding. Just be honest with us. Mom and Dad will support you, as will I, and Lizzie and the other members of the Bible study."

"More Neanderthal men," Ben said. "Haven't we had enough?"

"Well, when male politicians and preachers are calling for the repeal of the 19th Amendment, we women have to speak up or we will lose the freedoms we've enjoyed for a little over one hundred years," Reverend Sue Moyers said.

May added, "Women in the United States had to fight for more than a century just to be able to vote in national elections; now there're men who are working to take those rights away."

"Wow, I didn't know that," Ed said. "It's ridiculous, and they have to be stopped!"

"Sue, you got all of the names of the women's Bible study group from suffragists and women's rights leaders of the 1800s, isn't that so?" May asked.

"I did. Those women were brave and worked hard to obtain the right to vote. And today, let me repeat, today, there are Christians, politicians, and clergy who want to see those rights taken away. That's why I chose those names."

"I wonder if Juana has any Graham crackers and marshmallows to go with the chocolate she gave us." Billy interrupted the discussion on women's rights. "We could make s'mores over the fire."

"S'mores? Are you serious, Billy?" May was upset with the Baptist preacher. "This is a critical discussion that means a lot to us women, and all you can think about is s'mores."

"I can think about two things at the same time," Billy said, defending himself. "And I can think better if my stomach isn't growling."

"We're on a retreat," Ben said. "With all due respect, it would be nice to make s'mores over the fire while we talk about women's rights."

"You Baptists are hopeless," May said. "Go and get your crackers, chocolate, and marshmallows."

"They ain't heavy, but they're my brothers," Sue said with a chuckle. The other women got quiet for a second and then started laughing.

"May, I found your story very enlightening," Princeton said. "I had no idea that there were so many study Bibles for sale whose authors were working to roll back the hard-fought rights of women."

"I didn't either," Dave said. "It's both maddening and disheartening at the same time."

"There must be a lot of money to be made with these Bibles," Sue said. "It makes me so mad."

"We're on a retreat; let's live the anger when we get back home," May suggested. "We're in a wonderful village; we've had a wonderful meal, and soon we'll be touring an ancient church. Let's live this moment together."

"Thank you, May," Dave said. "I think we're ready for another story."

"There're no graham crackers or marshmallows," Billy reported.

"Well, there you go," May said. "Why don't you find another snack?"

"Who's next," Dave asked.

"I am," Reverend Bob Bending said. "My Scripture passage is Matthew 28:18–20, from Today's New International Version." He could see the room was a little tense after the inopportune insertion of s'mores into a serious discussion of the loss of voting rights for women. "I call my story *The Last Presbyterian Church*."

"Let's hear your tale," Dave said.

The Last Presbyterian Church

All authority in heaven and on earth has been given to me. Therefore go and make disciples of all nations, baptizing them in the name of the Father and of the Son and of the Holy Spirit, and teaching them to obey everything I have commanded you.

(Matthew 28:18–20 TNIV)

Beulah in August is frightfully hot and never popular with tourists. It's not popular in June or July, either. For that matter, tourists rarely pass through Beulah on any day of the year. Visitors who do see the small South Georgia town are typically lost or need to use the facilities at its one and only diner. The Georgia's Department of Tourism recorded five tourists in Beulah over the last twelve months. Oddly, all were from South Korea.

Beulah's historic visitors' bureau is the tallest, widest piece of furniture in Sheriff Bull Dookie's office. His wife, Butter Bean, polished it up two years ago and got it looking pretty professional. The earliest record of the bureau dates back to the 1920s when it was used as a base for the city's first stop sign. Once Roosevelt got the Rural Electric Cooperative running and the streetlight installed, Bull Dookie's dad used the bureau as a mini silo for a soybean experiment. Painted white in '53, it then served as a screen for the Beulah Drive-in Movie Theater. After that, it found its way to the roof of the Last Presbyterian Church, where it held up the steeple before the congregation could afford renovations. Beulah High School's football team used it for tackle practice until Hydrangea Splinter's son broke his collarbone trying to knock it down. It was sitting behind the bleachers when Butter Bean got the idea of putting it in her husband's office. Bull now keeps the brochures in the top drawer, fact sheets in the middle, and patriotic bunting in the bottom.

Beulah isn't unattractive. It isn't too small, and it isn't a place where folks are too busy to talk to everybody like they are up in Atlanta.

"That's the problem with this town," Mayor Acidophila Riley said to the council and those in attendance at their last meeting. "We can't just be an *isn't*. We've gotta be an *is*!"

"What the hell's she goin' on about?" Hydrangea Splinters whispered to Bull Dookie. "She's makin' no sense, like usual." Hydrangea, on account of her son's broken collarbone and a settlement from the county school system's insurance company up in Atlanta, was an unattached and not unattractive woman of not unmodest means. Having had to travel up to Atlanta to meet with the insurance company lawyer a dozen or so times, she came to dislike the city intensely. "I don't like it one bit!" she told Butter Bean. "It's too damn big, it's too darn confusing, and it's too doggone mean!"

"What do you mean we gotta be an *is*?" Bull asked loudly.

"There are two types of towns in this world," Acidophila replied. "There are *is's* and there are *isn'ts*." She was pretty emphatic.

"I take it you're thinkin' we's an *isn't*," Moses Duck said. Moses owned a family-style restaurant called Duck Diner in downtown Beulah.

"My point exactly."

"What does she mean?" Hydrangea whispered to Bull again. This time, she grabbed his shirt sleeve and shook it. Butter Bean, sitting on the other side of Bull, didn't like Hydrangea getting so close to her husband. She felt like punching her.

"I still don't get it," Bull said.

"How do you know if you're an *is* or if you're an *isn't*?" Moses asked.

"If you're an *is*," Mayor Riley replied, "your town's got a Yelp page with a list of attractions other than a public restroom. That means you've got something somebody's gonna want to see." The mayor waited a few seconds before continuing. "And not just a place for somebody to pee."

Bull looked puzzled. "And we need an attraction?"

"Exactly."

"That'd make us an *is*?"

"Exactly."

"Would people still come here to pee?" asked Moses. "Sometimes when they stop to pee at my diner, they order something to eat."

"Probably. But like I said, they'd stay longer if there was something to see," the mayor said. "And they might have two meals at Duck Diner."

"Are you suggesting we get us something somebody will wanna stop and look at?" Plutarch Johnson asked. Plutarch was the managing partner (and solitary partner) in the Law Offices of Plutarch and Johnson. He added the "and" to the firm's name to make it sound bigger.

"As a matter of fact, Plutarch," Acidophila said, "that's precisely what I'm saying."

"Whoa there, Acidophila," Moses interjected, "We already had some Koreans come through here. I stocked up on Peking Duck on account of the chance they might come back."

"Moses," Hydrangea said, irritated. "Peking Duck is Chinese."

"You sure about that?" Moses asked, concerned. Duck is mighty expensive, especially when you have to truck it in special order. He couldn't afford any mistakes.

"Can we get back on track here," Mayor Riley pleaded.

"I'm sure about that," Hydrangea said sarcastically, ignoring the mayor. "And what makes you think your Peking Duck's gonna draw Koreans back to Beulah?"

"Look, I . . ." Acidophila started to say.

"Five of 'em came through a few months ago," Moses replied defensively.

"Maybe what they saw could get us on Yelp," Bull noted. "They had to come here for a reason."

"You know, the Japanese built a Subaru plant next to my cousin's place up in Tennessee," Moses said, sounding hopeful. Maybe those Koreans are thinkin' of settin' up down here.

"I bet they came here 'cause they were lost," Hydrangea said. "Nobody's gonna build no plant in little old Beulah."

"I want . . ." the mayor tried to cut in.

"But if we treat 'em right, they'll come back," Moses said. He was anxious about the expensive duck he ordered. He didn't want to take a bath.

"Moses, they sure as hell won't come here 'cause you've got Peking Duck," Hydrangea replied. The room erupted in laughter.

"Don't knock those Koreans, my friends," the mayor said. "They've got bucks and lots of expertise."

"You know," Plutarch added, "it wouldn't be bad if we got one of their plants down here, like a Kia plant."

"Kia plants are from Korea?" Bull asked, surprised.

"What're Kia plants, anyway?" Moses asked.

"Those sheep things," Bull explained, "you know, with a plant growin' on it. Butter Bean's got one in the kitchen window."

Plutarch looked at Bull, puzzled for a moment. "Cars!" he said. "I'm talking about cars."

"Butter Bean's got a Chia Pet, Bull," Hydrangea said. "Kia's a car."

"I'm confused," Moses said. He pointed to Mayor Riley. "Are you sayin' we should get the Koreans to make Chia Pets down here in Beulah?"

"If y'all let me finish, you wouldn't be so confused," Acidophila said. "I'm only suggesting that we get us somethin' to put us in Yelp."

"You know," Plutarch said excitedly, "Moses might be onto something."

"Chia Pets?"

"Well, sort of," Plutarch replied. "Last summer, the wife and me, we went up to Callaway Gardens." Moses and Bull looked confused, not sure where Mr. Johnson was heading. "You know, those gardens near Pine Mountain. Tons of people go there, but it's real expensive."

"I think I know where you're going with this," Acidophila said, her interest piqued. "We might could do our own garden."

"Exactly, sort of," Plutarch said. "I'm visioning a huge topiary garden. Callaway doesn't have anything like that. If we do it cheaper, we might could get all the families on a tight budget."

"What's a topiary garden?" Moses asked.

"Plant-shaped animals and things," Plutarch replied. "Kinda like giant Chia Pets."

Moses nodded his head. "Like they got in Orlando?"

"When were you ever in Orlando?" Hydrangea asked.

"We could do scenes from scripture," Acidophila suggested. "Topiary Bible stories!"

"I've been to Orlando," Moses said, defensively. "A lot of times."

"The Ten Commandments," Plutarch said, "in kudzu."

"You ain't even been out of the county," Hydrangea said to Moses. "Don't you lie to me."

"We could call it, 'Ivy Land,'" Bull said, excitedly.

"I ain't lying," Moses said to Hydrangea.

"With a huge Moses!" Butter Bean added. "And a real burning bush!"

"Moses? Why would we want a huge Moses?" Bull couldn't see how a topiary version of the restaurant's owner would get anybody to come to Beulah.

"You are a liar," Hydrangea snapped at Moses.

"I don't mean our Moses. I mean *The Moses*, the one in the Bible." Butter Bean thought if her husband Bull wasn't paying so much attention to Hydrangea, he wouldn't have said something so stupid.

"I don't wanna distinguish our fire, but we got us a problem," Plutarch said. "Where are we gonna put this Ivy Land? We're gonna need a big piece of property."

"Moses's restaurant's on a good-size lot," Hydrangea suggested in jest. "After buyin' all that duck there won't be nothin' left."

Acidophila stood up and stepped over to a large wall map of Beulah. "I know exactly where we can put it." She pointed to a spot on the map.

Everyone was intently focused on the mayor. "Where?" they asked in unison.

"You know the old Last Presbyterian Church just outside of town? Nobody hardly ever goes there anymore; it sits on a hill and has pretty near two acres they're not using. If we got hold of it, we'd have plenty of room to start with a giant topiary Ten Commandments."

"I always wondered how it got that name," Moses said. "It's a terrible name."

"The hill was once owned by old Easley Last—he gave the land to the church back in '73," Plutarch said. "That's 1873."

"Can we rename the hill Mt. Sinai," Hydrangea asked?

"Don't see why not," Plutarch said. "I don't think anybody'd object."

"So, we get folks coming here," Bull said. "So what?"

"So what?" the mayor replied. "Visitors mean money, money for all of us. Maybe then we'd be able to get you a new patrol car."

"And you think tourists, heading to Florida, are gonna drive fifty miles out of their way to see a topiary Ten Commandments and then eat a greasy lunch at a diner owned by a guy named Moses?" Jean Crenshaw asked sarcastically. Jean was a retired physician from Albany who moved to Beulah with her partner two years earlier. Being new to the town, she had been quiet until she felt she couldn't be quiet anymore. "I think y'all are nuts." Her partner Leslie pinched her.

Bull Dookie preferred office work and not because he liked pushing paper. Nope, he just hated his old patrol car. The air-conditioning didn't work very well, the radio only had the AM band and couldn't pick up anything much beyond Cairo, it was too old to have Bluetooth, and the worn-out siren sounded a lot like Plutarch's pet donkey when she's hungry. He'd be drenched in sweat waiting for a speeder, and then every time he tried to chase one down, the speeder would think he was being chased by a wild jackass.

At the same time, there wasn't a whole lot to do at the office. So, most days Bull clocked out by 3:59 p.m. Preferring to keep the patrol car behind city hall, he always walked home, taking a leisurely stroll down Liberty Boulevard, the main street and only thoroughfare through Beulah. Along the way, he'd get some ice cream from Moses, check for mail at the post office/drug store/realty office/copy center, chat for a spell with Plutarch, and on Fridays, get some cash for the weekend at the town's only bank, now nothing more than a banged-up ATM owned by some big Atlanta financial institution.

The town itself was three blocks long going east or west, two blocks wide to the north, and one to the south. Only the middle block on Liberty was occupied; the buildings on the other two blocks were vacant, though some storefronts were used by politicians during election years. The northernmost block was largely covered in kudzu; there are plans to remove the weedy vines and clean up the one remaining building so they could move the tourist bureau out of Bull's crowded office.

While walking home on the Monday afternoon that followed the council meeting, Bull noticed a large white van parked in the Last Presbyterian Church parking lot. He could see the part-time pastor, Rev. John Spencer, and the church's three members speaking with a group of Asian men and women. Getting closer, he could see that the people were holding what looked like architectural drawings and maps. One of the women had a giant tape measure, and one of the men was setting up surveying tools. Getting even closer, he thought they might be the same Korean visitors who had been at Duck Diner several months earlier. Bull got very excited and called Butter Bean.

"Butter Baby, I think we're gonna get ourselves a Kia plant! Can you believe it? This could be great!"

"What makes you think so?"

"I think there's a group of Koreans talking with Reverend Spencer and his church members. They've got maps and drawings; they're taking measurements. It's gotta be a new plant for our town. They must be the folks who were here a few months back."

"Hang up and call the mayor, quick." Bull did just that.

"Hey Bull, what's up?" Acidophila could tell the sheriff was excited.

"You're not gonna believe this, mayor." Bull was talking unusually fast. "There's a bunch of Koreans up at Last Presbyterian talking with Rev. Spencer and his church members. They got maps and drawings. I think we're gettin' us a Kia plant."

"Are you sure about that, Bull?"

"They must want the church for somethin'. Why else would they be measuring and surveying the place?"

"I don't think you could fit a Kia plant on two acres. There must be another reason why they're there."

"Maybe they're gonna build a plant for small cars," Bull suggested.

"That's still not enough space."

"Maybe it'll be a Chia plant."

"That would fit." Acidophila found it hard to get excited about a Chia plant, both the plant itself and the plant in which they make the plants. Bull, on the other hand, was.

"Butter Bean loves Chia pets," Bull noted. "And if they make 'em here, we'd be an international *is*, just like you said."

"Bull, I'm gonna make some calls and see what's up with Last Presbyterian. After I find out more, you call me." Acidophila knew Bull wouldn't be able to figure out when to call her back, which was fine with her. She liked Bull but found the Dookies a bit tiring.

Bull was back on the phone with Butter Bean as soon as Acidophila hung up. "Butter Baby, we're gettin' a Chia plant!"

"I have one. It's on the kitchen windowsill."

"I don't mean a little plant; I mean a huge plant where they make all the little plants."

"You're kiddin' me. Really, for sure?"

"Darn right, Butter Baby. Beulah's gonna be known all over the world."

"This is great news, Bull Baby. I wish I could kiss you right now!"

Meanwhile, about an hour later, Acidophila was on the phone with attorney Plutarch Johnson. "Plutarch, Bull says there's some Koreans at Last Presbyterian checking out the place. Have you heard anything about this?"

"Yeah, I have. Hydrangea told me they're gonna build a Chia plant there." It was common knowledge that Hydrangea and Plutarch had a secret relationship that went beyond legal representation.

"And where did she hear that?"

"Moses called her a few minutes ago. He also told her that the Koreans were stopping by the diner for some of his Peking Duck. They're supposed to be there around 6:00."

"How did Moses find out?"

"Butter Bean told him."

"I know, Plutarch. Bull Dookie called Butter Bean," Acidophila said with a little sarcasm. She was feeling frustrated. "Plutarch, we don't know for a fact that a Chia plant is going to be built. The only thing we do know is that some Koreans were meeting with Rev. Spencer and his congregation at Last Presbyterian and that they were looking at drawings and taking measurements."

"So, do you think we need to do something about this?" Plutarch asked. "I thought we were gonna build a topiary Ten Commandments there."

"I get the sense folks are more excited about a Chia plant than they are about the Ten Commandments," Acidophila said. "The plant would mean a lot less work for us, and it might bring in more tax revenue for our town."

"That's true, mayor. Besides, most folks 'round here don't go to church much anymore. I don't think they were enthusiastic about the commandments in kudzu," Plutarch chuckled at that last comment.

"I'll call Reverend Spencer tomorrow, Plutarch, and I'll call you back when I learn more."

"Sounds good, mayor. I appreciate all you do for this town."

"Good morning, John." Acidophila was on the phone with Reverend Spencer from Last Presbyterian. "The rumors are flying all over Beulah."

"Rumors? About what?"

"Everybody thinks your visitors are from Korea and that they're gonna build a Chia plant or some other business on the Last Presbyterian property."

"What's a Chia plant?"

"It's a plant where they make Chia Pets."

"And, if I might ask, what's a Chia Pet?" Reverend Spencer thought the town was going nuts.

"It's a sheep-like planter for chia seeds." The mayor was feeling like a fool.

"I can tell you unequivocally there are no plans to build a Chia Pet plant at Last Presbyterian."

"What are your plans? Folks are wondering who your visitors were. They heard about the architectural drawings and maps and that people with surveying equipment were taking measurements." Acidophila felt the pastor was being evasive. "Something must be up."

"It's not public yet. So, I'm not sure what I can tell you."

"Oh, come on, Reverend. Your church is part of Beulah, and what happens to your facility and property affects everybody who lives here. And, besides, I want to stop all of the rumors."

"They're missionaries from Busan in South Korea," Reverend Spencer replied.

"And why are they here?"

Reverend Spencer paused and sighed. "Oh, what does it matter? They're missionaries, and they wanna buy Last Presbyterian for their new evangelism center. You and I know you can't have a big church building and two acres with only three members."

"I'll let people know. Hopefully, this'll put an end to the rumors."

An hour later, Acidophila got a call from Bull Dookie. "Mayor, I hear there's gonna be a Korean cult moving into the Last Presbyterian building. I don't like the sound of that."

"Who told you that?" the mayor asked.

"Butter Bean told me."

"And how did Butter Bean find this out?"

"From Moses."

"And who told Moses?"

"Hydrangea."

"And, let me guess, Plutarch told Hydrangea. Do I have that right?"

"Yup. So, what're we gonna do about it?"

"Wait, wait. How did Plutarch find out?"

"Butter Bean told me that Plutarch's cousin, who works for the county, told Plutarch that the lawyer who was researching the deeds for Last

Presbyterian said to her that the pastor of the Presbyterian Church told the lawyer that Korean missionaries were buying the property."

"It was a beautiful service," Jean told everyone who was attending the city council meeting several months after the Presbyterian Evangelistic Center of South Georgia was opened by five Korean missionaries. "They've renovated the church and cleaned up the property. Leslie and I were made to feel most welcomed. The preaching was excellent, and the music was spectacular."

"But was it Christian?" Hydrangea asked. Like most of the people present at the meeting, she was afraid of foreign religions.

"Yes, it was. The Koreans were very pleasant. They're also frequent visitors to Duck Diner," Jean replied.

"We don't want a cult in our community," Hydrangea said. "Even if they eat at Ducks."

Jean was getting frustrated. "It was as Presbyterian as Presbyterian can be. I grew up in a Presbyterian church, and the service, scripture, and creeds were all the same."

"Did they use the Christian Bible?" Butter Bean asked, still a little unsure about the presence of Korean missionaries.

"Yes. They use the same Bible that we use."

"I heard they all wear weird clothes," Butter Bean said. "I also heard they have secret orgies and worship idols."

"No, no, and no. Not true on all counts." Jean was doing her best to be patient. Since opening a small part-time medical clinic, most of the people in the meeting were her patients. "You know, Butter Bean, that's exactly what the Romans said about the early Christians."

"I heard they drink sake for communion." Hydrangea wasn't sure who told her, but she knew somebody did.

"Sake is Japanese. They use purple grape juice during communion." Jean hoped she shot that rumor down.

"I'm going on Sunday," the mayor told everyone. "Let's all go together and see for ourselves."

"It had been thirty years since I'd attended church on a regular basis," Jean said. "But after attending the Presbyterian Evangelistic Center, I am so at peace, and I feel at home with these Korean brothers and sisters."

"Same for me," Leslie said. "Jean and I fell away from the church, and we're thrilled to be back. It's been a long time since I truly felt I could be a Christian."

"Bull, Butter Bean, Hydrangea, Plutarch, Moses, will you come?" Jean asked.

"Nobody's gonna try to wash my feet, are they?" Bull asked.

"No, they're Presbyterian."

"They're not gonna anoint oil on my head are they?" asked Butter Bean.

"No, like I said, they're Presbyterian."

"I'm not taking my shoes and socks off," Plutarch was emphatic.

"I don't think anyone wants to see your toenails, Plutarch," Hydrangea said.

"So, we're all going to the Presbyterian Evangelistic Center on Sunday, right?" The mayor wanted a commitment from everyone. "No excuses."

"I want to welcome the missionaries from the Presbyterian Evangelistic Center to our council meeting this afternoon." It had been nearly a year since the center opened its doors, and Mayor Acidophila Riley wanted to acknowledge its work. "We are thankful for the investment you've made in our community, from renovating the old Last Presbyterian Church building to setting up a food bank for the folks in our community who've fallen on hard times. There are so many ways you've inspired us, and you've fostered so many new things that have benefited so many folks—like alcohol and substance abuse treatment, nutrition classes, and more."

"Can I say something, mayor?" Hydrangea asked.

"Please do." Acidophila was nervous about what she might say.

"Well, I didn't like the idea of foreign missionaries coming to our town," Hydrangea said. "Now, I wish you had been here years ago; maybe my husband would have survived his addictions." Her eyes teared up. Butter Bean stood up and gave her a hug, partly to comfort her and mostly to keep Bull from doing the same thing.

"It's my turn!" Moses stood up. "You made me realize that we didn't need a big Yelp spot to be an *is*. Not everybody's gonna become Presbyterian, but that doesn't mean your work's not been a success. It has, and I thank God you made us an *is*."

Butter Bean got up and faced the missionaries. "Me and Bull are glad you're here too. Maybe he won't get his new patrol car right away, but that doesn't matter. 'Cause like Moses said, we're an *is* now."

"If there are no other comments, Plutarch and I have a surprise for everyone." Plutarch got up and stood next to the mayor. "Most people don't welcome strangers to this country anymore. But all of us want y'all to know that we want you to stay; you've become part of us," the mayor said.

"I know that missionaries usually have to move on to another place," Plutarch added. "It goes with the work. In recognition of how you've given new life to Beulah . . ." He looked at Acidophila, who removed from a box a framed document that was signed by Georgia's Secretary of State. She held it up for all to see.

"Two months ago, we had a special council meeting to finalize a change to our little town." Acidophila said. "I received word from the state government that from this day forward, Beulah, Georgia, will henceforth be known as Busan, Georgia."

Applause and cheers erupted from the audience, for two reasons—because residents greatly appreciated the work of and the fellowship with the missionaries from Korea, and because they truly despised the former name of their town.

Moses stood up. "And one more thing. The Peking Duck is on me tonight!"

"We're not used to being on the receiving end for missionaries coming from other countries, are we?" Princeton asked rhetorically.

"We see ourselves as the 'city on the hill' and the place from where the church spreads the gospel to other parts of the world," May said.

"The folks in Beulah, now Busan, came a long way—they overcame their mistrust of outsiders, their stereotyping of foreigners, and the bigotry that undergirds those deeply held feelings," Sue said.

"They also accepted charity from the Korean missionaries; that was a big step for them," Ken added. "Bull Dookie and his fellow citizens did come a long way."

"Maybe with Koreans moving to their town, it'll survive. It seems like everyone was leaving and no one was coming," Sue said.

"It's hard to attract people if people don't want to come," Dave said.

"Same with our churches, it's hard for us to get people in the door because people today don't want to come anymore," Sue said.

"We could always welcome strangers and people new to our land," Billy said.

"And that shouldn't be a challenge for us," Ken said.

"Thank you for your tale, Bob," Dave said. "Who is next?"

"I'm next," Reverend Jim Mayer said. "My text is Luke 6:43–44. Like Ron, I'm using a version that's not used much anymore—it's The Wycliffe Bible."

"Is that one as old as the one Ron used?" Ed asked.

"Much older," Jim said. "It was finished in 1382. There is a reason why I chose this version, which you'll see in my story, if you're paying attention."

"I guess it's got those thees and thous," Ed said.

"And then some, Ed. I call my tale *The Great Repairaphrase*."

The Great Repairaphrase

It is not a good tree that makith yuel fruytis nether an yuel tree that makith good fruytis for euery tre is knowun of his fruyt. And men garderen not figus of thornes nethir men garderen a grape of a buyschre of breris.

(Luke 6:43–44 Wycliffe Bible, 1382)

"The floor is yours, Kimberly," CEO Sean Simonie said. Every member of the Bible Corporation of America's management team was present for this all-important, attendance-required meeting. They were there to hear from Kimberly Krankenstein, an expert in brand turnaround strategies hired to clean up the *Christian Rendition for All People* Bible fiasco. Mary Daniel, the former Marketing and Strategic Positioning manager, had fled the corporation after her humiliating experience marketing the most badly received, highly criticized version of Scripture since *Marcion's Bible* of circa AD 140. Fortunately for the weaselly CEO Simonie, Mary's departure provided an opportune place for the buck to stop, ensuring that he could keep the proverbial corner office.

"I hope everyone had a nice spring break." Kimberly jumped into her presentation without pausing; she did not want, nor did she expect a response. "As you all know, our *Christian Rendition for All People* Bible was fraught with problems. We should have used professional and academic scholars to prepare a scripture rendition and not a *King James Version* paraphrase done by a bunch of beer-guzzling, pizza-gobbling frat brothers. And it should have been proofread and edited more carefully. Furthermore, I don't think we should have sold spots on the Bible maps to travel resorts or study annotations to advertisers. At the risk of stepping on some toes,

I must be candid with you. You did enormous damage to your reputation, and you looked like a bunch of sophomoric idiots in the process. The task before us could very well be the biggest do-over of any Bible version in history."

"That's all in the past, Kimberly. I am sure there are lots of should-haves that we should have and shouldn't-haves that we shouldn't have." CEO Simonie knew the only way to avoid responsibility was to be intentionally flippant. So he chose his flippant words carefully. "We are paying you to move us forward and not to revisit the past." *The Great Bible Fiasco*, as it had become known throughout Christendom, was still a sensitive topic for him.

"That is what I fully intend to do." Kimberly was choosing her words very carefully, too. "We are in a deep hole with our Bible, and it will take a lot of digging to get ourselves out." Her original notes read "bottomless pit" and "incalculable digging," but she changed her words so she could appear more positive.

"You know what they say, 'Hope springs eternal,'" CEO Simonie said.

"Look, let me be frank. You don't have any money to fund the revision work, and lenders have all turned you down." Kimberly delivered the bad news in a very monotone voice. "Basically, your corporation is broke on account of that Bible you put out."

"So, I guess there won't be a Christmas bonus this year," Robert Beardless, Division Manager for Press Operations, said. "That stinks."

"I'm not done," Kimberly said. "I've been putting out feelers to the corporate community, and I'm convinced we can develop sponsors for the different books or groups of books for the revised Bible. This, in my opinion, will net us enough money for the project and even more funds for our bottom line."

"That sounds great, but who's gonna want to buy a Bible from us again?" Division Manager for Product Development John Flynch asked rhetorically. "We shot our wad."

She looked around the table and smiled. "Look, I don't think anyone is going to actually buy the *Revised Christian Rendition for All People*. Like you said, John, we shot our wad with the first go-around. But if corporations sponsor the new Bible, they'll give them out to customers, investors, and other stakeholders in things like swag bags. Think of this like massive bulk sales."

"Sponsorships?" asked Robert. "I hadn't thought of that. How do you envision this in real time?"

"It's simple. Let's say a big bank forks over a million to be the Gospel sponsor. We use some of the cash to pay Bible scholars to re-render Matthew, Mark, John, and Luke for our new *Revised Christian Rendition for All People*. Once that's done, we send a draft over to their PR people to make sure they're happy and to see if they have any suggestions."

"Luke and John," John said.

"What?" Kimberly asked.

"You said John and Luke. It's Luke and John."

"Whatever, John. I've made my point." Kimberly was getting irritated with Mr. Flynch. "Look, we're putting all of our eggs into the sponsorship basket. If they give us cash input, we'll give them the output they like."

"Whoa," said Robert. "Aren't we crossing a line here? Do we really want corporate input on the rendering of the text?"

"Yes, we're crossing a line, a line of creativity is how I'd spin it. Remember Robert, your last attempt at producing a Bible crossed several big lines, all of which were . . . how shall I say it, stupid. This time we'll be smart." Speaking to the group, Kimberly added, "Bible publishers routinely send drafts of a new translation to seminary professors, pastors, and church leaders. Why shouldn't business leaders have the opportunity to add their two cents? Don't you think their input is important, too?"

"If they're gonna give us cash and put their names on our Bible, then they deserve to have some say in how the thing is rendered," CEO Simonie said. "Besides, business leaders are important and can have valuable insight too."

"Pro quid pro," John said. "Makes sense."

"You mean, Quo pro quid," Sean Simonie said. "We'll bank on it."

"No, it's Quo quo quid," Robert said.

"Quid pro quo," Kimberly responded. "But I think y'all got the idea."

"You know, many CEOs go to church." Wilbur Iverson, Division Manager for Bible Derivatives, thought this was an important point to add.

"Come to think of it, a lot of them teach Sunday School, too." Robert was getting into the Bible-business symbiosis. "Bill Marriott taught Sunday School, and so did Truett Cathy."

"Don't forget Sam Walton and John D. Rockefeller!" Wilbur thought it important to highlight these two prominent businessmen to the who's who of Sabbath schoolteachers.

"I didn't know Rockefeller taught Sunday school," John said. "I knew about Sam Walton. Did I ever tell you about the time I saw Mr. Walton's office? It was really simple and . . ."

"I'm glad to hear y'all agree that businesspeople should have input into Bible renditions." Interrupting John's description of Sam Walton's office, Kimberly was ready to move on. "I think we're ready to talk about how we are gonna accomplish the revision of our Bible and the rescue of the Bible Corporation of America." She looked at the team with a very stern no-nonsense expression. "I have a potential sponsorship from GreenStone Capital Investment Partners. They might cough up $1.5 million for the Gospel sponsorship."

"1.5 million? Wow!" Robert sat up in his chair; his eyes were wide open. The mood in the room perked up. "We might could get a Christmas bonus after all," he said.

"I'll bet we can up their sponsorship to $2 million; after all, we're talkin' about the Gospels and Jesus. I think they're worth a whole lot more to us than what they're offering," CEO Simonie added.

"Soon we'll have a pro-forma contract in hand," Kimberly said. "And I think we'll be ready to discuss the terms."

"Terms?" Wilber asked. "What kinda terms are you talking about?"

"We'll offer a simple acknowledgement in the Bible's preface and a little sponsor logo on the first page of Matthew, Mark, Luke, and John," Mr. Simonie said. "I wouldn't be surprised if they wanted a tiny bit of rewording here and there, but it won't be a big deal."

"Speaking about wording, I have it on good authority that business leaders think everyone would buy more Bibles if it didn't have so much negativity. I think they're right." Kimberly looked at each person to make sure everyone understood. "Doom-and-gloom is out. Fun and prosperity is in."

"Kimberly, can you give us an example?" John asked.

"Don't you remember when Jesus talked about fasting, what did he say? Don't look like you haven't eaten in days, look like you're a walking success story! That's what our Gospel sponsor wants to see more of."

John nodded. "Makes sense to me. Nobody wants to read the Bible and feel down."

"I agree," Wilbur added. "People want to feel blessed and happy."

"Count me in." Robert was thinking about the Christmas bonus. "Our board needs to be happy, too."

"What about you junior executives?" CEO Simonie asked. "I've not heard from any of you." As a rule, new leaders at the Bible Corporation of America were afraid of Sean and rarely spoke up at meetings. "Rocky, Boris, Natasha, Dudley, Nell, are y'all on board?"

"Yes, sir!" they said together. "Let's make our sponsors happy!"

"Glad we're all of one accord," Mr. Simonie said. "Let's continue, Kimberly. I think our team is ready."

"Great, Sean. Right now, we need to create our sponsorship teams. Each of you will be a team leader, taking one of the eight sponsor groups." Kimberly got up from her chair and walked over to the electronic presentation board. "Here are the names of our sponsorship teams. Each of you will be the leader of one of them." She wrote the number 1 on the board. "Rocky, you've got the Pentateuch."

"The what?"

"The Pentateuch is Genesis through Deuteronomy," John said in a snarky tone.

"When did they start calling it that?"

"It's been a long time, Rocky."

Moving on, Kimberly wrote the number 2, "Boris, you're the History Books man, Joshua through Esther."

"Don't they have a name like Pentateuch?" Boris asked.

"They do, Boris. It's History Books." Kimberly shook her head in frustration.

"That's not very scholarly sounding. I bet they've got a different name for them; maybe something in Latin."

"Let's continue with numbers 3 through 8," Kimberly wanted to up the pace. "Poetry Books, Job through Song of Songs go to Natasha; Prophets are Dudley's; Gospels go to Nell; Acts is Robert's; Wilbur, you take the Letters, Romans through Jude; and finally, Revelation is yours, John." She turned to look at the leadership group to make sure everyone was paying attention. "John, put down your phone."

"AI says that some scholars use the term Deuteronomistic History books, but if we did that, we would have to change the Old Testament sponsor groupings," John said as he put his iPhone on the table.

"Thank you, Mr. Flynch, but we're not gonna do that," Kimberly said quickly. "What a schlemiel," she thought. "Mr. Simonie and I have already lined up prospective sponsors, and I will work with each of you to develop the sponsor agreement, get their money, coordinate the text revisions, and incorporate the sponsor text suggestions."

"What about the Apocrypha?" John asked. "It doesn't seem right to leave it out again."

"No one reads it. No one wants it. It's not worth it," CEO Simonie said. "Let's move on."

"But Catholic people like most of it," John countered. "I think we should consider it."

"Then go work for a Catholic publisher, John," Mr. Simonie said.

John blushed; his palms were sweating. "I only wanted to make sure we covered all of our bases, Sir," John said defensively. He couldn't understand why no one was willing to take up the cause for the Apocrypha.

"I think we're done here," Kimberly said, picking up her legal pad and tablet computer. She quickly walked out of the room, shaking her head. "These people are nitwits," she said to herself.

Sean Simonie left as well and caught up to Kimberly in the hallway. "I've got some whisky in my office if you need some."

"No, thanks, Sean," Kimberly said. "I have another appointment to get to."

"It's always there," Sean said. "I wonder who she's meeting with?" he thought to himself.

"The floor is yours, Kimberly." One month had passed since the last leadership meeting, and CEO Simonie was hoping to hear of great progress on sponsorship development for the *Revised Christian Rendition for All People* Bible. Kimberly had made a few cryptic remarks, both positive and negative, in recent weeks, and Sean was quite anxious.

"Good morning, team leaders! I trust y'all are ready to give us a sponsor update."

"Good M. . ." Everyone started to respond, but Kimberly cut them off.

"Let's start in the beginning." The turnaround expert did a laugh-snort. "I made a joke," she said, not something people thought she could do. "Pentateuch group, update please!"

"We have a million-dollar proposal from FilmFlam Motion Pictures," Rocky said. "They're ready to finalize a deal, but with two caveats. First, their legal team says a lot of the texts are way too misogynistic and racy. Their lawyers, however, would be willing to sign off on a deal if we use archaic language, like in the Wycliffe Bible. This will make the text incomprehensible and thus keep them free of any liability." Rocky was proud of himself for making this suggestion to resolve what had been a thorny issue for the valuable entertainment corporation.

"Won't we be violating a copyright?" John interrupted Rocky. "We can't just steal a text from another Bible."

Kimberly looked at John and rolled her eyes. "That translation is seven hundred years old. I'm sure the copyright has long since passed." Shaking her head, she thought to herself, "Not only is he a schlemiel, but he's a nudnik, too."

Rocky continued his presentation. "The second caveat is that their producers want to make a new movie about Moses, and they need the exclusive usage rights over the terms Ten Commandments and Exodus. They'd be willing to compromise and accept a time limit on the rights, say ten years."

"Done!" CEO Simonie said with magisterial authority. "We'll give 'em the rights."

"Wait," Robert said. "How can we do that? We don't own those terms."

"It doesn't matter," Sean responded. "I can't imagine anyone else wanting to do another remake of such a silly movie; it'd never come to trial. I want the one million, so let's give them what they want."

Kimberly looked at Rocky. "Get a copy of the Wycliffe Bible and give it to our editors. If there's nothing else from the Pentateuch team, let's move on to the Historical Books team. Boris, you're up!"

"The team Libido Histerico reports that defense contractor Southrup Corporation is happy, period. They love all of the battles and the palace intrigue."

"The what team?" Sean asked.

"I think he's trying to use Latin," Kimberly said. "Good god, another nudnik," she thought to herself. "Boris, I think you mean *Libri Historiae*."

"You sure about that?"

"Just give us what you got, Boris. We don't have all day," Sean said, getting testy with the team.

"Their PR person, Matilda, said those books remind her of dealing with people at the Pentagon. They've committed $2 million, but they insist on inserting a short article at the end of the Bible on the history of weapons, from a wooden stick to their new orbital space laser. I have a draft right here." Boris handed it to Kimberly.

"What if we decline the article?" Kimberly asked.

"Their sponsorship drops to $1 million."

"I say go with it," CEO Simonie said. "If we're not selling the Bible retail, who cares? Let's take the extra million. Besides, some Christians might find it interesting to see how weapons have progressed since the time of Cain and Abel."

"If you say so," Kimberly replied. "Okay, let's move on to the Poetry team. Natasha, you're on."

"Puffin Press is going for $1.5 million," Natasha reported. "But there's a big problem. The Song of Songs has too much sex and nudity for their PR and legal people. They want to end their sponsorship at Ecclesiastes."

"That would mean the Song of Songs won't be getting us any cash," Sean said.

"What do you think we should do?" Kimberly asked Natasha.

"Well, my brother told me about another business that wants to sponsor the Song of Songs. It's the St. Simon's Island Surf and Sin Gentlemen's Club. They'd do half a million." Natasha was a little uncomfortable bringing up this potential opportunity. "They see it as a way for Georgia's adult entertainment industry to become more faith-based and better positioned for growth across the Bible Belt."

"That's a mighty long bridge for us to cross for only a half a mil," CEO Simonie said. "What do you think, Kimberly?" The room got very quiet.

"Way too risky, Sean. I don't think it's wise to do a Surf and Sin sponsorship," Kimberly said. She looked at CEO Simonie while the other folks in the room breathed a sigh of relief. "Natasha, go back to Puffin's PR people and ask them if we removed all of the sex and nudity, would they be happy to move forward?"

"That should work," Natasha said. "That's all I have for my presentation."

"What if we sold copies of the Song of Songs all by itself; changed its name, updated it a little, and added pictures? I'd bet you dollars to donuts we'd make a fortune," Robert said, laughing.

"That's not a bad idea," CEO Simonie said. "I'll think about it."

"Whatever," Kimberly said, wanting to move on. "Dudley, the Prophets."

"Lackland and Water, Attorneys at Law, are happy to offer $1.25 million, but they would like us to remove Lamentations. They feel it's a real big downer of a book and that no one would notice if it were taken out of the Bible. They're not going to make an issue over it, however."

"Kimberly, could we remove Lamentations from the Bibles they get and leave it in on all the others?" CEO Simonie asked.

"Dudley, work with Robert and Press Operations to see how costly this might be. That would create two options: one, we tell Lackland that the book needs to stay in the Bible, or two, we make a counteroffer of $1.5 million with Lamentations removed." Kimberly thought she had a good compromise. "Let's you and I talk once you have the information from the printers. Nell, you're up!"

"GreenStone's ready to be the Gospel sponsor. Like I expected, there are a few things they like and a bunch of things they don't. First, the things they like: They love the Prodigal Son because it's about a wayward teenager who returns to his wealthy family. They like the Pearl of Great Price because their customers like pearls. They are okay with the beatitudes in Matthew—they can live with poor in spirit because even the greatest financier of all time, JP Morgan himself, became poor in spirit when his nose became disfigured. They love that parable where the vineyard owner pays all the workers the same thing no matter when they started because they think it's anti-minimum wage. Oh, I almost forgot, their favorite parable is the one where the master gives his servants talents and comes back to see how they invested the money; they want to use it in their 401(k) plan advertising. They like . . ."

"I get what they like," CEO Simonie interrupted Nell. "What don't they like?"

"Well," Nell said nervously. "Sometimes when Jesus talks about money, their PR people throw a fit, for one. They want us to tone that down."

"Can you give me an example?" Kimberly asked.

"They would like it if Jesus said, 'You can't serve God and money between 10:00 a.m. and noon on Sunday mornings.'"

"Okay, I can get their point," Kimberly said.

Nell continued. "They really dislike the beatitudes in Luke. They want them to be exactly like the ones in Matthew. The Widow's Offering story from Mark and Luke needs to go—that undermines their business philosophy. That part about paying taxes to Caesar makes them uneasy since they have a whole division dedicated to helping the wealthy avoid paying any taxes at all to anybody, so that would need to go. They don't like forgiving debts in the Lord's prayer. They want it worded differently."

"Did they have a suggestion?" Sean asked.

"Their preferred rendition is, 'Forgive us our debts as we collect the debts of others.'"

"Hmm. That's an interesting perspective. Anything else?"

"After their PR people finally read all of Luke's Gospel, they really soured on it."

"What part of it?" asked Kimberly.

"The whole thing, period. Every jot and tittle."

"Why, what's their problem?" Sean asked.

"They think it's a lot more extreme than Matthew, Mark, and John. They dislike . . ."

"I got it," CEO Simonie said, stopping Nell from continuing. "I thought this would be the easiest sponsorship; everybody loves the gospels, don't they?"

"Not if you read 'em, especially if you're a financier. I wonder if the banking and private equity business is not a good match for the Gospels," Kimberly said.

"GreenStone did offer to do a small $150,000 sponsorship on just the crucifixion. They said that there wasn't anything in the parts where Jesus was betrayed and executed that bothered them."

"You didn't mention the resurrection," John noted.

"Too sectarian," their PR person said.

"Oh, I almost forgot. They were wondering if the two people crucified alongside Jesus could be regulators instead of robbers."

"Let's get together first thing in the morning, Nell." Kimberly was ready to move on to Acts. "Clearly, we have a lot of work to do when it comes to the Gospels. Okay, Robert, tell me about Acts."

"Garden Depot is ready to move forward with a cool million, with one exception and one request. First the exception—the verses in chapters two and four where the Christians share their possessions need to be deleted. Their PR people said it smells of communism and they don't want anything to do with that." Robert looked at CEO Simonie. "Can we dump those verses? If we can remove Lamentations for Lackland and Water, can't we drop a few verses for Garden Depot?"

"I'm not against removing them. Scholars removed a whole lot of verses that were in the King James Bible so why can't we remove a few, too? What do you think, Kimberly?" Mr. Simonie said.

"Let's have a conversation about that tomorrow afternoon. I'll need to give this a lot of thought. I don't want to shoot ourselves in the foot. Is that all, Robert?"

"Don't forget their request. Garden Depot wants the exclusive right to use the name, Acts. Just the name and not the content. They're coming out with a new line of tools for organic gardeners that they're naming *Acts Naturally*."

"Done!" said CEO Simonie. "If we're gonna sell the naming rights to the Ten Commandments and Exodus, we may as well sell Acts, too."

"Wilbur, what do you have for us?" Kimberly wanted to get through the last two units quickly.

"We've got $1.65 million for all of the letters from Romans to Jude from IQ Technology. They don't care at all about what's in the texts. Instead, they want a tracking chip embedded in the Bible itself, in the spine or cover." Wilbur looked at CEO Simonie and then at Kimberly to gauge their reaction. "They think keeping tabs on where folks put their Bibles, if and when they read them, and what they were doing before and after, is worth a lot of money. They also want a note that indicates their sponsorship is purely research-based and does not imply any endorsement or belief in the content."

"That gives me an idea," Kimberly said. "What if we put the chips in the Bibles for IQ, get them to share their data with us, then we could resell that data to the other sponsors."

"Go to your IQ contact and see if they'll buy it," CEO Simonie instructed the team leader. "Get back to me and Kimberly ASAP!"

"I think we're done," Kimberly said.

CEO Simonie and Kimberly stuck their papers into their briefcases and got up to head for the door.

"Wait, you forgot about Revelation!" John shouted as the team members were packing up and getting ready to leave, too. "Interactive Games will agree to a $750,000 sponsorship. It's less than the other sponsorships, but we expected that the confusing book would command a lower price. While they don't feel a need to change anything, they do want exclusive rights to use the term, Great Tribulation, and the storyline that goes with it for a new video game."

"Sounds good," CEO Simonie said, walking out the door. He was tired, wanted to go home, and wasn't much interested in Revelation as he didn't care for the book anyway.

"Sean, this is Kimberly." The turnaround expert was on the phone with her boss late in the evening. "I just heard from Nell that GreenStone is backing out. I've called dozens of other banks, and I can't get even a nibble from anyone."

"No one?"

"No one. I keep hearing the same thing. They can tolerate the nativity story, and they like the crucifixion, but they hate all the stuff in between. Fred at Silibank told me flat out, 'How do you expect me to sponsor a book where the lead character tells somebody to sell all they own and give it to the poor?'"

"Damn!" Sean exclaimed. "Why did Jesus have to go and say that? We can't make a Bible without the Gospels, can we?"

"I hear you, Sean. I know you're frustrated."

"What do you think we can do? Maybe a defense contractor would take 'em?" Sean suggested.

"I doubt it. Prince of Peace, remember? And, besides, we already have a defense contractor for the history books."

"We could drop that Prince of Peace title."

"Be serious, Sean."

"What about an airline?"

"Nope, tried that. Jesus and first class don't mix, Western Airlines told me."

"An oil conglomerate?"

"They don't like the end-of-times stuff; it makes people think oil will run out."

"Okay, Big Pharma?"

"Too much healing. They don't like it when Jesus cures people."

"I got it! Fast food?"

"Too much religion in the Gospels. They serve all people."

"Schmidt and Weston, the gun manufacturer?"

"Don't think so, Sean."

"Well, do you have any ideas?" Sean was exasperated. "You were supposed to be my turnaround expert."

"There's one possibility," Kimberly said. "I've been meeting with a private equity business, and they're willing to buy the company outright."

"What company?"

"Your company, The Bible Corporation of America," Kimberly said. "With their resources, they can produce a new Bible all on their own. And they have the means to leverage a translation to generate a ton of cash."

"So, as CEO, who would I report to?"

"No one. They'll pay you $2 million to leave."

"Leave?"

"You know that this marks the end of the *Christian Rendition for All People*, revised or not," Kimberly said. She paused for a moment. "Sean, you never noticed your Bible rendition's acronym, did you?"

Sean picked up a copy of his Bible that was sitting on a coffee table. He looked at the spine. At the bottom was the letter C followed by an R, an A, and a P. He let out a big sigh. "It all seemed like a good idea at the time," he thought.

"I guess Mary Daniel had the last laugh," Kimberly said.

"What about the staff? They don't need a warning, do they?"

"They already know."

"What do ya mean, they already know?" Sean was shocked.

"Yesterday, your board accepted the buyout terms and your resignation. Your office is being cleaned out as we speak," Kimberly explained. "They'll deliver your personal belongings to your home in the morning."

"But I haven't resigned yet," Mr. Simonie protested.

"They just assumed that for two million you would."

Sean thought for a second. "Okay. I'll take it. You know, I really liked working with you; people like you always have their clients' best interest at heart. What are you gonna do, Kimberly?"

"I'm moving into your old office tomorrow afternoon. The corner office is mine now. And they're paying me a five-million-dollar signing bonus to take your old job."

"That's not fair!" Sean was suddenly angry. "You know, I really disliked working with you; people like you never have their clients' best interest at heart! I want five and a half million or I'm not leaving."

"Too late, Sean. You've already agreed to take two million."

"Then I'm not leaving."

"Too late for that, too. You've already agreed to resign. And there's no repairaphrase for that decision, my friend."

"What will Sean Simonie do now?" Princeton wondered. "Two million sounds like a lot, but it doesn't go as far as it used to."

"You of all people should know, Princeton," May said. "Didn't you pay for seminary with your debit card?"

"I did, but my grandaddy worked hard for that money."

"And didn't you use your debit card to buy the condo you lived in while at seminary?" May asked. "And a Lincoln Town Car?"

"Well, yes."

"I can see why you'd overlook the whole point of Jim's story. You're fixated on what would become of a man who was handed two million dollars all because he was a complete, disreputable bozo." May was seriously irritated with Princeton.

"Look, May, I think you're being a little self-righteous," Princeton said.

"Maybe we should make popcorn over the fire," Billy wanted to get folks focused on something else; he was worried that the twelve O'Postles would become the eleven O'Postles if things got too testy.

"We don't need popcorn, Billy. Let's enjoy the peace our surroundings provide to our fellowship," Sue said. "I love this place."

"I'd like to point out something from my tale," Jim said. "Sometimes an unscrupulous person or business will use scripture in such a way that he, she, or it benefits from believers not truly understanding the text."

"I don't follow you," Dave said.

"One publisher friend of mine told me to 'Follow the affinity group,' when talking about specialty Bibles sold for no other reason than to make money," Jim explained. "We have patriots' Bibles, and Bibles for golfers, Marines, businessmen, and for people who want to become wealthy entrepreneurs, to name a few. Affinity groups promote their views in the annotations and insert articles to ensure the text of the Bible is seen to support their cause, regardless of whether or not the text actually does."

"Imagine a Bible for billionaires that had a footnote instructing the reader to give away everything he or she owns and to become an economically poor disciple of Jesus," May said. "I'll bet that edition would sell really well," she said sarcastically.

"You can't serve God and money," Jim added. "Sean Simonie did everything he could possibly do to serve money, and he always failed."

"So why the Wycliffe Bible?" Sarah asked.

"One of the sponsors couldn't go along with what the Bible said in plain English, so they wanted to use an archaic form of English that was incomprehensible. That way, the sponsor could buy an affiliation with the Holy Scriptures that allowed them to have their cake and eat it too."

"Jim, last year you mentioned something the head of the Christian Booksellers Association said a while back: 'The Bible is the lead product from which all other products are spawned.'"

"And here we are," Jim said. "He was right."

"I hate to say it," Sue said. "I feel like the Bible has become a tool for making money and not the sacred text it was meant to be."

"On that note, I am certain that this is something we all can agree on, even Princeton and May," Sarah said.

Princeton smiled at May. "You're still my sister in Christ," he said. She gave him a faith-based thumbs up.

"Who's next?" Dave asked. "Come to think of it, that was a great rock album."

"Who was it by?" Princeton asked.

"Oh, never mind, I'm just dating myself," Dave said.

"I'm next," Ben said. "I call my tale, *Hash Wednesday*. It's a wild one, and I hope it doesn't get me arrested. My text is Luke 22:19. I'm using the TNIV Bible."

Hash Wednesday

And he took bread, gave thanks and broke it, and gave it to them saying, "This is my body given for you; do this in remembrance of me."

(Luke 22:19 TNIV)

Honey and Clutch Bigman's home is tucked into a leafy mountainside lot about a half mile from the entrance to Georgia's Tallulah Gorge State Park. Theirs is truly a famous home, largely on account of the fact that Eleanor Roosevelt stayed there when she came to witness the Baxley, Georgia strongman Earl Knoodle's historic 1935 tossing of a fifty-pound Hubbard squash across the 1,000-feet-deep Tallulah Gorge. Added to their modest but historic house is a big garage for the Bigmans' two Harley-Davidson Cruiser motorcycles and a four-door Ford F350 monster pickup and motorcycle trailer.

"Did you see this, Honey?" Clutch Bigman had a social media app on his smartphone open. His wife, Honey Bunch Bigman, was sitting next to him on their plush grey living room sectional couch; they were spending the afternoon binge-watching *Smokey and the Bandit* movies. Being purists, Clutch and Honey only recognized the first two *Smokey and the Bandit* films as authentic and the third as barely canonical since Burt Reynolds only made a cameo appearance. Though there were four more sequels, all of those were without Bert. Honey felt strongly that they were outside the canon and should be deemed pseudepigraphal.

"What is it that you're lookin' at, Clutch?" Honey asked.

Clutch moved closer to her so she could see the social media post better. "Says here that a church in Cartersville is offering free hash if you go to their Ash and Hash service." He then handed his phone to Honey. "Check this out."

"It's the week after next, and it's being hosted by Reefer Lutheran Church, ELCA," Honey said. "That's ten days from now. But I've got a question, Clutch. What's an 'Elca?' I've never heard that word."

"I don't know," Clutch replied. "What I do know is that a lot of Motorcycles America people are interested in going to the Ash and Hash thing; there were thousands and thousands of likes. Do you wanna go, Honey?"

"Yeah, let's do it, Clutch." Honey took a closer look at the announcement. "It says you drive to the Weed's parking lot, and the minister gives you the ashes, and then we get our hash."

"Since when is that stuff legal in Georgia? That Elca thing sounds suspicious to me, too," Clutch said. "And since when is a Lutheran Church getting named after a reefer?"

"Maybe the laws have changed, dear," Honey told her husband.

While Clutch and Honey were watching *Smokey and the Bandit*, three hundred and forty miles north, another Motorcycles America couple was catching wind of the Hash and Ash service at Reefer Lutheran Church.

"Free hash, man. It must be legal in Georgia now," Bumper Bender said to his girlfriend, Tini. "Says right here—show up, the minister gives you ashes, and then you get your hash."

"Cool," Tini said. "We goin'?"

"You bet, Tini!"

Tini and Bumper lived in a Wheeling, West Virginia, renovated brick storage building behind the downtown 7-Eleven. Converted into a single-family residence, it was just large enough to have space for their treasured Honda motorcycle; they knew, however, that once they had the money for a sidecar, they would need to find larger accommodations. Tini, who handles all of the finances for the couple, had been saving for a long time; she told her sister Tuni that they were about eighteen months shy of a really nice, fully-equipped, sleeper sidecar with a fold-out double bed and top.

About six hundred and twenty-four miles southeast of Wheeling, motorcyclist Jett Jettson, a Kawasaki man with a brand-new bright green Ninja model, was driving his bike down Highmarket Street in Georgetown, South Carolina. "Brummmm, Brummmm, Brummmm," Jett couldn't resist the temptation to rev the engine at each stoplight. At green, he zipped down the block and turned into the gas station to get lunch.

"Hey Jett," Hamid, owner of the filling station, said. "How's that Ninja?"

"It is great! Got anything fresh today?"

"Egg salad, tuna salad, and pawpaw pie."

"Sounds good, my friend."

"Did you hear about the church near Atlanta that's giving away free hash?" Hamid looked around to make sure no one was listening. "Do a search for 'Reefer Lutheran Church.'" Hamid, a Triumph man, was also a member of Motorcycles America.

"Reefer church? You've got to be kidding me."

"Yeah, I saw it on a social media post. It's gonna happen the week after next. I'm taking a few days off, and I'm planning on goin."

"I'm off that week, too. Mind if I join you? I'm ready to get my Ninja out on the open road!"

"Sure, man. But your Ninja ain't no match for my Triumph Rocket 3!"

"Yeah, right. We'll see about that." Jett grabbed some chips, an egg salad sandwich, a slice of pawpaw pie, and a bottle of water. He paid Hamid and headed back to his green Ninja.

At the same time that Jett and Hamid were discussing the Ash and Hash event at Reefer Lutheran, Bess and Tessa, both Honda people, were at home in Memphis, Tennessee, looking at the same social media post. Bess clicked, "I will attend." In Birmingham, Alabama, Clarkston, a Yamaha man, was at his desk when he too saw the post and clicked "I will attend," as did Dave and Maggie, both people of the Harley-Davidson persuasion. They were from Huntsville, Alabama. Also reading the post and clicking "I will attend," were the BMW men Marvin and Robert from Lookout Mountain, Tennessee; Abbot, a Kawasaki man from Lexington, Virginia; Leslie and Don from Frederick, Maryland, both of the Suzuki denomination, and the dual Ducati couple Mary and Tamara from Dover, Delaware, all clicked "I will attend." By day's end, motorcycle club folks from Maine to Florida and from Delaware to Missouri and beyond had seen Reefer Lutheran's Ash and Hash post and clicked the "I will attend" button.

Four months before the Ash and Hash social media post was sweeping the motorcycle club world, the leadership at Reefer Lutheran Church, a congregation named after War of 1812 hero and Lutheran pastor Gustavus

Adolphus Reefer, were having a Sunday-after-church meeting. Top of the agenda was a discussion about ways to improve upon the Ash and Dash model.

Ash and Dash had become a popular Ash Wednesday liturgy that added fast food drive-through convenience to the very solemn occasion. Not only could more people enjoy the imposition of ashes, but they could do so at any time of the day from the comfort of their car, SUV, or motorcycle. Participants could then display their forehead markings with great pride once they were back at work, out shopping, or eating at a restaurant—indeed, the ash-cross-on-the-forehead look was quickly becoming a veritable faith-based fast fashion and a trendy way for Christians to display their inward humility. Prior to Ash and Dash, busy believers simply did not have time for this ancient ritual.

"I think Ash and Dash is a good idea," Reverend Mary Jane Beaver, pastor of Reefer Lutheran Church, said. "But I think we can come up with a way to make it even better."

"I've got a great idea to deal with the Ash and Dash lines," Jason Dollar said. Jason was a Technology Sales Representative and a member of the church's group of elders. "I travel a lot and I got myself a TSA PreCheck number, so I don't have to wait in line at the airport much anymore. We could do something like that."

"Not a bad idea, Jason," banker Martha Gelterson said. "In exchange for a 'donation,' (Martha made quotation marks with her fingers) busy businesspeople could get a secret code which gets them access to a special premium imposition line. What do y'all think?"

"We could set the minimum donation at, say, one hundred dollars," Jason added. "I'd pay that for a code if it meant I could avoid a long line."

"Ash and Cash," Martha said, half joking. "If someone couldn't afford the fee, they could pay in installments; we could charge interest too."

"I think that's a horrible idea," Mary Jane said. "We are one congregation, not two with one that serves mammon and one that wishes it could."

"I wasn't serious," Martha said. "We could keep the fee pretty low, like fifty bucks."

"Why don't we give 'em something to eat instead, like brunch food," Za Za Gabor suggested. Za Za was a distant cousin of the once-renowned Gabor sisters. "I can make my Hungarian smoked hash. We could hand it out in plastic containers with a plastic spoon and napkin as folks drive by."

"That's a great idea," Jason said. "You know, we've still got cases and cases of sporks that no one wants. Let's use those instead of buying more spoons."

"Tell everyone what's in your hash, Za Za," Mary Jane said. "It's absolutely heavenly!"

"It's got mashed potatoes, chopped smoked Hurka sausage, onions, carrots, and turnips, plus my secret spices."

"I love it," Jason said. "And folks won't mind waiting in line if they knew they were getting Za Za's hash."

"I for sure wouldn't," Martha said. Several others in the meeting nodded their heads in agreement.

"I think we've got ourselves a consensus. This year it will be Ash with Hash then Dash," Mary Jane suggested.

Martha made a pained face. "It sounds like the hash will make you dash to you know where. Maybe say mash instead of hash."

"Mash and Ash?" Mary Jane said. "Or Ash and Mash?"

"No, that sounds disgusting. It sounds like you're mixing mash with the ashes," Jason said.

"How about 'Ash and Hash,'" Za Za said. "Everybody loves my hash." Her recipe for Hurka hash was from a very old Hungarian family tradition. "I'll bet you didn't know my cousin Ava got the writers of *Green Acres* to have her character Lisa make a batch for Fred Ziffle and Arnold the pig. They cut the scene anyway."

"We did know, Za Za," Jason said.

"You've told us that before," Martha added. "Maybe Arnold wouldn't eat the stuff." She started laughing.

"That's not funny, Martha." Za Za was now upset. "No one's making you eat my hash."

"I'm sorry, Za Za. I shouldn't have said that."

"All right, let's move on. Any objections to Ash and Hash?" Mary Jane asked. "Seeing none, we have a name! 'Ash and Hash.'"

Hardware store owner Henry Weed then raised his hand. "Yes, Henry."

"I'll close Weed's Hardware, and we can use the parking lot for the day. My lot is three times larger than the church lot, and it's got easier access to the highway."

"That's very generous of you, Henry," Jason said. "You're most kind."

"Okay, everyone. We're calling our Ash Wednesday event, 'Ash and Hash.' We'll be using Henry Weed's parking lot, and we'll be serving Za

Za's Hurka hash in plastic cups with the plastic sporks that we have in the storage closet. Is there anything else?" Wendell Weezell, a budding social media entrepreneur and newest member of the council, raised his hand. "Yes, Wendell."

"I'd like to send out a social media message. We might could reach some of the unchurched people in our community." He didn't mention that the unchurched market upon which he was focused was the motorcycle club crowd, a group he had recently joined.

"Maybe we'll get some churched people to come our way too," Za Za said. "My Hurka is famous."

"Sounds good, Wendell. Does anyone have any objections?" Mary Jane asked. "Hearing none, we've got ourselves a plan. Have a great evening!"

On the Fat Tuesday before Ash and Hash Day at Reefer Lutheran Church, Wendell Weezell booted up his computer to see how his social media posts were doing. He figured that if they did well and had lots of people clicking "I will attend," he'd tell Reverend Beaver how well his social marketing efforts had performed; he envisioned a nice spiral-bound glossy report that could be presented to the church council. If they didn't do well with only a few affirmative clicks, he wouldn't say anything if she forgot to ask. Wendell gasped when he saw the tabulated numbers. "That can't be right." He called his sister Wendy, an expert data analyst and numbers cruncher at Enhancement Consulting, a firm dedicated to helping its clients squeeze more profit from consumers with stagnant or declining incomes.

"Wow, Wendell. Those numbers are outstanding; you did really well."

"Way too well, Wendy. 80,000 is a lot of people saying they want to come. How many people do you think will actually show up?"

"That's hard to tell. Given how little information you've gathered, I would think fifteen percent might be a good guess."

"Fifteen percent?" Wendell started sweating. His hands were shaking.

"Look Wendell, I'd love to talk with you, but you got me at a bad time. I've got to go."

"Where are you off to?"

"Billings."

"Montana? What'd ya have goin' up there?"

"No, the billings department. I've got a customer in Arkansas who's broke and can't pay. See ya."

Wendell switched to his cell phone calculator app. "Let's see, eighty-thousand times point one-five," Wendell mumbled as he entered the numbers. "That can't be right." He redid the calculation four times, always coming up with the same number, 12,000. Wendell decided it would be best not to tell Reverend Mary Jane Beaver how well his digital marketing did. He also decided to take the week off and go alligator watching at the remote, dark-sky, no-cell-coverage Okefenokee Swamp.

"You gave me the ash, now where's the hash for my hookah?" Clutch asked Mary Jane. He was getting a little irritated. Clutch was on his blue Harley and Honey was on her pink Harley just behind him. They were the fourth and fifth people in line at the Ash and Hash event.

"You can't smoke our hash," Mary Jane tried to explain. "You eat it."

"Your social media post says you've got Hookah hash that comes from zaza that's being served in the weed parking lot. He handed his cell phone to Mary Jane. "Read this."

Mary Jane took the phone and was shocked at what she saw. Instead of Hurka, the post read hookah when describing the hash. "That must be an auto-correct typo. I'm so sorry."

"You mean Honey and I aren't getting hash for our hookahs and that we rode all the way down here from Tallulah for nothing?"

"Well, the hash is very good. Please try it. We'll give you four servings."

In a huff, Clutch and Honey rode to the next station in Weed's parking lot. "That lady over there said we could have four of those hash cups," Clutch said, pointing at Mary Jane. They rode over to a corner of the lot and tried the Hungarian Hurka hash.

"Baby, this stuff is amazing," Honey said. "Think we can get some more?"

"Whoa, you're right. It's really good. To get more, we'd have to get in line again," Clutch said. "Let me see how long the line is." He rode his Harley to the end of the driveway. He looked up and down the highway and returned to the spot where Honey was waiting.

"Well. Baby. Can we get some more?" Honey asked.

"The lines go on as far as I can see, in both directions. There must be at least several thousand motorcyclists out there."

"Maybe if we joined the church, they'd give us more hash," Honey said. She rode her bike over to the person handing out the cups of hash. "If my husband and I joined Reefer Church, could we have two more cups of the hookah . . . oops, I mean Hurka hash?"

Za Za Gabor was in a good mood. She enjoyed handing out the cups of hash to people who appreciated her recipe. She was, however, completely unaware of the sheer number of motorcyclists waiting for the free hash. "I don't see why not," she said, handing Honey two more cups. "I'm Za Za."

"You're Za Za?" Honey asked. "Boy, did we ever get that wrong," she said to herself, heading back to where Clutch was waiting.

"They're sure nice at this church," Honey said to Clutch. "They gave me two more cups of hash. I'd take the Hurka over hookah any day."

"Me, too, Baby."

"And I met Za Za," Honey said. "Za Za is a woman who makes the Hurka hash and not something that we would have smoked." Honey was laughing.

"We sure got that wrong," Clutch said. "It's very funny. Not in a million years would I have thought Za Za was a person."

Meanwhile, back at the imposition station, Officer Dale Dimwittie was speaking to Reverend Beaver. "It's not very funny." He was pointing at Tini and Bumper who were wearing handcuffs. "Those two people came all the way down here from West Virginia to procure hashish from you."

"It's all one big mistake," Mary Jane tried to explain. "We're giving out Hurka hash made by Za Za but somehow word got out that we had hookah hash made with zaza."

"So, you think that explains why there are over ten thousand motorcyclists clogging every road and highway for as far as the eye can see?" Dale said.

"What are you talking about?" a shocked Mary Jane said.

"I don't think all those motorcycle clubs would ride for hundreds of miles to get a small cup of your hash casserole. You need a better explanation, Reverend."

"But I don't have a better explanation, Dale."

"Then I'm going to have to take you to the station."

As Officer Dimwittie was getting ready to handcuff Reverend Beaver, Za Za came running towards them. "We're out of hash! I filled 500 cups, and they're all gone," she cried. "Somebody stole my hash!"

"I haven't done the imposition of ashes on more than fifty or sixty people," Mary Jane said. "I don't know what happened to all the boxes of your hash, Za Za."

"We seized 'em," Officer Dimwittie said. "That's why you don't have no more."

Za Za turned beet red. "You're crazy." She kicked the police officer in the shin. "Give me back my hash, now!" Then she noticed that he was trying to handcuff Mary Jane. "Hey, why are you putting those handcuffs on my pastor?" She kicked Officer Dimwittie in the shin again. "Let go of her, you jerk!"

"Za Za, they think your Hurka hash is hookah hash," Tini said.

"What did you say?" Za Za asked.

"Marijuana. Za Za, they think your hash is made from marijuana."

Meanwhile, standing at the driveway entrance, Jason Dollar was becoming concerned about the vast sea of impatient motorcyclists waiting to enter the Weed parking lot. He also noticed several police cars with lights flashing driving towards them on the sidewalk and on the shoulder, trying to get through the completely clogged highway. "I better tell Mary Jane about this," Jason muttered as he was running to tell her what was happening.

"What's going on here?" Jason asked when he arrived at the Imposition Station.

"We're arresting Reverend Beaver," Officer Dimwittie said.

"Why? What on earth did she do?" Jason asked. Before the officer could answer, he said, "You need to be dealing with the mess of motorcycles on the highway; that's what you should be doing!"

"I need backup; they should be here any minute. And this woman is distributing marijuana. That's why she's getting cuffed. My officers over there are testing that stuff she put into the cups." Dale pointed to a picnic table where several uniformed men were eating cups of Za Za's Hurka hash.

"They are in no way testing my hash!" Za Za said. "They are eating it, and they've no right."

"Chip, get over here." Dale yelled at one of the officers who was testing the hash. He turned to look at Za Za. "And don't you try to kick me again."

"You're making a big mistake," Jason said.

"We'll see about that." When Chip arrived at the Imposition Station, Dale asked him, "It's hashish, isn't it?"

"It is hash, and it is good hash," Chip said, with a big emphasis on the last two words.

"That does it. Mary Jane Beaver, I am arresting you . . ." Officer Dimwittie started to say.

"Wait" Chip said. "It's not hashish, it's plain old hash."

"Plain old hash?" Za Za said. Her face turned beet red again. "It's my Hungarian family's Hurka hash recipe. There's no other hash like it in the world." She raised her hand as if she was going to slap Chip. "You insult my family; you insult my people!"

"I'm sorry, ma'am," Chip said, apologizing to Za Za. "I didn't mean your hash wasn't the best hash I have ever had in my entire life; I was only telling my fellow officer, who is a complete fool, that your hash wasn't illegal."

"Okay, you can have more if you like." Za Za was calmer.

"Will one of you please remove my handcuffs!" Mary Jane said.

"Ours too," Tini demanded.

"There's still the matter of the motorcycles; they're everywhere, like an infestation of cicadas," Dale said as he started to remove Reverend Beaver's cuffs. "I can still arrest you for that."

"No, you can't," Mary Jane said. "It's not our fault that so many people showed up. So, take them off now!"

"Now!" Jason added.

"Now!" Tini said.

"Right now!" Bumper demanded.

"Now, or Chip gets no more Hurka hash, and I'll kick you again!" Za Za said.

Clutch, Honey, and now Jett and Hamid were standing near the Imposition Station observing the hash ruckus. The four bikers all knew each other and had been talking about Za Za's Hurka hash. They wanted to speak with Mary Jane once the handcuffs were removed.

"We have an idea, Reverend Beaver," Hamid said. "Do you have a second?"

"Do I have a second? You're kidding!"

"We all loved Za Za's Hurka hash. We all agree that it's the best thing we have tried in years," Honey said.

"Hamid owns a convenience store, and we want to try selling cups of Za Za's hash to see if people will buy it," Jett added.

"The four of us will front the money," Clutch said. "If the Hurka hash does well, then who knows where it could go."

"It's a good idea," Mary Jane said. "I'll talk to Za Za about it. But in all honesty, this is a bad time. I have to deal with our Ash and Hash Day and the 10,000 or more bikers clogging the roads from here to kingdom come."

"We'll call you in a few weeks after all this mess is settled, if that's okay."

"Tini and I wanna join you," Bumper said. "Wheeling might be a good market, too."

While they were talking about the market for Hurka hash, Jason was on a telephone call with his brother, Harold, who works in the FBI office in Atlanta. Mary Jane could see a look of concern on his face.

"Is something wrong?" Mary Jane asked.

"The FBI's coming; they think we started an insurrection."

"An insurrection, over what?"

"My brother told me Washington thinks you are trying to overthrow the duly elected government of Cartersville."

"Overthrow the government in Cartersville?"

"Apparently, FBI and CIA satellites picked up unusual traffic patterns. The pictures were sent to Quantico, and Homeland Security has been notified."

"Okay, what else can go wrong?" Mary Jane asked. "All we wanted to do was observe hash Wednesday, I mean Ash Wednesday."

"If everyone will go home, there'll be no one here by the time the helicopter arrives," Jason said.

"Helicopter? I'm not going anywhere." Mary Jane was defiant. "If they want to talk with me, then they're getting the ashes first. I'm gonna stay put."

"But they're gettin' no Hurka hash," Za Za said.

"We have to offer the hash," Jason said. "That's what we committed to do as a congregation. You do the ash; you get the hash."

"Just because we're angry or don't like someone, we can't refuse our hospitality," Mary Jane added.

"Humph," Za Za muttered. "Maybe I'll sneak in some canned corned beef hash and make them eat it with a plastic knife."

"Ma'am, you must come with me." An unidentified man sporting a bright white earphone with a wire that went into his collar was standing behind Mary Jane. "Ma'am, you must come with me," he said again, in a very firm, emotionless voice.

"Yeah, right. I heard you the first time," Reverend Beaver said, in a very irritated and impatient voice. Mary Jane looked at the person speaking to her. "Now, who are you?"

"I'm from NSA and my name is not important," he said. "You must come with me." The man pointed to a shiny black suburban parked in the Weed's lot.

"I'm not going anywhere, Mr. Not Important. I've had it with all of you."

"Ma'am, you must come with me."

"You already said that. You want ashes? Fine. I'll say a prayer, make the cross on your forehead with the ashes, give you a cup of Hurka hash and a spork, and send you on your way. If you want anything else, today is not the day."

"The NSA believes you have instigated an insurrection over the internet."

"Does this look like an insurrection to you? I've got oil and ashes," Mary Jane said. She pointed to Za Za. "She's got Hungarian Hurka hash in plastic cups with sporks." She pointed at the street and continued, "and a lot of people who for some reason known only to God and to my technology entrepreneur elder who, incidentally, is on vacation in the Okefenokee Swamp watching alligators, believed that the Hurka hash we're serving was hashish for their hookahs. But a whole bunch of other people came here because it was Ash Wednesday and the day meant something to them."

"It's kind of hard to attack the Cartersville government armed with these," Jason added, laughing, waving a plastic spork in front of the NSA agent.

The unidentified man turned away from Reverend Beaver and, looking around, noticed that a very, very large crowd of believers, bikers, and believer-bikers had surrounded the Imposition Station and were quietly watching.

One of the bikers stepped from the crowd, walked over to Reverend Beaver, and silently knelt at the Imposition Station.

Mary Jane dipped her thumb in the ashes and made a cross on the biker's forehead. "Remember that you are dust, and to dust you shall return. Repent and believe the gospel," she said. The biker rose to her feet and started back to the crowd. Officer Chip stopped her.

"You're supposed to get one of these." Chip handed the biker a cup of Hurka hash and a spork from one of the boxes that he had taken from Za Za.

"Thank you," the biker said.

One by one, people in the crowd walked to the Imposition Station to receive the ashes and to get a cup of hash from Officer Chip. A few minutes later, a contrite Officer Dale received the ashes, too. Seeing the several thousand people who were now gathered in the Weed's Hardware parking lot, Mary Jane said, "This is so much better in person than doing it drive-by; we're a community again." Mary Jane then looked at the unidentified man who stood quietly watching. "What about you? Do you believe the gospel?"

The unidentified man had not expected to face such a question. He looked at the shiny black Suburban and the two waiting, assistant-unidentified men, and then at the motley crowd of penitents.

"Who are you, anyway?" Mary Jane asked the unidentified man. There was total silence in the Weed's parking lot; not one person spoke or whispered, and some even stopped breathing, waiting to hear what the unidentified man would say. The birds were quiet, too.

"Don't you want to try my Hurka hash, Mr. Not Important?" Za Za broke the silence, and a few people laughed.

The unidentified man walked to the Imposition Station and reached for his gun. People in the crowd gasped; Mary Jane, Jason, Chip, Dale, and Za Za remained calm.

"I believe the Gospel, and my name is Harry Bronson." He removed his gun and handed it to Mary Jane. "I can't repent with this thing on my belt." He knelt at the station, and Mary Jane made a cross on his forehead with the ashes.

"Remember that you are dust, and to dust you shall return. Repent and believe the gospel," Mary Jane said to Harry. He stood up, and Mary Jane gave him his gun.

"I'd like to try the hash," Harry said. Chip gave him a cup and spork, and Harry returned quietly to the shiny black Suburban. The driver started the vehicle, and the NSA agents left the parking lot, weaving through the motorcycles.

"How far do you think we can stretch the hash," Mary Jane asked Jason. They were looking at a veritable sea of penitents.

"We've got five hundred cups and four thousand sporks," Jason replied.

"Maybe we can use paper sippy cups for the Hurka," Za Za suggested.

Within minutes, an FBI Bell 407 helicopter was flying above Weed's parking lot.

"Now what?" Mary Jane cried, looking up at the hovering helicopter.

"FBI, I told you they'd be here," Jason said into Mary Jane's ear. The noise was so loud it was hard to hear anything. "I tried to explain to my brother what we were doing. I guess he didn't listen." As Jason was talking, a long rope and basket descended from the helicopter. Everyone in the crowd stayed calm and watched.

"What on earth?" Mary Jane said.

Being the bravest individual in the group, Za Za stood underneath the descending basket, waiting to see what it contained. "It's an envelope addressed to you, Reverend Beaver," Za Za yelled at the top of her lungs.

"Bring it to me," Mary Jane yelled back. Za Za brought the envelope to her. The basket was not raised back to the helicopter, a strong indication to everyone that the agents in the sky wanted something from Reverend Beaver. Revered Beaver opened the envelope. "There's a note," Mary Jane yelled. "'We want to test the hash. Send some up,' it says." Mary Jane looked at Jason.

"This is what I think you should do," Jason yelled. He handed her a pen and a notecard. Write, 'No ash, no hash!' and send it up." Mary Jane did as Jason suggested. Za Za took the note and dropped it into the basket and back up to the helicopter it went. A few minutes later, another note descended from the hovering aircraft.

Za Za brought the note to Mary Jane, who read it aloud. "Send some ash up so we can get the hash," it read.

Mary Jane looked at Jason. "I'll send them a note explaining that the imposition of ashes must be done by an ordained minister in person and cannot be delivered as if it were some sort of prescription." That note was sent up to the FBI agents. Nothing happened for about fifteen minutes. Then an agent, attached to the rope, was lowered to the ground. The crowd and the birds were again silent.

Standing at the Imposition Station, the agent looked directly at Mary Jane and yelled, "I believe in the gospel." Being unarmed, he then knelt. And with the ashes, she made the sign of the cross on his forehead.

"Remember that you are dust, and to dust you shall return. Repent and believe the gospel," Mary Jane yelled to the FBI agent. He stood up and looked around at the crowd.

"Now, how about that hash? I hear it's great!"

"Harold?" Jason shouted. "It's you. What are you doing here?"

"It's Ash Wednesday, and I need to receive the ashes, bro. And when I heard the field office was sending agents by helicopter to your church, I wanted to make sure they didn't make a mess of things. So, how about some of that hash?"

Officer Chip handed Harold a cup of Hurka hash and a spork in a plastic grocery bag. "Enjoy," he said, saluting the agent.

"Harold, I can't believe you did this. Thank you for taking charge of the agents."

"God bless you all," Harold shouted as he was raised back to the helicopter.

Two months later, the first batch of the Za Za's Hungarian Hurka Hash was ready for distribution, with batches going to the Wheeling, West Virginia's downtown 7–11, Hamid's convenience store in Georgetown, South Carolina, and to the visitor's center at Tallulah Gorge State Park, in Tallulah, Georgia.

"I'm so excited about this," Za Za said on the phone to Hamid. "And the tee shirts? You guys never said anything about them."

"They're a surprise," Hamid said. "Remember, bikers always want a new tee shirt, and we've got three!"

The tee-shirts came in several colors, all with Za Za's image on the front with a tagline. One read, "Trade Your Hookah for Hurka," another read, "Za Za's Hash Is Better," and a third read, "Hurka Makes Me Happy."

"And Za Za, we agreed that the profit from the sale of tee shirts will be donated to a fund that supports people injured in motorcycle accidents."

"Thank you, Hamid. That's what I wanted."

Meanwhile, back at Reefer Lutheran Church, Reverend Mary Jane Beaver was having a heart-to-heart conversation with Wendell Weezell.

"Wendell, you shouldn't have waited so long to talk to us about your social media posts," the pastor said in a stern voice. "Our Ash and Hash Day was about as close to an apocalyptic disaster as you could get."

"I'm truly sorry, Reverend." Wendell was very apologetic. "I was afraid to tell you; I knew you'd be mad."

"You got that right," she said. "What really makes me angry is that you waited two months to tell us that you knew beforehand how many bikers were gonna show up."

"Is there anything I can do to make this up to you?"

"It's not me, it's the church that you offended, Wendell," Mary Jane explained. "Remember what Jesus said when he began his ministry?"

"Umm. Wasn't it the Sermon on the Mount?"

"No, after Jesus was in the wilderness for forty days and after John the Baptist was imprisoned, he began preaching. In Matthew's Gospel he says, 'Repent for the kingdom of heaven has come near.'"

"So, I need to apologize to everyone at the next worship service?"

"Not exactly, Wendell. If all you do is apologize, it's because you feel guilty and you wanna let people know how bad you feel." Mary Jane thought for a moment. "And you hope they'll feel bad about how you feel or, perhaps, they'll feel glad that you feel bad."

"Isn't that what I wanna do?" he asked.

"That's up to you. But when you repent, you do so because you think differently about your actions and you want your life to be more aligned with the Kingdom of Heaven." Mary Jane smiled at Wendell. "Repentance is a much bigger deal than we realize. It takes a lifetime to fully understand it."

"So, how do I repent?"

"Share with our faith community where you believe you have let us down; in this case, it's quite obvious. 12,000 motorcyclists are a lot. Then you set your mind on the right path, or as Paul writes in Romans, 'be transformed by the renewing of your mind.'"

"I'm not sure I understand."

"Philippians is one of my favorite books of the Bible. Remember where it says, 'whatever is true, whatever is noble, whatever is right, whatever is pure, whatever is lovely, whatever is admirable—if anything is excellent or praiseworthy—think about such things."

"I was trying to impress the council about what a great tech entrepreneur I was, and I made a mess of things."

"Because you were focused on your own self-importance. If you were focused on things that were right, pure, lovely, or admirable, you would have told us that you grossly underestimated the number of bikers for the event and that they might be coming, not because it was Ash Wednesday, but because they wanted to get high."

"That makes sense."

"I too have had to repent. I was focused on getting more people to the imposition of ashes because I wanted more people to be there, not because I wanted the people to have a more meaningful experience. We all traded our faith for a cup of hash and a plastic spork."

"I've got a lot to learn about being in a faith community," Wendell said.

"Wendell, we all do."

"For some reason, Ben, your story makes me think of Bonhoeffer's *The Cost of Discipleship.* Reefer Church was offering God's grace along with drive-through convenience and Hurka hash," Sue said. "Cheap grace."

"We Baptists are new to the Ash Wednesday tradition, if and when we actually do it," Ben said. "But I was surprised when I read about the Ash and Dash movement."

"Does it seem to cheapen grace to any of you?" Ken asked. "Ash and Dash is popular with Lutherans."

"I'm of two minds," Sue said. "Connection is important to Methodists, but Ash and Dash is so modern American, individuals sitting in their individual cars. I do see that work puts so many demands on our members that making things more convenient is a plus."

"Fast Faith," I would call it," Jim said. "I don't like it."

"What if someone thinks receiving ashes is cool but is not involved with the church and doesn't know the first thing about what the ritual means?" Sue asked. "Should we turn them away? I mean there's no opportunity for a brief homily to explain things."

"To me, your story shows how misinformation about something as simple as the imposition of ashes can infiltrate the community of believers," Princeton added.

"Ben, you've raised many questions for us to think about. Thank you for your funny and thoughtful tale," Dave said.

"I don't think my Baptist church will be doing Ash and Dash next year," Ben said. "We'll work hard to find ways for people to gather with each other, instead."

"Okay, we're ready for the next tale." If Ken is last, that leaves you, Sarah."

"Sarah Brewster is back! She's a year older and a year more precocious," Sarah laughed. "I call the tale, *Thus Asked Sarah Brewster*, and my text is Luke 18:16–17. I'm using the New English Translation Bible.

Thus Asked Sarah Brewster

"Let the little children come to me and do not try to stop them, for the kingdom of God belongs to such as these. I tell you the truth, whoever does not receive the kingdom of God like a child will never enter it."

(LUKE 18:16–17 NET)

THE REVEREND LUCIUS KYLE does not like Sarah Brewster. No, not one bit. It's because of that "young lady," a derogatory title throughout South Georgia, that membership at his church declined by fifty-three percent in the months since she put a stop to the special perks that the city council and businesses of Cedar Springs afforded him. He lost his cherished siren and emergency light atop his church-provided brown Ford Tempo, and gone were his exemptions from parking and speeding tickets, his special fountain booth at Grady's Apothecary, the free home-delivered subscription to the *Cedar Springs Spigot*, and his fifteen percent discount at Wheeler's Grocery Store, to name a few. Spigot reporter Jay Walker titled his front-page story about Sarah's triumph, "Preacher's Perks Popped," and he referred to the "young lady" as the "Great Perk Popper." Deep in his soul, Lucius believed that the lack of respect afforded him by Sarah and the *Spigot* led a lot of the members of his First Baptist Church to drift over to the First Methodist Church, where Sarah and her mother worshiped.

"We're making things happen at First Baptist!" Reverend Kyle declared to his congregation on a recent Sunday morning. Standing in the old white oak pulpit, he spoke in as bold a voice as he could muster. "Starting on Monday, the Holy Ghost will be back, and those drifters will drift back home, too!" Lucius stood erect with his hands on his hips. He waited a minute for the news to reach into the hearts of his flock. "Going forward, the First Baptist Church of Cedar Springs will henceforth be known as Ignition Church of Early County. We're still Baptist, but we'll have the fire of rocket ignition; we're still in Cedar Springs, but our mission will thrust us forward throughout the whole county!"

"Amen," grocer Houston Wheeler growled. He stood up and uncharacteristically raised his hands in the air as high as he could, which was not much past the top of his ears. Earlier, Reverend Kyle had asked Houston to give his Ignition Church announcement a resounding, heartfelt Holy Ghost-inspired "amen." He did the best that he could, but the gravelly-voiced grocer sounded more like he was coughing.

"Are you coming down with something?" Pharmacist Lamar Grady was seated next to Houston and scooted further away, fearful of getting sick.

"Do ya need a Kleenex, Houston?" Sheriff Barker's wife Rhonda asked, leaning forward from the pew behind Houston. She pulled one from her purse and tried to hand it to him.

"I'm fine, Lamar; and Rhonda, I don't need a damn Kleenex!" He disliked drawing attention to himself and wished he had never agreed to being the one to give the Holy Ghost-inspired amen.

"Ya need to change your shirt, too." Rhonda was peeved at Houston's shortness with her. "Either that or get yourself a new deodorant—your armpits are yeller." Houston glared at her.

"Thank you, Houston, for your hearty amen!" Reverend Kyle said. "Everybody, say Amen!" The sanctuary was silent.

"We don't do that in this church, Lucius." Delmar, Lamar's brother and Grady Apothecary soda fountain manager, said. "And we don't raise our hands, either."

Undeterred, Reverend Kyle continued, "My first project as the Ignition Church pastor will be to bring the Bible back to the schools of Cedar Springs." He looked over the congregation; a few were nodding off.

"How long's your sermon gonna be today?" Delmar asked. "We're not doin' communion, are we?" He was feeling irritable and didn't want to miss the Falcons pre-game show.

"I'll be done when I'm done," Reverend Kyle responded. He, too, was starting to feel irritable; he disliked being interrupted. "Hear me now, brothers and sisters. The first place Ignition Church is going to ignite its Holy Ghost rocket fire is in our schools." Lucius pounded his fist on the pulpit. Now he had everyone's attention. "And Cedar Springs Middle School is where we will make our first launch."

"How you gonna do that, Reverend Kyle?" Rhonda asked, interrupting the sermon.

"Yeah, Reverend, them lawyers won't let you do that," Emit Dooly said. He owned three popular convenience stores in Cedar Springs. "Those nitwits at that Civil Liberty Union ain't gonna let you fire your holy rocket in no school that I know of."

"I have a plan, and my plan is constitutional," the Reverend replied.

"But you ain't no lawyer," Delmar said. "How can you be sure?"

"I got a kit from some experts up in Washington who say it is. And they know the law better than anybody, even the Civil Liberty Union." Lucius explained. "And once we take a stand for the Word of God, believers will be streaming back to First Bap, I mean, Ignition Church!"

"Amen," Houston grumbled.

"Streaming?" Rhonda asked sarcastically. "Creeping, I'd say. I'm still mad at 'em; they should be on their hands and knees when they come back here."

"So, in conclusion, I want to see all of you at the Wednesday School Board Meeting," Reverend Kyle said, ignoring Rhonda's comment. Finally, he felt ready to take on his arch-nemesis, Sarah Brewster, and he didn't want anyone to spoil the moment. "Barbara, let's sing hymn number 659." Lucius stepped down from the pulpit and stood facing his church members. For the first time in months, he felt the power of the Holy Ghost.

Music Director Barbara Slingsteen got up and faced the congregation. "Join me in singing hymn number 659, "Guide Me, O Thou Great Jehovah."

"Sometimes our members drive me bonkers," Reverend Kyle said to Lamar Grady after the service. "I don't like it when they ask me questions while I'm preaching."

"It's okay, Lucius," the pharmacy owner said. "Some folks just don't like change; they get used to the way things are and don't see why anything needs to be different.

"You're right, Lamar. But wait 'till they see our old members drifting back from Sarah Brewster's church!"

"Amen to that, brother," Lamar said. "You're number two on the agenda and don't forget to make the handouts. And, Lucius, I'm sorry my brother Delmar is so obnoxious."

The first day of the school year in South Georgia, a region known for its astonishingly hot and muggy summers, is during its most hot and muggy week. No one seems to know why the school year starts during the worst part of South Georgia's climatological inferno.

Cedar Springs entrepreneur Adam P, a self-described visionary change-agent who changed his last name to a single letter, offered to focus his artificial intelligence program on this very question and to use his proprietary technology to figure out the best new school year start date and schedule. Adam was at the Wednesday school board meeting to make what he hoped would be a lucrative proposal.

"I'll be able to use AI to pick the absolute best day of the year to start school," Adam P said, making a bold promise to the board.

"When can you start and how much will it cost?" Chairperson and Pharmacist Lamar Grady asked.

"Not much. But I have top-secret work to do for the Pentagon. They want my AI program to solve pi to its final decimal point before the Chinese do. It's an urgent project that must take absolute priority," Adam P replied. "But as a gesture of appreciation to the school board, the hard-working teachers, and the students, however, I can hold the next spot in my project calendar in exchange for a reasonable monthly placeholder fee."

"I tink y'all sood do dis," Mayor Fogg said from the back of the room. His tongue was swollen, and his voice was a little slurred. "He's got my endorphins."

"I think you mean endorsement," Lamar told the Mayor. "I'll bet he's on pain killers," Lamar whispered to Rhonda. "He's been to the dentist."

"Wait a minute, everybody," Cedar Springs Middle School science teacher Javon Bunsen said. He knew Mr. P was nothing but a fraud. "Pi is a transcendental number and not the root of any non-zero polynomial equation," he explained. "That means Mr. P's program will not reach a final decimal point until the end of time itself. Don't give that man one dime!"

"Transcendental, you say?" grocer Houston Wheeler asked. "I don't see what being a dentist has to do with Armageddon."

"Houston, did you forget your hearing aids?" Rhonda, herself a retired teacher, asked. "He wasn't talking about the Great Tribulation or dentists; he was talking about pi. And besides, the Rapture comes first, so we don't need to worry about the sun exploding."

"What kind of pie?" Houston asked.

"I don't understand, Houston, what do you mean what kind of pi?" Javon asked.

"What do you mean, what do you mean what kind of pie?" Houston asked back. "There's lots of kinds of pie." He pointed to his wife, Jessie. "She makes the best pear pie in Early County. She got the top prize at the fair last year."

"Rhonda, you're wrong about the Rapture," Delmar said, ignoring the pi-versus-pie discussion. "Most theologians say it comes after the Great Tribulation." The soda fountain manager had been listening to a series of end-of-times sermons by an up-and-coming Tulsa evangelist known as Dr. Elmer Didactikle.

"It was peach pie, and I got third place." Jessie worried Houston was getting more confused lately. "I want to ensure there's been no misunderstatements about my pies."

"No, you're wrong, Lemar," Rhonda snapped. "The Bible says it's before!"

"I'm not on Ensure anymore," Houston said. "The doc says I'm getting enough vitamins now."

"Don't you mean misunderstandings?" Rhonda asked. "And Houston, put on your hearing aids or go home. Jessie wasn't talking about that stuff you used to drink."

"Stop, everyone! Stop!" Lamar Grady said, raising his voice and hitting the table with his gavel. "Nobody gets to say anything unless I say so."

"Well, since when did you get to be in charge of the meeting?" Rhonda was very snippy.

"Since you elected me to be the board chair!"

Rhonda's face turned red, much like the way left-behind people look in pictures of the Rapture. "Well, I, I, I, never!"

"We need to move on with the next agenda item, and then we're leaving." Lamar was getting tired. He looked at his watch. "We've been talking about I-don't-know-what goin' on forty minutes. Reverend Kyle, you have the floor."

"Good evening, everyone."

"Good evening to you, Reverend Kyle," Rhonda said.

"Rhonda, I said no one says anything, and I mean anything."

"I was just being respectful of the minister," Rhonda shot back. "It's been a long time since . . ."

Lamar slammed the gavel on the table. "Revered Kyle, please continue."

"Our county wants us to include the Bible in the school curriculum. I propose that we do exactly that." Reverend Kyle looked at the school board members. "Students will need to use their own Bible; that way, we won't be spending tax dollars on Bibles." Lucius could see that Sarah Brewster was in the audience. He knew that the precocious middle schooler would have raised a First Amendment objection.

"Jessie, you have copies of Reverend Kyle's proposal, is that so?" Lamar asked.

"Yes, I do, Mr. Chairperson."

"Can you pass out the proposal to everyone?"

"Yes, I will, Mr. Chairperson."

Lucius then continued his presentation. "I am recommending we use the Bible in three subject areas: science, civics, and art." *Cedar Springs Spigot* reporter Jay Walker raised his hand.

"Yes, Jay," Reverend Kyle said.

"Does this mean we would be having creationism taught in our schools?"

Lucius had anticipated this question. "No, we will not change our current curriculum." The teachers let out a sigh of relief. "We will, however, be dedicating one week of each semester to student-led discussions involving the Bible in those classes I mentioned. They'll then prepare a summary report that they'll share with y'all after they're done."

"So, the teachers won't be leading the discussions; the students will."

"Yes, Jay, it'll be student-run. The teachers can make suggestions, but they can't offer conclusions."

"Does it have to be the Bible? I mean, could a student choose to use the Qur'an or another holy book?"

Reverend Kyle had anticipated this question, too. "Yes, Jay. They can." Lucius was feeling confident he had prevented all possible First Amendment objections to getting the Bible into the classroom. "Are there any other questions?" Sarah Brewster raised her hand. "Here we go," he thought to himself. "Sarah, you have a question?"

"I do, Sir. What Bible do we have to use?" she asked. "In Oklahoma, it had to be the King James."

"That's a good question, young lady." Lucius knew Sarah Brewster would be at the meeting and that she would point out some critical issue or barrier. "Whichever one you want to use—King James, Living, New International, it doesn't matter."

"I'm using the NET Bible Full Study Notes Edition. It's got sixty thousand notes from the translators on word choices, variant readings from the Hebrew, Greek, and Aramaic texts; it's so huge that my Mom will have to get me a bigger book bag!"

"That's very nice, Miss Brewster. I'm glad you use that version," Lamar whispered to Houston, "What an obnoxious know-it-all."

"I used the 'One Year Bible for Men' with the New King James Version translation," Sheriff Barker said from the audience. "It's great 'cause you get through God's word in a year, then you're done with it. I think . . ."

"Thank you, Sheriff," Lamar said, cutting him off. "Are there any more questions or comments?" Lamar waited for a minute. "Seeing none, is there a motion to approve Reverend Kyle's proposal?"

"I second the motion," Gas Station owner, Emit Dooley, said.

"We need a motion before you can second it," Lamar said.

"I make a motion and I second it," Emit said.

"You can't do both. You have to pick one."

"Geesh," Rhonda said. "I'll make the motion."

"I second it," Emit said.

"Wait, Emit. Rhonda hasn't made the motion yet," Lamar said.

"I move that we approve Reverend Kyle's program," Rhonda said.

"I second it," Jessie said.

"Hey, I was gonna do that!" Emit complained.

"You took too long," Lamar said. "All in favor, please raise your hand, and those opposed, don't raise your hand."

"What if you're abstinating," Emit asked.

"I don't know, Emit. Touch your nose," Lamar said.

With a majority voting in the affirmative, the Cedar Springs School Board adopted Reverend Kyle's Student Bible Discussion Project. The members of Ignition Church cheered, all fourteen of them, those in the audience, and those on the board. (Lamar, who, as chair, felt he needed to display his decorum and did not cheer out loud.)

"Are there any other questions, from the board or from the audience?" Lamar waited two seconds. "The meeting is now adjourned," Lamar continued, ignoring Adam P, whose hand was still raised. Mayor Fogg was with Adam P. "What a bunch of sleaze bags," he mentioned to Lucius.

"I did it," Reverend Kyle said to Houston Wheeler, "Houston, we have ignition—the Bible will be back at the Cedar Springs schools!"

"Good morning, Javon," Civics teacher Lisa Colquit said to her colleague as he entered the Cedar Springs Middle School faculty lounge. She and art teacher Vincent Dali-Hopper were in the smallish but comfortable room having coffee. They were anxious to hear how the student-led Bible discussions had gone in Javon's science class the previous afternoon and were waiting for him to arrive. The civics discussions were set to begin at 9:30, immediately following Home Room, and the ones for the art class, the following day.

"Hey Lisa. Good to see you, Vin," Javon said.

"So, how did it go?" Vincent, or Vin as he was known, asked.

"We've gotta know," Lisa was eager to hear something from Javon.

Walking over to the coffee machine, Javon said, "Lamar told me that the school board assumed science would be the most controversial, you know, creation versus the big bang and evolution. They were wrong, very wrong. In fact, it was fun."

"Using the Bible in a science class was fun?" Lisa was dumbfounded.

Javon sat down at the table with his colleagues and continued. "Well, my students chose to discuss the creation story in the Bible," Javon said. "Some believed the universe was created by God. Some thought it happened with the Big Bang, and some said they believed in the Genesis story. We do have one Muslim student who shared creation stories from the Qur'an. And our Buddhist student told us the world was an illusion. Then my students started talking."

"And?" Lisa said.

"Well, Sarah Brewster, you know she's one smart kid. She walked up to the big marker board and drew a picture of the universe from a Neil deGrasse Tyson book on one side. On the other side, she drew a picture of the world envisioned in the Genesis creation story that she took from the notes in her Bible." Javon stopped and enjoyed a sip of his coffee. "This coffee is really good."

"And?" Lisa said again.

"And then Sarah led the class in a discussion about the Mars rover, the Webb space telescope, and the TV series, *Star Wars: Andor*."

"So, what about the diagrams?"

"They decided that the Genesis diagram was a small part of the big universe diagram. Everybody was happy with that, though there were disagreements over some of the details." Javon smiled at Lisa and Vin. "I thought it was going to be a rough day, but it wasn't. I had fun and they had fun, and we all learned more about each other in the process."

"So, did the Mars Rover, the space telescope, and *Star Wars* discussion go anywhere?" Lisa asked.

"Sarah drew the path of a spaceship leaving Earth's orbit, or the dome in the Genesis diagram. The Genesis-believing students realized the rocket had to go somewhere; otherwise, there would be no Webb Space Telescope pictures, no Mars Rover, and no Star Wars." Javon looked at his watch. "It's your turn soon, Lisa."

"Finish the story, please," Vin said.

"You remember Burke Herbert. He's on the football team; he got up to the board and drew a line from the Genesis picture to the Universe diagram and said, 'This must be part of this.' Everyone cheered, though the Buddhist student was quiet the whole time."

"They were that enthusiastic about astronomy?" Lisa wanted to know. "I had no idea."

"Like I said, they had fun."

"If only the parents were as wise," Lisa said. A second later, the bell rang. It was 9:25, and time to head to first period. Lisa, Javon, and Vin headed to their classrooms.

"Good morning, class," Lisa greeted her students. "I heard you had a good discussion in Science yesterday."

"It was far-out," Burke said.

Sarah looked at the football player. "Far-out? Is that new?"

"No, that's what my gramps said he and his friends would say when they thought something was cool. "It came after groovy."

"So, class, what do you want to discuss today?"

Sarah Brewster raised her hand. "Yes, Sarah, do you have a question?" Lisa said, feeling a little uneasy. "Here we go," she thought to herself.

"Yes, ma'am, I have a question." All eyes in the classroom were directed towards Sarah Brewster, curious about what she was going to ask. "Ms. Colquit, is God a communist?"

"Is God a communist?" Lisa repeated Sarah's question. "It's not for me to say. This is something y'all need to discuss."

"Why would God be a communist?" Sally Pinpoint asked.

"I didn't say God was a communist. I asked *if* God was a communist." Sarah picked up her NET Bible and started reading: "'The group of those who believed were of one heart and mind, and no one said that any of his possessions was his own, but everything was held in common.' Acts 4:32. That sounds like communism, if you ask me."

Omar Al-Jabari raised his hand. "Can I say something?"

"Yes, Omar, you can," Lisa said.

"I know that the Qur'an also states that everything on the earth belongs to Allah."

"Wait a minute. The earth is God's, not Allah's," Sally said. "Who's Allah, anyway?"

"Sally, why don't you look up 'Allah' in the dictionary," Lisa suggested, hoping to avoid religious confrontation, if not conflagration. She could see Omar was looking a little upset.

"Yes, ma'am." Sally said. She grabbed the *Merriam-Webster's* dictionary and looked up Allah. "Oh, I see. It says that Allah comes from Arabic and means 'The God.'" Sally was much calmer. Sally smiled at Omar. "Sorry."

"It's okay," Omar said.

Sally raised her hand. "Yes, Sally."

"My Torah has some verses about why God might be a communist. Can I read them?"

"Okay, let's hear them," Lisa said. Looking at the class, she added, "I want to make sure everyone knows that this is a student-led discussion. The school board will not allow us teachers to take any sides or express our opinions in any fashion."

"Okay," Sally said. "Deuteronomy 10:14 from my Torah reads, 'Behold, the heavens and the heavens of heavens belong to the Lord your God, the earth and all that is in it;' and in Exodus, 19:5 God says, 'for all the earth is Mine.'"

"That's what the Qur'an says, too," Omar exclaimed. He smiled at Sally.

"Sally, why don't you look up communism in the dictionary?" Sarah said.

Sally picked up the dictionary and flipped through the pages until she found the word. "Okay, found it. Let's see. Hmmm . . . It does sound a little like what Sarah read in her Bible: 'A system in which goods are owned in common and are available to all as needed; a theory advocating elimination of private property.'"

Sarah Brewster raised her hand. "Yes, Sarah."

"Thank you, Ms. Colquit. What about socialism?" Sarah asked. "I heard someone say he was a Christian socialist."

"Sally, how does *Merriam-Webster's* define that?"

"Give me one second. 'Socialism, any of various egalitarian economic and political theories or movements advocating collective or governmental ownership and administration of the means of production and distribution of goods.'" Sally looked at the teacher. "That doesn't seem to describe what's in the Torah."

"Not the Qur'an, either," Omar said.

"Look up capitalism, Sally," Burke said. "What does it say about that system?"

"Let's see . . . 'An economic system characterized by private or corporate ownership of capital goods by investments that are determined by private decision, and by prices, production, and the distribution of goods that are determined mainly by competition in a free market.'" Sally put the dictionary down and thought for a moment. She looked at her notes. "That goes against the Torah, big time. Leviticus 25:23 says, 'The land shall not be sold in perpetuity, for the land is Mine and you are strangers and resident aliens with me.'"

"Somebody can rent land for a while but not forever. Is that what it's saying, Ms. Colquit?" Burke asked.

"Class, what do you think?"

"Who would they pay the rent to?" Sally asked.

Sarah raised her hand, again. "Yes, Sarah."

"This is so complicated to me," Sarah said. "Jesus said, 'No one can serve two masters,' and that 'You cannot serve God and money.' That's a lot simpler."

"Jesus didn't say that," Burke said. "My pastor says Jesus was in favor of capitalism."

"He did too, say that." Sarah handed her NET Bible to Burke. It was open to Matthew chapter six. "Here, look at this."

Burke read the text silently. "Hmmm," he muttered. "You've got a modern liberal Bible. I'll read from mine. I got the original Bible, the King James, that's the one we use in my church." Burke opened his Bible. "Okay, here we go, Matthew 6:24, 'No man can serve two masters,' wait let me get to the important part, 'Ye cannot serve God and mammon.' See, I told you so. You can serve God and money. It's mammon that's bad."

John Bradshaw raised his hand. "Here we go, he'll be wanting to use the bathroom. He always does this," Lisa said to herself. "Yes, John."

"I use the NIV Bible. My pastor says it is the best one, even better than the King James. Can I read something?" Lisa was surprised that John was really engaged in the discussion.

"Go ahead, John."

"My Bible says, 'You cannot serve both God and money.'"

Sally raised her hand. "What's mammon?" Sally asked.

"Look it up, Sally," Lisa Colquit said.

Sally picked up the *Merriam-Webster's* dictionary and found the entry for mammon. "It says, 'Material wealth or possessions especially as having a debasing influence.'"

"You mean wealth, mammon, and money are the same thing?" Burke asked, feeling very troubled.

"Seems so to me," Omar said.

"Ms. Colquit," Sarah said, raising her hand. "I have a question."

"Go ahead, Sarah."

"Thank you, Ms. Colquit. If God's not a communist or a socialist, and God's not a capitalist either, then Burke's pastor can't be right, don't you think so?"

"Like I said, it's not for me to say. This is your project."

Sarah got up and walked to the large wall dry board; her classmates watched as she started writing. When she finished, she turned to the class and said, "I've made a summary of everything we're talking about. One: God is not a communist, a socialist, or a capitalist. Two: God owns everything. And three: God thinks wealth or riches are bad for us." She turned and faced the class again. "Okay, raise your hand if you agree with me."

First, Sally raised her hand. "I agree with Sarah," she said.

Next, Omar raised his hand. "I don't know what's in the Bible, but I think the Qur'an is the same on this."

Then, John Bradshaw raised his hand. "Can I use the bathroom?"

"No, John. You can wait until everyone has voted," Lisa said. "I knew he would do this," she thought to herself.

"Okay, then. I think Sarah is right. Now can I go?"

"You can wait another minute, John."

"What about you, Burke?" Sarah asked, looking at her classmate. It was obvious to everyone that she was feeling impatient.

"Come on, Burke," Sally said. "What do you think?"

"Oh, I don't know," he said. "I don't know." He was blushing.

"It's okay if not everyone agrees," Lisa said to her class. "Remember, people have been arguing about this topic for hundreds and hundreds of years. Burke, do you want to tell us what you think?"

"What if Sarah wrote, 'God thinks wealth or riches can be bad for us?'" Burke said.

"I'm okay with that," John said. Omar nodded.

"What about you, Sarah?" Omar asked.

"Oh, I'll go along with it," she said. "I think that's being wishy-washy." She made the change on the dry board. "Okay, this is what we've got. One: God is not a capitalist, a communist, or a socialist. Two: God owns everything. And three: God thinks wealth or riches can be bad for us."

Mya Aung raised her hand. "Yes, Mya. We've not heard from you yet. Do you have something you want to add?" Lisa asked.

"Number One doesn't mean anything to me. Number Two needs to say, 'nobody owns anything 'cause everything isn't anything.'" Mya paused for a moment. "Three, should say 'wealth or riches lead us away from enlightenment.'"

The room got very quiet. John raised his hand quickly.

"Yes, John. You can take a bathroom break." John darted out the door.

Sarah raised her hand. "Ms. Colquit. What do you think we should do?"

"I cannot help you. But find the one thing everyone can agree on."

The room was very quiet as the students thought. Sarah stood at the dry board again and erased everything they had written. She thought for a moment and started writing again. When she finished, she turned to face her classmates. "How about this, 'Wealth or riches lead us away from God, what truly matters, and each other.'"

"I can accept that," Mya said, smiling.

"Me too." Omar was in agreement.

John, returning from the bathroom, looked at the board and said, "Cool, I like it."

"I think I'm okay with it." Burke was looking calmer now as he didn't think his father or pastor would get angry with the statement.

"Me too," Sally said.

The remaining classmates were happy with the new statement. And, within two minutes of the vote, the bell rang, announcing the end of first period Civics class. "Thank God that's over," Lisa said to herself.

The following morning, Lisa, Vin, and Javon were in the teacher's lounge, enjoying their coffee.

"I am dying to hear how it went," Vin said to Lisa. "Give me the details."

"All I can say is that I am glad it's over and done with," Lisa said. "There were a couple of times where I thought we'd have some confrontation. Sarah and Burke were poles apart; Sally is Jewish, Mya is Buddhist, and Omar is Muslim. As to the other students, I don't think they were interested in the discussion or, maybe, they aren't involved in a congregation. They were largely quiet."

"But did you survive?"

"Yes, surprisingly. By the end of the class, they came up with a values statement that everyone could agree to."

"I heard that Burke Herbert's dad called the School Board chair last night," Javon said.

"Oh dear, should I get my resume out?"

"No, no," Javon said. "He was just a little concerned about how negative the class was regarding wealth and riches. Lemar brushed him off, telling him, in so many words, that it was the students' project and the teachers weren't allowed to be a part of the discussion."

"Live with it," in other words.

"Yeah. I don't think Mr. Herbert was overly concerned anyway. I believe he was simply trying to ensurethe discussion didn't get too anti-business."

"In a little over four hours, it's your turn, Vin. I hope it goes well, my friend," Lisa said.

The bell rang, homeroom was over, and the three teachers headed to their classrooms.

As soon as Vin walked into the room for his 2:00 class, Sarah, Sally, and Burke had their hands raised. Omar and John were looking very embarrassed. "Burke, what do you have to say?"

"If my sister watches TV next to my dad, say for a long movie, is she gonna get pregnant?"

Vin froze. "Say that again."

"Is my sister gonna get pregnant if she watches TV with my dad?" Burke seemed a little angry.

"No, I don't see how." Vin was very uncomfortable with the course of the conversation. "I'm an art teacher, not a sex ed teacher," he thought to himself. "We're here to talk about the Bible, Burke. Sally, you had a question?"

"It can't be possible for Burke's sister to get pregnant just because she's watching TV with her dad, isn't that right, Mr. Dali-Hopper?"

"This class is about the Bible and art, not sex ed. You'll need to talk to your parents about that," Vin suggested. "Sarah, you had your hand raised."

"If you commit incest two times and don't know about it and your kids get pregnant, shouldn't you go to jail?" Sarah seemed angry, too.

"Where is this coming from?" Vin thought to himself. "It's hard to imagine you wouldn't know about it, and yes, you should go to jail," he told the students.

"The Qur'an does not allow sex between a father and a daughter," Omar said.

"Look class, let's take a break. Find something to read for a minute. I need to text someone." Vin took out his cell phone and sent the following text to the school social worker: "One of the girls in my class may have been the victim of incest. We need to get the police here ASAP." He waited for a response.

"On it, Vin," the school social worker texted.

"Thx!" Vin texted back. Two minutes later he had a response.

"Police on way. 5 min. Got name?"

"Not sure. 1 of 3."

"Will rept when pol r here."

"Class, we have some people coming to the class in a couple of minutes. So, do some reading or homework until they get here." Vin took a seat at his desk and waited. "I always knew this was going to happen," he thought to himself.

A few minutes later, there was a knock on the classroom door. Vin walked to the door and peered through the window. He opened the door to a county police officer and a plain-clothes detective; after speaking with Vin for a few minutes, they entered the room and took seats at the front of the class.

"Everybody, these women are here to help us with the conversation that we started at the beginning of the class."

"You mean about incest and getting pregnant?" Sally asked. She looked at the officers with a surprised look on her face.

"Yes, Sally. These people are experts and can help us," Vin said.

Sarah raised her hand. "Yes, Sarah."

"Can I ask the officers a question?"

"Yes, you can, Sarah."

"Did you go to seminary?"

"Seminary?" Vin asked. The officers looked at each other, puzzled.

"Maybe she wants to know if we're qualified counselors," the plain-clothes detective, Janet Gordon, whispered to her partner.

"If they're experts on the Book of Genesis, then they should have gone to seminary," Sarah said, emphatically. "Did you go to seminary?"

"No, neither of us has been to seminary," Marla Monroe, the uniformed officer, replied. She looked at her partner; both were confused.

"Burke, read the story we're talking about," Sally said.

Burke took his King James Bible and opened it to the book of Genesis. "It's a bit long."

"Go on, Burke," Sarah said.

Burke started reading 19:32–38: "Come, let us make our father drink wine, and we will lie with him, that we may preserve seed of our father . . ."

"You were all talking about Lot and his daughters," Vin said. "That's why you were asking me about pregnancy and incest?"

"Well, yeah," Sarah said. "One of the art pictures on the wall is Dürer's painting of Lot and his daughters. You told us you liked Dürer, so that's what we decided to talk about."

"That's why I was worried about my sister watching TV with my dad," Burke said.

"I think I can help a little," Janet, the plain-clothes officer, said. "Your name's Burke, right?" she said, looking at the eighth grader.

"Yes, ma'am."

"It is impossible for your sister to become pregnant just by watching TV next to your dad."

"That's what I thought," Burke said.

"If any girl becomes pregnant from a relationship with her father, then that's something we'd get involved with," Marla added.

"It's illegal, right?" Omar said. "It would be punished?"

"Yes, the father and not the daughter," Marla replied.

"The daughter is the victim," Marla, the uniformed officer, said.

Sarah raised her hand. "Do you have a question, Sarah?" Vin asked.

"Yes, Mr. Dali-Hopper. Let's say the daughters get the father drunk and then they sleep together and the daughters get pregnant, do you still become involved?"

Janet turned to Vin and asked him. "What on earth are these eighth-grade children reading? I don't think this is appropriate material for a middle-school class."

"They're reading the Bible."

"The what?"

"The Bible. Genesis, to be exact."

"That kind of stuff's in the Bible?" Marla asked.

"Sure is," Sarah said. "I'm surprised we're even talking about it in school."

"Me too," Burke said.

"I agree. It's gross," Sally said, scrunching her nose and making a grossed-out look. "Whose idea was this, anyway?"

Sarah raised her hand. "Yes, Sarah."

"I have a question, Mr. Dali-Hopper. Can we propose having the Bible removed from the school library? I don't think this kind of stuff should be available to us children."

"Yeah, I had a nightmare about Lot last night," Burke said.

"The story made me afraid to sit anywhere near my dad," Sally added.

Sarah stood up and faced her classmates. "All in favor of removing the Bible from the Cedar Springs Middle School Library, please raise your hand." The vote was unanimous.

"What about the Qur'an?" Sally asked.

"Lot is in the Qur'an," Omar replied. "But I don't think it has him sleeping with his daughters."

At the school board meeting the following week, chair Lamar Grady was anxious to rush through the students' report about their experience with Reverend Kyle's Bible project. Neither he nor Reverend Kyle, however, were pleased with their choice of Sarah Brewster as the eighth-grade class spokesperson.

"Good evening, ladies and gentlemen," Sarah began. She was seated at the long rectangular table as a guest of the Cedar Springs School Board. "My report on the Bible discussions for the fall semester will be short and to the point." Each school board member had a copy of her summary, as did everyone watching from the audience. Reverend Kyle was feeling uneasy. Seated on the side of the room, Sarah's mother was feeling very proud.

"Per the guidelines that you approved at the beginning of the semester, we had three Bible discussions. The first one was in our science class, the second in civics, and the third in our art class." Sarah and her classmates prepared a bullet point display board that summarized what she called "their proceedings." Using a laser pointer, she started with the first one. "Regarding our science discussion, we concluded that if some students believed the creation story in Genesis and others did not, we could still be friends. This is because, based on *Star Wars*, the Webb Space Telescope, and the Mars Rover, the creation story in Genesis covers a small part of the whole universe. We all agreed on that." She looked up at the school board members who seemed to be squirming a little. "But we never talked about fossils or how you could get two 115-foot-long, 70-ton Patagotitan dinosaurs on an ark plus two Argentinosaurus at 131 feet and 80 tons. We'll be talking about that next semester."

"Thank you, Sarah, for the presentation," Lamar said. "I am sure you and the other students will figure that out."

"Wait, I still have parts two and three."

Lamar and several school board members moaned. "Go ahead, Sarah."

"In our Civics class, based upon our discussions of the Torah, Bible, the Qur'an, and Buddhist principles, we concluded that wealth or riches lead us away from God, what truly matters, and each other."

"You did, did you!" Lamar said. "Did Ms. Colquit put you up to this?"

"No sir, she didn't." Sarah was upset with his question. "She gave us no opinion or input other than telling Sally to look up certain words in the dictionary. Next semester, we'll discuss the Song of Songs." She looked at Lucius. "We followed Reverend Kyle's plan exactly."

"Thank you for your presentation . . ."

"I still have one more section, sir. In our art class, we looked at a picture of Lot and his daughters by an artist named Dürer. Then we read the story in Genesis, in five different Bibles plus the Qur'an. The Buddhists don't have a Lot story. With the help of the Cedar Springs Police Department, we unanimously adopted the following request: 'We, the eighth-grade art students at Cedar Springs Middle School, without input from our teacher, do hereby request that the Bible, in any translation, be removed from the school library. We believe the stories of rape, incest, decapitation, sex, nudity, and other adult themes are not appropriate for middle school students.' We also want to thank Officer Marla Monroe and Detective Janet

Gordon of the Early County Police Department, Special Victims Unit, for their help with our discussion." The room was silent.

"What in Heaven's name was the Special Victims Unit doing in your classroom?" Lamar asked, breaking the silence.

"We were talking about incest and getting pregnant by your dad, Sir," Sarah replied. "At first, Mr. Dali-Hopper didn't realize we were discussing the Bible, so he called the police. When they came, he and the officers figured out we were talking about Lot."

"And that's what led you to recommend we remove the Bible from the library?" Lamar asked.

"Well, that plus all the other bad things I mentioned—rape, decapitation, nudity, you know, stuff like that."

"We can't do that," Houston said. "The community would throw a fit."

"According to the policies you adopted last year, the library cannot have materials that, wait . . ." Sarah looked through her papers to find the minutes from the meeting at which the library book standards were set. "Here it is, 'the library is banned from having any materials that depict sex acts.'" She looked at Lamar directly and continued. "Not only did the story from Genesis that we read include two sex acts, but they were also between a drunk father and both of his daughters."

Lamar froze for a moment. "Those stories were in the Bible, you say. I don't remember reading them, and I've read the Bible many times."

Sarah handed Lamar one of the Bibles from the middle school library. "Please read out loud so everyone can hear, Genesis 19:30–38."

Lamar looked at the text and read to himself for a minute. "It says they lay with their father. That doesn't mean they had sex, young lady."

"Keep reading, please."

Lamar continued reading. He stopped and looked at Sarah. "They got pregnant."

"My point exactly. We have here a story in which a father lives with his two daughters in a cave because he doesn't want to live near anybody else, and then he gets them pregnant."

"It's only one story, Sarah," Rhonda said.

"Ma'am, with all due respect," Sarah said, "we could be here all night if we read all the other stories with sex and violence."

"Well, if we remove the Bible, then the Qur'an's gotta go, too," Rhonda said.

"That is not our recommendation," Sarah said, in a monotone voice.

"And why is that, young lady?" Houston asked.

"We didn't find the same adult content in it that's all over the place in the Bible."

Lamar looked at Reverend Lucius Kyle, who was seated in the audience, squirming. "Lucius, you're the one who proposed this Bible study stuff. What do you think?" Sarah turned to look at the minister, as did everyone else in the meeting room. "And, let me add that because of you, we might have to ban the Bible from the Middle School Library but not the Qur'an. How does that look to the community?"

"I, uh, I uh. Hmmm . . ." Lucius wasn't sure what to say.

"We'll all be booted off this school board if that happens," Houston said.

"Uh. Hmmm, I uh, the Bible in the library? I hadn't thought of that," Lucius said.

Lamar looked at Sarah. "Thank you for your presentation. As always, you've given us adults a lot to think about." Sarah took her papers and returned to her seat along the back wall.

"Fellow board members, we're in a pickle. Let's think about this and bring Sarah's proposal up at the next meeting." Sarah stood up, waving her hand in the air. "Yes, Sarah."

"It's not my proposal, sir. It's the eighth-grade class proposal from Cedar Springs . . ."

"Yes, I know, from Cedar Springs Middle School. We'll take up the proposal at the meeting next month. I'll also wanna talk about removing the Bible discussion projects from the school curriculum." Lamar hit the table with his gavel and declared the meeting adjourned.

Lamar got up from the table and walked straight to Reverend Kyle. "Lucius, you got us into a big mess. Why couldn't you have left things alone?" Not waiting for a response, he left the room, muttering something under his breath.

As the other folks exited the room, *Spigot* reporter Jay Walker was laughing, Rhonda Barker was fuming, Reverend Kyle was feeling deflated, Houston Wheeler was grumbling, and Sarah and her mother were talking about ice cream. In the back of the room, teachers Javon Bunsen, Lisa Colquit, and Vincent Dali-Hopper were speculating to each other that the whole fiasco might be over, for now at least.

"Good morning, sweetie," Mrs. Brewster said to her daughter. "You did great last night. I'm so proud of you."

"Thanks, Mom. Is that bacon?"

"Yes, and pancakes. But eat quickly, I don't want you to be late for school."

Sarah ate her favorite breakfast, grabbed her book bag, and headed out the door. Along the way to school, she passed Grady's Apothecary and Wheeler's Grocery store, both of which had not opened. She saw Sheriff Barker in his car at the intersection where she would cross the street and head towards her middle school.

"Good morning, Miss Brewster," the Sheriff said.

"Good morning to you, Sir."

"I heard about last night's School Board meeting. You're a force to be reckoned with in this town."

"Thank you, Sheriff Barker." Sarah blushed a little.

"When you're finished with school, maybe you could enter the police academy. I sure could use someone as smart and as brave as you."

"Thank you, Sir. I'll talk to my mom about that. I think I'd rather be a Bible scholar," she replied. "I hope you have a good day."

"You, too." Sheriff Barker chuckled. "I've really grown to appreciate Sarah. I'll bet Reverend Kyle hasn't," he thought to himself.

Once in the building, Sarah walked past the teacher's lounge. She waved at Javon, Lisa, and Vin, who were at a table having coffee together. Javon called out to Sarah, "Come here for a second, Sarah." Sarah, not wanting to enter a restricted room, stuck her head in the doorway. "Did you see the *Spigot* headline this morning?" Javon asked.

"No, Sir," she replied.

Lisa held up the newspaper for Sarah to see. The headline read, "Bible Bumped from Bookshelf?" A subtitle read, "Did Kyle Caper Cause Holy Kick?"

"Jay Walker has a way with the headlines," Vin said.

"I hope we didn't get Reverend Kyle in trouble," Sarah said.

"He'll survive," Vin replied.

"Sarah, your class did what you were supposed to do."

"Javon, tell her about Mayor Fogg," Vin said.

"There's another article at the bottom of the page. Mayor Fogg and Adam P were arrested last night, too."

"Money laundering, contract fraud, and a bunch of other charges. Mr. Bunsen, your science teacher, steered the School Board away from Mr. P's company two months ago. They were trying to cheat the school system!" Vin told Sarah. "We're so proud of him."

"Thank you," Javon said.

"Our Civics class was right, Ms. Colquit," Sarah said. "Money and riches can lead us away from God and each other."

"You and your classmates did a good job, we're proud of you."

"I am so glad you brought Sarah Brewster back," Dave said. "I've missed her this past year!"

"Don't you think the middle schoolers were learning that there are two ways people approach the Bible?" Sarah asked. "One group focuses on the first clause of 2 Timothy 3:16, believing that because scripture is inspired by God, it's inerrant: cherishing it as an object to revere. The second group emphasizes the second clause, using the Bible, like Paul says, for its usefulness in teaching us how to 'walk the walk,' sometimes never coming to terms with the Greek text, 'god breathed.'"

"And never the twain shall meet," Jim added.

"If you're in the first group," Princeton said, "you're gonna have to figure out how to get the Patagotitan dinosaurs on the Ark." He chuckled at the thought.

"And if you're Methodist like me, Wesley's Quadrilateral pulls you towards the second group," Jim said.

"We Lutherans traditionally put the gospels above the other parts of the Bible. That makes it easier to not feel threatened by science," Ken said. "The other parts of the Bible point you to the gospels which reign supreme."

"Same with us Episcopalians," Sarah said. "And we only stand when the Gospels are read and not the other parts."

"Ditto for us Lutherans."

"But all of us still need to deal with many, many texts about wealth, with or without having the dinosaurs on the Ark," May added.

"True, but don't overlook how the students learned to remain friends," Sue said. "Whether they took Genesis literally or not, or if they believed in the Qur'an or were Buddhist, they figured out a way to be friends and to study together."

"And for Reverend Kyle, getting the Holy Bible into the school was his objective," Ben said.

"No, it wasn't," Ed replied. "He was using the Bible as a means to enhance his standing in the community. That's why he wanted to get it into the classroom. In the end, they'll have to remove it from the school altogether."

"Now people want to attack those who don't believe like they do," Sarah said. "The Bible's become a veritable gun; its texts are used like bullets to harm folks people don't like."

"So true. It's not at all in line with how Paul describes Scripture's purpose in Second Timothy," Ed added.

"Sarah and her classmates should be a model for us all," Dave said.

"Hola," Juana said, interrupting the conversation; she and two servers walked into the lounge holding several trays. "We have some tapas for your refreshment." They placed the trays on a coffee table that sat directly in front of the fireplace. "We have *quesos mixtos, patatas bravas, y chorizo*. To drink, we have *agua o sidra*."

"I'd rather just have some small appetizers and a glass of water," Billy whispered to Ken.

"That's what she just brought us," Ken said. "Remember, we're in Spain and they speak Spanish."

"There's nothing weird, is there?" Billy asked.

"No, she's given us some pretty typical appetizers," Ken said, looking at the tapas.

Dave looked at Juana and said, "Thank you so much, this is absolutely marvelous! I'm sure we'll all enjoy these dishes."

"I was getting pretty hungry," Ken said. "You know in Spain sometimes the dinner hour's not 'til 10:00 p.m."

"10:00 p.m.?" Ben asked with a frightened look on his face. "That's nuts!"

"Hence the tapas, my brother."

"And it's not nuts; it's another way of life," Ken said. "I lived in Spain for a few months as a volunteer. I loved their lifestyle. You probably didn't notice, but while we were all telling stories, Juana, Father Alcuin, and everyone else were taking their siesta."

"Speaking of telling stories, we have one more. Ken, it's your turn."

"Thank you, Dave. I call my story, *Root, Branch, & Twigg*. My text comes from Matthew 11:29–30. And like most of you, I am using the TNIV."

Root, Branch, and Twigg

Take my yoke upon you and learn from me, for I am gentle and humble in heart, and you will find rest for your souls. For my yoke is easy and my burden is light.

(Matthew 11:29–30 TNIV)

The Most Highly Reverend Potentate Axel J. Cleaver, CEO, Chair, President, and Supreme Ruler of his independent church, the Whole Bible Prophecy Church of God's Impending Judgement, liked big things—big Lincoln SUVs, big gold rings, big Swiss watches, big steak dinners, a big house, and big audiences. He was also proud of the fact that he knew the Bible, and especially the Book of Revelation, better than any other human being on earth, or so people were compelled to tell him. To the Potentater, as he liked to be called, Revelation was the most authoritative book in the Bible and the source of his absolute power. And he used that book and its chilling visions and prophecies to instill fear in the hearts and minds of everyone who lived within his domain, Pleasantville, Georgia, and the surrounding county of Affable, for which it was the seat.

Axel was a man disliked by everybody, too. His first wife hated him, as did his second, and his third. His children also hated him. Axel, Jr. thought his dad was a total jerk. His second son told friends that his dad was meaner than a pitbull, and his youngest son said he was the backside of a mangy moose with an intestinal disorder. Axel's two daughters despised him; the oldest thought him totally vile, and the youngest called him "the Big Creepster." The mayor of Pleasantville and the seven town council members disliked the Potentater with equal intensity; so did the local pharmacist, banker, grocer, car dealer, sanitation engineer, realtor, haberdasher, postmaster, school principal, physician, hotelier, sheriff, restaurateur, and all of their employees, customers, volunteers, and directors. Not one single person in Affable County harbored any positive thought or memory about the Most Highly Reverend Potentate Axel J. Cleaver.

Five years ago, Axel borrowed a lot of money from the Affable County Bank in order to build a seven-story mountain of a tower next to his church. He brazenly refused to make any loan payments and told bank president David DeMure to "shove off" when he was already six months in arrears. Axel wouldn't pay for his prescriptions, drove a new Lincoln SUV off the lot at Pleasantville Motors without letting anyone at the dealership know about it; yelled and screamed at the school principal each time one of his children did not get the highest grade in his or her class; and regularly filled his cart with groceries at Crowger's Food and then walked out the door without stopping to pay. One Sunday, after a frighteningly apocalyptic sermon, Crowger's Food manager, Clay Coy, mentioned to the Potentater that he ought to pay for his groceries. "Your end is nigh, so shove off," was his reply. Larry LaShy also got the "shove off" message and angry glare from Axel when he tried to get paid for the Lincoln SUV. Indeed, Potentate Cleaver was truly a hateful man.

If all of this were not enough reason to harbor ill feelings toward that man, everybody grumbled over the fact that if you wanted to run a business in Affable County, you had to be a member of the Whole Bible Prophecy Church of God's Impending Judgement. If parents wanted to enroll their child in a school, they had to have paid Potentate Cleaver to perform a baptism for everyone in the family—infant, child, teen, and adult—it didn't matter if they had already been baptized before. Lastly, before you were allowed to go out to eat, go bowling, or see a movie (or spend any money on anything), you were expected to have satisfied your monthly financial pledge to the Potentater's church, whether or not you were a member. Shunning, expulsion, and humiliation were all tools Potentate Axel Cleaver used to ensure that his church, and his church alone, was the absolute and all-encompassing foundation for every aspect of life and human activity in Affable County.

On a positive note, if you named your male child Axel or your female child Axela, he or she would be guaranteed a high school diploma with honors upon turning seventeen.

In the decade since the Most Highly Reverend Potentate set up shop and infiltrated, or as Clay Coy would say secretly, "infected" Pleasantville and Affable County, people learned to live in a world far less pleasant than the one they had known before. And with each year that passed, the more folks grew accustomed to life under the iron fist of the Potentater, the less they broke bread in fellowship with their friends, neighbors, and fellow believers, and the less they would go out of their way to help someone in need. It is said that even the bees and butterflies had stopped pollinating the flowers of Affable County. The city council members and county commissioners had all come to rue the day when they accepted Potentate Cleaver's offer to build a new mega church and evangelism center, and gave him tax incentives, land grants, and his own streaming Bible commentary TV channel (which Axel named "Leave It to Cleaver") with the hope that church attendance would increase and more jobs would come to their county.

Two hundred miles northeast of Pleasantville at the Annual Conference offices of the Methodist Churches of Georgia, the Bishop and Evangelism Committee members were listening to a group of consultants they hired to help them come up with a new evangelism strategic plan.

"Good morning, Bishop Farro and Evangelism Committee members, both clergy and laity. We have the phase one results of our research, and we are happy to present our report to you," Elaine Root said, welcoming everyone to the meeting.

"What about me?" Missy Millet asked. "I'm here, too." Missy, thanks to her grandmother, was the Conference Administrative Assistant and maintained a seat on each committee. Her grandmother, Martha Magnum Millet, was the largest benefactor to the Methodist Women of Georgia. "Everyone always forgets to welcome me."

"I apologize, Missy; let me start over. Good morning, Bishop Farro, Evangelism Committee members, and Missy Millet."

"I have a title in case you didn't notice," snipped Missy.

"Okay, one more time. Good morning, Bishop Farro, Evangelism Committee Members, and Conference Administrative Assistant Millet."

Michelle Branch handed a thirty-page, spiral-bound, glossy document to each person sitting around the table at the conference center meeting room. Michelle's partner, Elaine Root, was leading the discussion while the other partner, Eleanor Twigg, took notes. Their firm, Root, Branch, and Twigg, was Georgia's leading faith-based consulting and investigation business, helping Protestant and Catholic organizations become lean, mission-focused, and better equipped to carry out the Great Commission. Methodist Bishop Shirley Farro and her team had contracted with the firm to help them determine those areas of Georgia that would be most fruitful for evangelism.

"The Methodist Churches of Georgia Conference is well represented in every county and community in this state." Elaine displayed a map with little blue dots, one for each church. "That is, in every county except one." This piqued the committee's interest—several people had been nodding off; lunch had been only an hour earlier, and the room was a bit on the warm side. But now all of the members were wide awake and listening.

"Well, Elaine, I am dying to know what county it is," Bishop Farro said.

"Affable County. There are no Methodist Churches in Affable County and . . .

"None?" Attorney Wilson Wheatly asked, interrupting Elaine. Wilson was a longtime member of the Evangelism Committee. "Where is Affable County, anyway? I've never heard of it."

"Neither have I," Reverend Reginald Rye said. Reginald was a popular minister and very supportive of the cooperative efforts of churches from different denominations (which he hoped would, at some point, be a part of their evangelism plan).

"Me neither," Beverly Barley, the president of Humble Bank, a small community bank based in Humble, Georgia, said. Like Wilson Wheatly, she had served on the Evangelism Committee for many years, ever since she had received her first promotion.

Insurance agency owner Roberto Bulgar had to add his two cents. "I've not heard of Affable County, and I know Georgia better than anyone here."

"I think Affable County is in South Georgia, somewhere." Missy Millet was curt; she was still miffed at being overlooked during the greetings. "I need two copies of the report, one goes to me and one goes to my grandmother," she said, as if this should have been obvious to the consultants.

"Okay, we have a long way to go with our presentation. So, if there is anyone here who has heard of Affable County, please raise your hand." Looking around the room, Elaine could see that no hands were in the air. Another chart was on the screen. "Missy is correct. Affable County is in South Georgia, in far, far South Georgia, and as best that we can determine, not only are there no Methodists, but there are also no Presbyterians, Lutherans, Episcopalians, Baptists, or Roman Catholics."

"What about Orthodox Christians?" Missy saw a documentary about them on the local PBS station. "There are Greek, Russian, Serbian, Bulgarian, Antiochian, Ethiopian . . . let me think, I can't remember the other versions."

"We did not find any Orthodox Christians of any kind," Elaine said. "Okay, let's move on to the next slide."

"What about Mennonites or Amish?" Missy had a cousin who lived in Lancaster, Pennsylvania.

"We found no Mennonites or Amish; neither did we find any Disciples, Brethren, Pentecostals, Mormons, Christian Scientists, Jehovah's Witnesses, Muslims, Buddhists, Zoroastrians, Jains, Hindus, or pagans in Affable County."

"What about Swedenborgians?" Missy asked. She saw an article about them in the most recent issue of *National Geographic* while standing in line at the grocery store.

"None," Elaine responded. "Not a single one."

"They have a really interesting history. They were founded in the eighteenth century by Emanuel . . ."

"Can we move on, please?" Beverly was getting impatient with Missy.

"Elaine, this is unbelievable!" Bishop Farro said. "Affable County is the most unchurched county I've ever heard of."

"I didn't say that it was unchurched," Elaine responded. "The county has only one church. It's independent, unaffiliated, and has a mouthful of a name: the Whole Bible Prophecy Church of God's Impending Judgement."

"As part of our preliminary research, we conducted telephone interviews with residents of the county," Eleanor said. "Our team reached out by telephone to 100 people chosen at random. Not one single person was willing to engage in our survey, not one."

"Isn't that unusual?" Wilson asked.

"Unprecedented," Michelle said. "Usually, we have a response rate of about forty-five to fifty percent."

"While that's considered high," Elaine added, "we find people in Georgia are typically very happy to talk at length to our researchers about their faith."

"But not this time," Eleanor said. "So, for the next step in our research, the three of us are going to spend a week in Affable County, meeting people for coffee or having lunch at restaurants, talking to folks waiting in line at stores, or in any other way we can engage the residents."

"And, we plan on visiting the independent Whole Bible Prophecy Church of God's Impending Judgement and its pastor, the Most Highly Reverend Potentate Axel J. Cleaver," Michelle added.

"Oh dear, it sounds like they'd better bring armed escorts," Roberto whispered to Bishop Farro. He was a little worried about the consultants' safety.

"We will present Phase Two of our report at the next Evangelism Committee meeting."

"Don't forget I need two copies," Missy said. "One for me, and . . ."

"Yes, Miss Millet, and one for your grandmother," Elaine said.

"Can you send Missy to an out-of-state training when we have that meeting?" Beverly whispered to Bishop Farro.

"Holy moly," Elaine said. It was her turn to be the driver. "There's no way to get to Affable County from anywhere in Georgia, unless you're on foot or in a balloon. It's gonna take us a while to get to where we're going."

"My map app says we gotta go to Jakin," Michelle said. "Then we cross into Alabama, and once we get to Pansy, Alabama, head south for about fifty miles 'til we get to Greenwood, Florida."

"I'm glad we left at five this morning," Elaine said. "It's gonna be a long drive."

"Let's not stop for lunch 'til we get there," Eleanor said. "I've got some munchies we can share."

"And let's pray no one has to pee along the way," Elaine added. "I don't think I wanna stop anywhere if we don't have to."

"Okay, Elaine. We'll do our best," Michelle said. "Now, once we're in Greenwood, we head east to Two Egg, and I'm not kidding, then we go thirty miles more or less 'til we get to Sneads. That's when we look for the spot where Lonesome Pine meets Jinks Crossing, then we can head north back into Georgia."

"Do you really think I'm gonna remember those directions?" Elaine started laughing, then Michelle and Eleanor joined her.

After about six hours of driving, Michelle, Elaine, and Eleanor crossed into Georgia from Florida and saw their first billboard from the Whole Bible Prophecy Church of God's Impending Judgement.

"Oh dear, look!" Eleanor pointed to the first sign.

On the billboard was a very large human ear and these words in bold capital letters: "HE THAT HATH AN EAR, LET HIM HEAR WHAT THE SPIRIT SAITH!"

A mile further, they passed a second sign. It read, "THOU ART WRETCHED, AND MISERABLE, AND POOR, AND BLIND, AND NAKED." Depicted were several men and women weeping and wailing; some were kneeling. "YOU ARE WARNED!" was at the bottom.

A third sign appeared about a mile from the second one. "THE GREAT DAY OF WRATH IS COME!" Potentate Cleaver was pictured holding a big black Bible in one hand and grasping a torn U.S. flag in the other. "YOU ARE JUDGED!" was in bold red letters across the bottom of the sign.

"I honestly don't know what to say," Michelle finally said. The three consultants had been speechless since seeing the first sign. Yet, just outside of Pleasantville, there was one more billboard to come.

"IS YOUR NAME IN THE BOOK OF LIFE?" A mushroom cloud from a nuclear bomb explosion was pictured on the billboard. "OR WILL YOU BE THROWN INTO THE LAKE OF FIRE?" appeared in the middle of the cloud. Along the bottom were the faces of dozens of screaming people.

Finally, past the billboards of the Apocalypse, the consultants entered Pleasantville; the highway narrowed and became Main Street once they passed Division Road.

"Lord Almighty, we're here," Eleanor said. "I'm one hungry consultant."

"I could use some food too, but I'm not so sure I'm hungry for this contract anymore," Eleanor said.

Pleasantville's Main Street was in bad shape. It needed repaving, dearly; the original concrete surface was cracked and filled with potholes. At the first stop sign, on the right side of the street, there was an old, faded sign that originally read, "Welcome to Pleasantville;" you could barely see the happy children that were once prominently depicted. On the left side of the street was a newer, much larger sign, with the words, in bold capital letters, "GO TO MY CHURCH ON SUNDAY!" plus a black and white image of Potentate Cleaver holding a sword with JUDGMENT written on its blade.

"It's mid-afternoon on a weekday, and there's no one anywhere," Michelle said. She was exceedingly nervous.

"I guess the Great Day of Wrath's already occurred here by the look of the place," Eleanor said sarcastically. "We're doomed." She and her partners started laughing.

"Let's find a place to eat," Elaine said. She parked the car at one of the dozens and dozens of empty parking places, barely marked by faded white lines.

"This is weird, did you notice that not one building has a sign? How do you know what anything is?" Now Elaine and Eleanor were feeling nervous, too.

Getting out of their car, they walked down the cracked and crumbling Main Street sidewalk. The first building they passed did have a sign above the door, but it was so faded you couldn't make out what it once read; little bits of red, blue, yellow, and green paint were still clinging to the old sign. In the middle of the door was a sticker with the word "SAVED" in bold gold letters. Eleanor noticed a 4x8 card taped to the picture window upon which someone had written "Realtor." She peeked through the window and could see a man seated at a desk, sound asleep. They passed two more shops with the same "SAVED" sticker on the doors. The fourth shop they passed had a 1x3 card taped to the glass door on which someone had squeezed, "OBGY." The window had a sticker on it with bold red letters that read, "WARNED." The next building they passed had the same red letter sticker on its glass front door. On a window there was a 1x3 card that read, "Rx." Above the door there was a rotting frame that once, long ago, held a sign.

"What's with these stickers?" Michelle wondered.

"Did you hear that bell ringing?" Elaine asked her partners. "It sounded more like a gong." She looked at her watch and realized it couldn't have had anything to do with the time.

"If we don't pass a restaurant in ten minutes, we're going home," Eleanor said. "This place gives me the heebie-jeebies."

"I've got the heebie-heebie-jeebies!" Michelle was more nervous than either of her partners.

"Hey, look across the street! People are coming out of that building. Maybe it's a restaurant!" Eleanor said. "It looks like they may have been eating."

"They don't look so happy," Elaine said. "But let's check it out, anyway."

Elaine, Eleanor, and Michelle crossed the empty street; just before reaching the other side, a large shiny black Lincoln SUV came from out of nowhere and sped by. It had an odd-looking license plate that read, "UR SEEN." An old dog that had been sleeping in the street had to jump out of the way to avoid getting run over.

"What a jerk," Michelle said.

"This looks promising." Elaine was looking through the front door. "I can see tables and chairs and a few booths on each side; two people are in one of the booths."

"Look at the window," Eleanor said to Elaine. "What does that 4x8 card say?"

"Food," Elaine replied. She looked up and she noticed there were a few pieces of an old neon sign still hanging from the weathered eave. In the middle of the glass door was a sticker with bold brown capital letters that read, "MILK."

Michelle, Elaine, and Eleanor cautiously entered the building. They were glad to see that it was indeed a restaurant, which to their surprise, though very stark, was also very clean.

"Sit down and I'll get you split pea soup," a young woman wearing a clean though faded red and white checkered apron told them. "I'll get your water and saltine crackers, too." She had short scissor-clipped auburn hair and was sporting a pair of spotless worn-out sneakers. After several minutes, the server returned with the soup and crackers.

"I'd like something else, if you don't mind," Michelle said. "Can't we get a menu?" They were seated in one of the clean but tired-looking booths.

"Split pea soup, crackers, and water is what we're serving today. Take it or leave it."

"Is there another restaurant in town we could go to?" Elaine asked the server.

"No," the server replied, yawning. "We're it, for miles." The Root, Branch, and Twigg team members were so hungry that they decided to take the soup and be done with it.

"Can you believe this?" Elaine said to her partners. "I doubt they'll be any Michelin stars for this place anytime soon. Eleanor and Michelle were equally shocked.

A few minutes later, the server returned carrying a big tray. "Here you go," she said, placing one very large ceramic tureen of split pea soup in the middle of the table along with three small, mismatched spoons, an opened box of discount-store-brand saltine crackers, and a partially used roll of paper towels. "I'll be back with the water." Michelle, Elaine, and Eleanor sat staring at the large bowl in total silence for several minutes.

"I'm afraid to try it," Michelle said. "I've never seen so much soup in one bowl."

Eleanor took a spoonful of the soup and smelled it. "It seems safe," she said. She slowly put the spoon in her mouth. "It's not bad; it's just bland." She consumed several spoonfuls before Michelle and Elaine joined her.

"Stale. No crunch." Michelle had taken a bite from a cracker out of the box.

The server returned with three half-filled glasses of lukewarm tap water and set them on the table.

"Could I get some ice and a slice of lemon?" Elaine asked the server.

"No," she said, showing no emotion. "Ice machine don't work, and we don't bother with lemons anymore." She yawned loudly and let out a long sigh.

"I have a question for you," Michelle said to the server. "What does the MILK sticker on your door mean?"

"The Potater put that there. It means the owner ain't a fully tested Christian yet. There's somethin' in the Bible about not bein' ready for solid food."

"Is that why you're only serving split pea soup?" Michelle asked.

The server shrugged her shoulders. "I dunno. I just serve what the owner gives me."

"I noticed the WARNED signs across the street. What are they about?" Eleanor asked.

"That means the owners aren't Christian, they don't go to church, and they're bad people. The Potater says we should avoid them."

"Who's the Potater?" Eleanor asked.

"That's the Reverend Potater Cleaver; he's the CEO of the church."

"I see," Eleanor said, not wanting to correct her.

"I noticed three stickers: SAVED, WARNED, and MILK. Are there others?" Elaine wanted to know what to expect as they prepared to explore Affable County.

"There's a purple one that says "SHUNNED." That means they were once Christian, but they stopped goin' to church."

"By the way, I'm Michelle, and this is Eleanor, and that's Elaine." The three partners were smiling at the server. "What's your name?"

"Why you asking?" The server suddenly got nervous and looked around to see if anyone was listening. "You're not with the Potater, are you?"

"We're just being friendly." Michelle held out her hand. "We work for a bishop, but a very kind and humble one. She lives pretty far from here."

"I'm Alice." She wasn't ready to shake Michelle's hand. "Your Bishop's a woman, and she's nice?" Alice asked, surprised there was such a thing. "Is she a Potater?"

"Yes, she's a woman and nice, and no, she's not a Potater. Now tell me, do you like this town?" Michelle asked.

"Oh, I dunno." Alice got very quiet and looked around again. She bent over to get closer to the three consultants. "It's not a place for smiling," she whispered. "That's all I'm gonna say."

"Thanks, we won't push," Eleanor said, paying for the meal.

"Wait, you left too much," Alice said as they were starting to leave.

"We left you a tip, Alice."

Alice looked at the money, puzzled. "What's a tip?"

"It's for you," Eleanor said. "For being our server."

"What do I do with it?" Alice was still confused. "Should I give it to The Potater?"

"No, don't." Eleanor couldn't believe she was having this conversation. "If I got a tip, I wouldn't give it to my bishop. It's none of her business."

"Really?"

"Alice, the money is for you," Elaine said.

Having left the restaurant, the consultants from Root, Branch, and Twigg decided to check into their hotel. It was across the street from where they left their car. Along the way, they passed several other businesses, each one having a sticker on the window marked with "SAVED," in gold, "WARNED," in red, "MILK," in brown, or "SHUNNED," in purple. The one exception was the Affable County Bank, which had two stickers, "SAVED," and "WARNED."

"Let's go by the bank first thing in the morning," Michelle said. "We have to see why they've got two stickers." As they crossed the street to get their suitcases from the car, the same large shiny black Lincoln SUV sped by. The dog, now resting on the sidewalk, growled at the vehicle as it passed him.

Like all the other businesses in Pleasantville, the hotel had a bold, all-cap sticker on the front door. It read, "SAVED." They entered the lobby and walked up to the counter. Seated in a chair, reading a magazine hidden within the pages of a larger newspaper, *The Affable End Times,* was the manager, Alfonse DeMure, the nephew of the bank president.

"Hello," Michelle said to the manager. "We have reservations."

The manager got up, accidentally dropping his magazine onto the floor. It was a copy of *Forbes*. "I thought he was looking at a porn magazine," Eleanor whispered to Elaine. "Why is he hiding *Forbes*?" Embarrassed, the manager pushed it out of sight with his foot.

"You've got the double-deluxe-sleeper-room with a king-sized bed and a sleep sofa." Alfonse handed an envelope with three keycards to Michelle.

"We'll need breakfast in the morning," Elaine said. "Do you serve it here?"

"Just a moment," Alfonse said. He reached below the counter and retrieved a large box of store-brand corn flakes. "Here," he said, handing the box to Elaine. "That should be enough for the three of you. There might be some milk in your room's refrigerator. If not, I might have more." Elaine was a bit stunned, both at the size of the corn flakes box and the lack of other offerings for their breakfast.

"What about coffee?"

Alfonse reached below the counter again and found three packets of instant coffee. He handed them to Elaine, too. "We're out of sugar and creamer. If you really want some, feel free to go and get it at the store. I won't mind." Alfonse then yawned and scratched the back of his neck. "Get some extra for me, too."

"I have one question. Why do they call Reverend Cleaver The Potater?" Eleanor asked.

"You must have been talking with Alice. She can't ever seem to get it right. It's Potentater."

"I thought that's who she was referring to," Eleanor said. The three then headed down the hallway towards their room.

"Did you notice this hotel doesn't even have a name?" Eleanor asked her partners.

"I'm not feeling very good about this place," Michelle said.

"Here's our room. Maybe I should say a prayer." Michelle entered the keycard into a slot on the door. A little light turned green, and she opened the door to room number 7.

"Oh, my." First Michelle, then Elaine, and finally Eleanor entered their room. Above the bed was a larger-than-life silhouette of the Potentater and the words, "REST HERE AND DON'T SIN."

"At least the room is clean," Michelle said.

“I am curious, why does Affable County Bank have two different stickers on its door?” Michelle asked its president, David DeMure. Michelle, Elaine, and Eleanor were meeting with David in his traditional 1930’s CEO office at the bank’s main and only remaining branch.

Seated in his brown leather executive chair with gold rivets behind a large traditional-looking desk, David seemed uncomfortable responding to the question. “I thought about fighting the WARNED sticker,” he said. Not wanting to make eye contact, he looked at the pictures on one wall of his office. “Wanda, our Head Teller . . .” David paused for a moment; he was trying to sound positive. “Her husband, who had Alzheimer’s, needed stomach surgery. She had to care for him, so she stopped going to church.” While they were talking, they heard the great bell that sounded like a gong. “Someone’s sticker must have changed,” David thought without saying anything.

“Let me make sure I understand what you’re saying. Wanda didn’t go to church because she wanted to stay by her husband’s side.” Eleanor had a look of disgust on her face.

“Did anyone at the church try to help her?” Elaine asked.

“Well, no. Wanda and her husband were at a hospital over in Jacksonville.”

“Wait, Wanda was in Jacksonville at the hospital with her husband while he was getting treatment?”

“You got it,” David said, still looking at the wall of pictures.

“That’s almost two hundred miles away! So, the only way for Affable County Bank to have avoided a WARNED sticker was for Wanda to drive two hundred miles to attend a church service in Pleasantville and then drive two hundred miles back to be with her husband?” Michelle was not able to hide her astonishment.

“When did all this happen?” Elaine asked.

“Oh, two months ago,” David replied, looking at Elaine.

“So, are Wanda and her husband back in Pleasantville, now?” Eleanor asked.

“Wanda is, but her husband passed away.”

“Why the WARNED sticker, then?” Michelle was having trouble keeping her composure.

“The Potentater didn’t perform the funeral service, and they didn’t buy a plot at his church cemetery—Wanda’s husband was cremated. She was so upset at how the Potentater was treating her that she stopped going to his church." He spoke very quietly. "I shouldn't have told you about this."

"That's why you have a WARNED sticker on your door?" Eleanor had just about lost it.

"The Potentater's waiting for her to apologize to him and to beg for forgiveness."

"Why didn't you fight for her? This is ridiculous!" Eleanor raised her voice. She felt frustrated with the bank president. "What a coward," she thought to herself.

"I did. He was going to put a SHUNNED sticker on our door. That would've been worse for Wanda and for us, don't you think?"

"What I think is that we're done here, Mr. DeMure," Michelle said. "Thank you for your time." The three partners were much too exasperated to continue.

"You should be aware that the Potentater knows you're here asking questions," David said as they were leaving his office.

Once outside, they decided to walk over to the building with the "Food" 4x8 card. Once at the door, Eleanor noticed there was a new sticker on the door. The "MILK" sticker was gone, and a "WARNED" sticker was in its place. The 4x8 card was gone too. In its place was a 3x5 card, with "Eat" written on it. Given the mandated writing size, food did not fit on the smaller card.

They entered the restaurant and sat down at a booth. After a few minutes, Alice wandered over to their booth and put a plate of peanut butter sandwiches on their table.

"Here's your lunch," Alice said. She seemed much sadder than the day before. "This is what we've got today."

"Are you okay, Alice?" Michelle asked.

"They put a WARNED sticker on the door this morning; all because I spoke with you." A tear fell to her cheek. "They said if it happens again, they're gonna change it to a SHUNNED sticker and take away the "Eat" 3x5 card. They also took the tip you gave me."

"My God," Eleanor said. "How dare they!"

"Please don't ask me anything. I'll go get your water."

Eleanor leaned forward so as not to be heard. "I think I'm done interviewing people. After lunch, let's go to that church and speak with this Impotentater!"

"Weren't we were gonna visit with Mr. LaShy at Pleasantville Motors?" Michelle asked.

"I agree with Eleanor," Elaine replied, agreeing with her partner. "We're done with these interviews."

"Okay," Michelle said. "After lunch, we'll go to that Church of God's Impending Judgement."

Alice was back at the table with the water. "Here you go." Putting the glasses on the table, she asked, "Is there anything else I can get you, not that there's anything else I could get you?" Eleanor noticed a tiny hint of sarcasm in Alice's voice.

"Thank you, Alice. We don't need anything else," Eleanor said.

"I'm sorry we got you into so much trouble," Michelle said.

"It's not your fault," she replied, looking exceedingly downtrodden. "That's just the waythings are in Pleasantville."

Michelle, Elaine, and Eleanor finished the sandwiches and paid for the lunch, leaving Alice another tip, plus the amount they had given her the day before. Once in their car, Eleanor called the church office and made an appointment with the Potentater for that afternoon.

Heading to the Whole Bible Prophecy Church of God's Impending Judgement, they passed through several residential neighborhoods of typical southern bungalows with perfectly cut and trimmed weed-filled lawns. It took just a few minutes to notice that something was very strange—each house had an identical metal signpost in the middle of the yard.

"What on earth are those signs?" Michelle asked. "Pull over, I've gotta see what they are." Eleanor stopped the car alongside a curb; Michelle got out and wandered into the nearest yard to look at one of the signs. She hurried back to the car with an unusual combination of facial expressions—shock, anger, disgust, and horror. Getting back in the car, Michelle said, "Every house in Pleasantville has one of those SAVED, MILK, WARNED, or SHUNNED stickers on a metal sign in the yard! Can you believe this?"

"That's really sick," Elaine said. "Let's get going. I can see people looking at us through their windows."

Eleanor pulled away from the curb and headed toward the church; she could see the large building straight ahead. "There it is," she said to her partners.

The closer they got, the weirder it looked. They were also surprised to see a seven-story, mountain-sized windowless stone tower. It was attached to the side of the large, nondescript windowless, aluminum-sided sanctuary that looked like a massive data center, a sanctuary big enough to have a seat for every person who lived in Affable County. In fact, each seat had the name of one of the people who lived in the county plus that person's current status, SAVED, MILK, WARNED, or SHUNNED.

"What's with the tower?" Eleanor wondered out loud, knowing full well that neither Michelle nor Elaine could answer the question.

"We'll see," Eleanor said, parking the car in a lot big enough to have a space for every car registered with the Affable County Department of Motor Vehicles, data which regularly was supplied to the church staff.

When they got to the front door of the Whole Bible Prophecy Church of God's Impending Judgement, Eleanor realized that this would be the only building in Affable County that didn't have one of those stickers on the door. "This kind of church is always the judge and never the judged," she said to herself.

Elaine, Eleanor, and Michelle were greeted at the church's main door by a tall, pasty-skinned man with deep-set eyes. He was wearing spotless white overalls and a white baseball cap with the word "SAVED" in the middle.

"I'm here to take you to the Potentater." His name tag read, "Virgil Lickspittle."

Just before they entered the church, the bell gonged twice. While they looked up at the bell, Virgil said, "One SAVED, One WARNED." He pulled the door open and said, "Let's go inside."

Virgil and the consultants walked into an expansive lobby with plush red carpeting. On one wall, there were life-sized photographs of the Potentater doing different things in the community—accepting awards; being applauded; being thanked by large numbers of men, women, and children; petting puppies who were wagging their tails; and being praised by important people. There was a red door in the middle marked "gift shop." Another wall had a picture window through which you could see a garden with a large fountain where dark-red colored water flowed through seven stone bowls. To the left, there were twelve white doors that led to the sanctuary, and to the right was a pair of glossy black doors leading to the seven-story stone tower.

"We're going into the tower," Virgil said, opening the black doors.

"I hope we're able to get out of here when we're done," Michelle whispered to Eleanor.

Inside the first floor of the tower was a stone reception desk, staffed by three armed and masked muscular men. They were wearing white and ochre camouflage overalls and white SAVED baseball-style caps. In front of the elevator door was a metal detector and an x-ray conveyor belt, similar to the ones used at airports. The consultants placed their purses on the conveyor belt and walked through the metal detector. One of the armed guards took their cell phones, saying, "These are not permitted in the tower." Virgil led the consultants into a pure-white elevator.

Stopping on the second floor, the door opened to an ochre-colored room used as a training facility and as a gathering place for the church's army of community informants. There was a group of twenty-five men with buzz haircuts listening to a lecture by the church's trainer. On one side of the room were seven large commercial laser printers; a few individuals were removing freshly printed documents and putting them into various baskets.

"These people are our eyes and ears in the community," Virgil said. "We call them Truth Seekers."

"Can we observe the training for a minute?" Michelle asked.

"Let's continue the tour," Virgil said without answering the question.

The elevator took them to the third floor, where the three consultants and Virgil stepped into a deep-purple-colored room. "This floor is for the SHUNNED," he said. There were dozens of computers and servers. The church staff, all wearing purple overalls, were busy at work, visiting various websites and downloading information. One individual was managing what appeared to be a database; it was displayed on four large screens for all to see. There were several purple file cabinets in the middle of the room. *A German Requiem* by Brahms played in the background on a continuous audio loop.

Michelle, Elaine, and Eleanor started to look around, but Virgil stopped them. "You can go no further." He led them back into the elevator. Virgil pushed a red button marked, "WARNED." The elevator doors closed and slowly rose to the fourth floor.

When the door opened, the consultants could see that, aside from the color (red versus purple), the room was identical to the one below; an equal number of computers, servers, filing cabinets, and workers, though those on the fourth floor were wearing red overalls. Instead of the Brahms music, *Gloomy Sunday* was playing on a continuous audio loop. Eleanor noticed that a purple ceiling light in the middle of the room started flashing.

"What's that light mean?"

"A WARNED is being downgraded to a SHUNNED," Virgil explained. "The electronic file will be transmitted to the SHUNNED floor server, and a new sticker will be printed on the second floor. One of the Truth Seekers will take the sticker and pull the cord for the tower bell. Then, he'll go to the appropriate address and apply the new sticker, either to the door for a business or the yard sign for somebody's house."

"What about that music? It's really depressing," Michelle said to Virgil. "How can people stand it?"

"They get used to it," Virgil said as he led them back into the elevator. "To work hard and feel good about their jobs, the staff on the WARNED floor need to feel gloomy. It's kind of reverse psychology."

Next, the elevator took Virgil, Michelle, Elaine, and Eleanor to the fifth floor. The doors opened, and Virgil led the consultants into the brown "MILK" room. Again, dozens and dozens of workstations filled the room; all were staffed by workers wearing brown overalls. A gold ceiling light was flashing.

"This is good news," Virgil said, without even a smidgen of emotion. "Somebody earned a SAVED sticker. Their data file is being transmitted upstairs to the SAVED room server; the new sticker will be printed on the second floor," he explained. "And, oh yes, the tower bell will be rung."

"I don't see anyone celebrating," Michelle observed. "You'd think they would be."

"No, not really," Virgil said. "Even though this person is getting a new sticker today, he or she might be dropped to a lower level sticker by month's end."

"Why's there no music playing?" Eleanor asked. "I don't hear anything."

"There is music playing," Virgil corrected her. "They're playing John Lennon's track *Two Minutes of Silence* from his album, *Unfinished Music Number 2*. It's also on a continuous loop. I think it's a perfect choice for this floor, don't you agree?"

Michelle, Elaine, and Eleanor did not respond to Virgil's question.

"Let's go to the sixth floor," Virgil said. "There's nothing else here to see."

The sixth floor was the most popular room in which to work. It wasn't dark and dreary like the third and fourth floors, nor was it dull like the fifth. The walls were painted yellow-gold, and the staff wore overalls of a similar color. As was the case with the other floors, the room was replete with computers and servers. In the background, a Christian country music version of the *Battle Hymn of the Republic* was playing on a continuous audio loop.

"The staff seem happier on this floor," Eleanor said to Virgil.

"Wouldn't you be? It's a lot more fun to associate with SAVED people than it is with MILK, WARNED, or God forbid, SHUNNED people."

"Do people get knocked down to a lower level frequently?" Elaine asked.

"Yes, of course they do. The average SAVED person keeps their top-level sticker for about six weeks. Invariably, our sixth floor team will catch SAVED people sinning, and they'll be dropped to a lower level."

"What happens to those people?"

"Losing the SAVED sticker does affect a person's credit score, so they can expect to pay higher interest rates on their car loans and more for car insurance. We up their church pledge, too. That's why we don't fully rejoice when a person or business reaches the SAVED level, especially those with higher incomes."

"So, I guess people don't worry about losing their SAVED sticker altogether," Eleanor said with a little sarcasm. "Looks like they've a vested interest in people losing salvation," she whispered to her colleagues.

"I think the financial penalties and the social embarrassment are enough to keep most people afraid of going all the way down to the tower basement."

"You never said anything about a basement. Will it be on our tour?" Elaine asked.

"Certainly not," Virgil said. "I will not speak of it again." Virgil hit the elevator call button. "Let's head to the seventh floor. I think the Potentater is ready for you."

The elevator arrived at the seventh floor, and the doors opened. Virgil and the consultants stepped into a ginormous, light-filled, high-vaulted ceiling, white oval room. A multitude of gold medallions bearing coats of arms, angels, open Bibles, crosses, and other symbols filled the walls. Directly in front of them, about three yards away, was the Potentater's shiny gilded desk that sat high on a marble platform encircled by golden barbed wire. And seated at the desk was Axel himself, looking rather grumpy and wearing a bright white shirt with a red Roman collar and a blue surplice. He was glaring straight at Michelle, Elaine, and Eleanor, all of whom had expected to enter a reception area before they had to encounter the Potentater face-to-face.

Standing next to the Potentater on the platform was his personal assistant, Sebastian Clinker. Sebastian, an exceedingly tall, immaculately groomed man, was wearing a gleaming white tuxedo with a glossy top hat that had a gold cross in the middle. He opened his mouth and said unto them, "This is the Potentater." Axel said nothing.

"Good afternoon, Pota . . . Potentater," Michelle said, almost calling him Potater. "We appreciate you taking the time to speak with us about your ministry."

"We do have a few questions for you," Eleanor added. "She took her notepad out of her purse, ready to read the questions.

With one finger, bearing a big gold and emerald ring, the surprisingly small, round-looking Potentater motioned for Sebastian to move closer and to lean towards him. He then whispered something into Sebastian's ear.

Sebastian straightened up and looked at Michelle, Elaine, and Eleanor. "You may not ask the Potentater any questions."

"That's it?" Eleanor said, feeling exasperated. "We've come a long way to learn more about your ministry here, sir."

"Answering questions is rarely something the Potentater does," Sebastian said. "He only wanted to pass judgement upon the three of you."

"But we want to learn more about your church and its ministries," Michelle told Axel.

Axel motioned for Sebastian and again whispered into his ear.

"He knows who you are. He knows your credit scores. He knows the temperature settings on your home thermostats," Sebastian said. "The Potentater wanted me to relay that to you."

Axel pointed to the elevator door with a different finger that bore an even bigger gold and sapphire ring and said, "Shove off!"

"I think we'd better go," Virgil said to the consultants. He pushed the elevator call button, and when the doors opened, he led Michelle, Elaine, and Eleanor out of the room.

Just as the elevator door was closing, they heard Axel yell, "This steak's not big enough!"

"Well, I never. . .," Eleanor said, unable to complete her sentence.

"What a creep!" Michelle said.

"Potater!" Elaine added.

"I don't think it's wise for you to remain in Pleasantville for too long," Virgil said, with an ominous tone in his voice. "But before you go, please visit our gift shop on the first floor. We have a big sale going on."

For a moment, Michelle stared at Virgil in disbelief at what he had just said. "We're heading back to our offices in Atlanta this afternoon," she responded coldly.

"I don't think we have time for the gift shop," Eleanor added.

When they got to the first floor, Virgil returned their cell phones and led them from the tower building back to the main lobby.

"Let's hold hands and say a prayer together," Virgil said before the consultants exited the building.

"That's okay," Elaine said. "We'll be on our way."

Six months after Michelle, Elaine, and Eleanor had their fateful meeting with the Potentater, they were back in Pleasantville to see the new house churches that missionaries from the Methodist Churches of Georgia had established.

"I'm glad you didn't try to start any new church building construction," Michelle said to Bishop Shirley Farro. "I think the evangelism plan worked out really well."

Shirley also was visiting Affable County to see how their work was progressing. "The house church was a good model. Our new members have suffered a lot of traumas at the hands of Axel Cleaver, and the safety and intimacy of a community-based home church proved crucial," Shirley Farro said. "We already have twelve house churches in Pleasantville, and thirty more are being set up in other parts of Affable County."

"We're so proud of your team," Michelle said to Shirley.

"They're not all Methodist," Shirley added. "Some are Presbyterian and Episcopalian, a bunch are Baptists, one is Lutheran, and a few are Roman Catholic. We've got a new synagogue opening. I've heard that a mosque might be needed as well. I'm thrilled at how we were able to work together for the benefit of everyone in Affable County."

"Any Swedenborgians?" Michelle asked, half-joking.

"No," Shirley replied. "I'm sure Missy will be disappointed."

"Hi, Bishop Shirley!" Alice walked up to the bishop and Michelle. "Hi, Michelle!"

"Hello, Alice. It's so good to see you," Bishop Farro said.

"Thanks for holding your meeting at the restaurant yesterday evening. We were so happy to see you there." Alice had a renewed sense of calling about her work in the food service business.

"Your food was wonderful. I've heard nothing but rave reviews."

"No soup in a tureen?" Michelle asked, laughing. "No pile of PB&Js?"

"We don't do that anymore." Alice was a little embarrassed. "We've got too much self-respect to do that now. And there's a new restaurant opening down the street, so we'll have competition."

Eleanor wandered over to join the conversation with Alice and Bishop Farro. "Did you bring Missy with you?"

"No, she's at a conference in Ohio. I've also convinced her to take a statistics class at the community college followed by multiple courses in accounting. She'll be busy for a long time."

Eleanor smiled. "Of all the people we met on our first trip to Affable County, the biggest transformation we've witnessed is with you, Alice." Eleanor took Alice's hand. "You're so different now."

"I lived in fear every day," Alice said. "When Reverend Rye showed me in the Bible what Jesus was like, I didn't believe him at first."

"His burden is light, indeed," Shirley said.

"I cried for two days when I heard that. I was so tired of worrying about being watched by the Potater," Alice smiled.

"His title was Potentater, Alice," Michelle said. "I never knew if I should have corrected you."

"I knew it was all along. I just liked calling him the Potater. That way I could rebel without getting into trouble because people always thought I wasn't very bright."

"Hello, Alfonse!" Eleanor said as the hotel manager joined the conversation. "It's good to see you. If we stay at your hotel, you're not gonna give me a big box of corn flakes, are you?" she asked with a smile.

"Oh, gosh, how embarrassing. I can't believe I did that," Alfonse said. "But you know, I didn't care. I was so downtrodden."

"What is it that King David said in Psalms, 'restore to me the joy of your salvation?'" Eleanor asked.

"I've got the joy back now," Alfonse said. "Life is hard for me, but my faith brings me joy. And I don't have to hide my *Forbes* magazines."

"Shirley, let me introduce you to David DeMure. He's the president of the Affable County Bank," Eleanor said. David, too, was joining the conversation.

"I'm so pleased to meet you," Bishop Farro said.

"You wouldn't have been pleased to meet me six months ago," David said. "I was such a miserable coward."

"You, a coward?" Bishop Farro asked.

"Yes," Michelle said, "he was a miserable coward." She smiled at the bank president. "But now he's neither miserable nor a coward."

"Thank you, Michelle," David said. "That means a lot to me."

"Oh, by the way, David, I heard that your bank foreclosed on the Whole Bible Prophecy Church of God's Impending Judgement property." Elaine was thrilled at seeing the news in *The Georgia Business Times* newspaper.

"The Potentater never made any payments on the loan for that ridiculous tower."

"I guess the court made the final judgement on that project!" Elaine started laughing.

"The day you visited me, I felt like such a coward. The first thing I did after you left was to remove those blasted stickers from the bank's front door."

"Good for you," Michelle said.

"I felt so free after I did that."

"We did the same thing," Alice said. "When my boss saw that the bank stickers were gone, she removed ours, too. Now she's ordered a real, honest-to-good neon sign that will have our new name on it."

"And the new name is?" David asked.

"Potater's," Alice joked. Everyone was shocked. "No, the new name is 'Pleasant Place Diner.'"

"Hey Larry," Eleanor said. Larry LaShy was now a leader of a home church and wanted to say hello to the consultants. "Did you ever get paid for the Lincoln Axel stole?"

"No," he replied. "It was a big loss for me. I just have to move on. I did finally file a police report, but I doubt anything will come of it."

"I hope you know, Bishop Farro, that this community has come together with a new spirit of faith, hope, and love." Alfonse was speaking from the heart. "Not everybody responded to your evangelism, but I feel we have a newfound appreciation for the many different people who make their home in Affable County."

"Not everyone has to conform. And do you remember those metal signposts that were in the front yard of every home?" David asked Michelle, Elaine, and Eleanor. "The business community put together the funds to pay for an artist. She'll be creating a large sculpture for the park in front of the county courthouse."

"It's gonna be called, *A Great Community with Many Different Faces,*" Larry said.

"What happened to the Potentater?" Michelle asked.

"I don't know; he disappeared about three months ago, just after the foreclosure proceedings began," David said.

"He must have seen the writing on the wall," Michelle said, laughing.

"I pity the folks wherever he ends up," Eleanor said.

"Ain't that the truth," Alfonse added. "He should be in jail!"

People are surprised that you can't drive to Amigo County, Texas, from anywhere in Texas. To get there, you must first cross the border into Mexico at Eagle Pass. You then take a left turn and drive approximately two hundred and seventy-five miles on the *Carretera No Confíes en el Estadounidense.* Once you reach the town of *Americano Tramposo*, you turn left, cross the Rio Grande, and there you will find the smallest border crossing in all of Texas. Go through immigration and customs, and then drive north on the only road for twelve miles until you reach Alegre, the county seat of Amigo County. It took Axel, Virgil, and Sebastian fourteen hours to make the drive from Eagle Pass to Alegre.

Axel heard about Alegre and Amigo County and its leadership's goal of attracting non-immigrant Christian families. Now known as the Right Reverend Father Anderson, he developed a proposal for a new network of what he called wholesome house churches. The former Potentater promised to bring in new residents, filling the churches with real God-fearing, American families from Utah, build a faith-based business complex and education center, and host a streaming family values program he called, *Father Knows Best.* The city and county governments were so taken with the proposal that they gave Alex land grants, tax incentives, and hundreds of thousands of dollars in well-below-market-rate loans.

"I can't wait to see all of the godly people you'll bring into our county, Father Anderson," Mayor Henry Maccus said to Axel. "Where are your assistants, by the way?"

Before Axel could respond, County Detective Clara Santos walked over to where he and the Mayor were talking. "Excuse me, sir," Clara said. "You need to come with me." Two of her partners, officers Kwafi and Thao, were looking at a large black Lincoln SUV with odd-looking tags.

"That's the stolen SUV," Kwafi said, walking over to the detective.

"That vehicle you were driving is stolen, sir," Detective Santos said to Axel. "You'll need to come with me now."

Axel turned and faced the detective. "Shove off!" he said, ready to draw his gun. In the distance, he noticed Virgil and Sebastian skedaddling away. Three county peace officers were running after them.

"I'd leave that gun alone, if I were you," Clara said. She handcuffed Axel and read him his Miranda rights, something the former Potentater had experienced several times before. "You're going back to Georgia tonight."

"Henry," Peace Officer Afia Kwafi said to the mayor. "You're gonna need to get yourself a new partner, especially one who's honest and trustworthy."

"Ditto," Detective Santos added. "Someone who's gonna make y'all appreciate the great things we immigrants are bringing to Amigo County."

"Amen," Officer Kwafi said. "The last thing you need is a scumbag like this guy. We heard about the mess he left in Georgia."

Mayor Maccus was stunned by the sudden turn of events. "Clara, you thinkin' we'll be able to get our money back from this guy?"

"Not before the next election day," she said, shrugging her shoulders. "Wait till he hears I'm running against him," she whispered to Kwafi who laughed, uncontrollably.

Maccus wept.

"Thank you, Ken, for your tale, I think," Dave said. "It was really depressing, but it did end well for the folks of Affable County. You didn't tell us if Axel and his cohorts ended up in jail!"

"Yeah, I wanted to see them incarcerated," Jim said.

Ken looked at the other O'Postles with a sly look. "Maybe they got him, maybe not."

"Why are we so attracted to scoundrels like Axel?" May asked. "It happens all the time."

"And why are they usually men?" Sarah asked.

"They make me angry!" Sue said. "They suck the life out of us, individually and as members of a community."

"It's always fear they use," Ken said. "Fear of foreigners, minorities, the poor, anybody who is different."

"Ain't that the truth," Ken said. "Axel thrived on fear, and once he was in control, he made everybody in Affable County afraid of his wrath."

"People like that are really scary," May said.

"Ken, you made me think of the First Letter of John where it says, 'There is no fear in love, but perfect love casts out fear; for fear has to do with punishment,'" Princeton said.

"Exactly," Ken responded. "If life as a believer makes you afraid, then something is clearly wrong. Then your yoke is never easy, and your burden is never light!"

"Maybe the old Potater will get his due!" Billy said.

"Okay, gang," Dave said. I think we need to finish the tapas and get ready for our tour. I see Father Alcuin standing at the door."

"I'm so glad we stayed in this little Santiago. I cannot imagine having the same pilgrimage and fellowship in a place filled with thousands upon thousands of tourists," Bob said.

"Amen to that," Princeton said. "I apologize for being so pushy about the directions. We ended up where we needed to be."

"You know what's scary?" Bob asked, rhetorically. "If we say that God led us to this place, then was God working through AI?"

"Oh, please don't go there," Dave said. "I don't want to even think about that."

"Me either," Sue said. "Let's just be thankful for where we are."

Epilogue

"Is that the finger you wouldn't give to the folks at the big Compostela?" Dave asked. He was pointing to what looked to be bones resting on an ancient cloth and encased in a thick glass box with a gold border. It sat on an ornate shelf above the main altar. He and the other O'Postles were in a dark, candle-lit, early Romanesque church. Many paintings and statues of the Virgin Mary with the baby Jesus, St. James, and other saints from history lined its walls and chapels. The smell of recently burned incense filled the air.

"My predecessor, Father Francisco, told me that long, long ago our church had an entire hand of Santiago," Father Alcuin replied. "Soldiers of El Cid seized the blessed saint's hand and gave it to the big Santiago in exchange for gold and silver. They dropped this little finger as they fled."

"And they still want that finger?" May asked. "Even after what, ten centuries?"

"Five years ago, we sent a delegation to Santiago de Compostela while we were preparing for our millennium anniversary, hoping they would lend us a hand." The Father seemed sad. "We wanted the hand that was missing our finger—the hand El Cid's men stole. Instead, they again demanded we give them the finger, the one you see before you."

"That's the way it is when you're a small church," Sue said. "Usually, you get stuck with the leftovers. In your case, a finger." She stopped herself. "I don't mean to say that the finger of the blessed saint isn't worth anything, mind you."

"We have what we have, and we are thankful for that."

"I love the rounded arches and thick walls of your church," Princeton said. "Very different from the arches in Gothic churches."

"It makes the church feel very cozy and spiritually warm, even though it's pretty big," Sue said. "It's beautiful."

After explaining everything he knew about the altar, Father Alcuin led the twelve O'Postles around the church, showing them the twelve small chapels that lined the walls, the artwork, sarcophagi, and the floor ledger stones. "Those two paintings are by Huguet. They're very important," Father Alcuin said, pointing up at a portrait of Mary and the baby Jesus, and next to it, a portrait of a long-forgotten benefactor."

"They're amazing," Sue said.

"A big museum in Madrid wants them," Father Alcuin said. "They don't think we can take care of them properly. They offered us free lifetime museum memberships for the citizens of our town plus free framed posters of our paintings."

"What did you say?" May asked.

"I gave them the finger," he said, laughing.

"You didn't," May said, shocked by what Father Alcuin said.

"No, I didn't." He was laughing. "We politely declined their offer."

"It is such an amazing experience being in your church, Father," May said. "I feel like I've walked into a timeless place where the days and lives of the past surround me."

"I agree," Ed said. "I don't know how else to describe it. I feel at peace like I've never felt before."

"This is how I experience 'the communion of saints,'" the Father said to the twelve O'Postles; his voice was very gentle and soothing. "Being here makes it easier for me to be a part of those who came before me."

"I can almost feel life everlasting," Sarah said.

Father Alcuin gave his guests a few minutes to their own thoughts and then said, "It's time for our dinner; we'll head to the rectory where our meal and your rooms await. Please follow me."

The priest led the group to a side door in the sanctuary that led down a long, ancient hallway, the stone floor of which was well worn by the footsteps of the many people who had gone before. They passed through another door and entered into a large room with a big, rectangular, centuries-old, wooden refectory table in the middle. "Please take a seat at our table." After everyone was seated, Father Alcuin asked Sarah to lead the group in a prayer of thanksgiving, for the food they were about to receive and for the faithful who had gone before them.

"I'm famished," Ed said. "I wonder what we'll be having for dinner."

"It won't be hamburger and French fries," Dave said. "I could really go for that."

“Me too,” Sue said. “Sometimes you just crave some comfort food like good old macaroni and cheese.”

“Look, here comes our food,” May could see Father Alcuin and two other priests entering the room, each carrying ornate, silver-covered platters which they carefully placed at the center of the table.

“We’ve prepared a special feast for you, Father Alcuin said. The three priests removed the platter covers; the first had a plate of hamburgers, the second a pile of what resembled French fries, and the third, a plate of macaroni and cheese. “I thought you could use some comfort food after your long journey. Father Pedro did an internet search of ‘comfort food’ for your hometown, and this is what he came up with.”

“We’ve never made what you call ‘buns’ before,” Father Pablo said. “I hope they meet to your liking. The bread we make is normally coarse and wide.” The priest held his arms out for emphasis. “We didn’t think you would like a wide hamburger.”

“And the *patatas* we grow aren’t long like yours, so the French fries don’t look like the ones on the internet, but I hope you like them.” Father Alcuin pulled a small, round potato from his cassock pocket to show everyone. “This is our *patata*.”

“We didn’t have what you call ‘Kraft cheese,’ either,” Father Antonio said. “I had to use *Zamorano*. But I was lucky to find short noodles at a shop down the street.”

Just then, Juana and the remaining ten members of the *Doce Saludadores* committee walked into the room and joined the group at the table.

“I’ve never had a hamburger,” Fernando Sanchez said. “I’ve seen them in movies, and I’ve always wanted to try one.”

Bob took a bite of his hamburger. His eyes lit up like he had seen a vision from on high. “Oh my God, this burger is amazing.”

“Does that mean he likes it?” a nervous Father Pablo asked.

“Yes, Father. It means he likes it, mucho.”

“And the French fries are perfect,” May said.

“Amen! ”Ben, Billy, and Bob said in unison.

“You hit a home run with the mac and cheese,” Sue said.

“Hit a home run?” Father Antonio asked. “Does she mean they are bad?”

“No, Father, she means they couldn’t be better,” Ken said.

“Tomorrow, if you are not going to leave us for the big Compostela, I want to show you the catacombs of our church. We recently discovered the remains of a Roman town that rests beneath this village," Father Alcuin said.

"And if you stay a little longer, I can show you the *Zamorano* cheese how to make," Father Antonio said.

"Oh, you must see old Casa de Huguet. It's one of the oldest homes in our town," Fernando said. "It's older than old."

"How old?" Ken asked.

"In 1450, Señor Huguet lived there when he did the paintings in our church you saw. It was very old when he stayed there."

"Then I take you to my farm. You must meet my sheep," Farmer and *Saludadores* committee member Valeria López offered. "They give milk for the *Zamorano* in the macaroni. It is said that El Cid's men crossed my field on their way to steal our hand of Santiago."

"I think I can say, speaking for everyone in our group, that we are overwhelmed by your hospitality, and we definitely want to see the sites and experience life in your community," Dave said. The twelve then applauded.

When the meal was finished, the twelve O'Postles and the *Doce Saludadores* committee members cleared the table, cleaned the dishes, and swept the floor. Then Valeria, Fernando, and Juana picked up their musical instruments—an old guitar-like *vihuela*, a *zanfona*, and a *gaita* bagpipe—and shared the music of their homeland. They even taught the more musically inclined O'Postles, Sarah, Dave, and Ken, how to play their instruments.

"We want to perform something for you that's probably never, ever been done by anyone, ever," Sarah said near the end of their evening together. She smiled at Dave and Ken, while the other O'Postles looked on suspiciously. "Okay, ready? One, two, three." Using the *vihuela*, *zanfona*, and *gaita*, the trio played a very awkward rendition of *All You Need is Love* while everyone clapped along.

Following the music, Father Alcuin led everyone in a prayer for peace, fortitude for where there is no peace, and thanksgiving for their all-too-brief communion of saints. The *Doce Saludadores* Committee members then headed home, and the Twelve O'Postles had a brief conversation before heading upstairs to their rooms.

"Ken, my brother, I'll have to admit that your obedience to our bus AI directives was most fortunate for us all," Princeton said. "This has been a truly amazing experience, and I'm sorry I doubted your ability to get us to where we needed to be."

"But think of the theological implications, everybody," Ben said. "We all believe it was the Holy Spirit that led us to the little Santiago and away from the big one."

"Truly mind-boggling," May added. "Did God intervene in the machinations of that little dashboard box?"

"If that's true, where was God when Ron got locked in the bus loo?" Billy asked. "That must have been really scary."

"It only happened because Ken disconnected the AI box from its docking station," Jim said. "And I bet it was scary for him."

"It's a brave new world we're heading into," Sue added. "I don't think we're ready."

"Methinks we have stumbled upon fresh material for future theologians!" Dave said. "And it all scares the hell out of me."

"Where is Ron, anyway?" Billy asked. "Has anyone seen him?"

"Help! The door's stuck and I can't get out!"

www.ingramcontent.com/pod-product-compliance
Lightning Source LLC
LaVergne TN
LVHW050626100826
845148LV00011B/1749
* 9 7 9 8 3 8 5 2 7 4 5 9 8 *